The stranger w

He was leaning ag   shadow among the   hanging minstrels' gallery. Nell didn't see his face clearly to know he was watching her. He'd been watching her since she'd first noticed him standing there a little over an hour ago, tall and powerful and unsmiling.

Despite the heat of the room, an odd little chill tiptoed down Nell's spine. There was something about the man's stillness, about the way he just stood and watched. Something leashed and waiting. Something. . .predatory.

Julia Byrne lives in Australia with her husband, daughter, and two overgrown cats. She started her working career as a secretary, taught ballroom dancing after several successful years as a competitor, and presently works part-time in the History Department of a Melbourne university. She enjoys reading, tapestry, and playing mah-jong.

Recent titles by the same author:

MY ENEMY, MY LOVE
GENTLE CONQUEROR

MISTRESS OF HER FATE

Julia Byrne

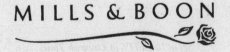

MILLS & BOON

MILLS & BOON, the Rose Device and LEGACY OF LOVE are trademarks of the publisher.
Harlequin Mills & Boon Limited,
Eton House, 18–24 Paradise Road, Richmond, Surrey TW9 1SR
This edition published by arrangement with
Harlequin Enterprises B.V.

© Julia Byrne 1995

ISBN 0 263 79290 0

Set in 10 on 11½ pt Linotron Times
04-9508-85388

Typeset in Great Britain by CentraCet, Cambridge
Printed in Great Britain by
BPC Paperbacks Ltd

CHAPTER ONE

Langley Castle, near Stratford, September 1464

HAD there ever been a time when she had enjoyed the colourful spectacle of a banquet? The music, the dancing, the constantly shifting crowd of chattering guests? If so, it was beyond the reach of her memory, Nell decided as she edged past the last of the trestle tables that had been set up along both sides of Langley Castle's great hall. She paused before one of the deep window embrasures and measured the distance to the door.

A discreet exit was not going to be easy. Though the hour was growing late, the room was still crowded, and ablaze with light from the flaming torches in their iron cressets high up on the walls and the candles flickering in their table-sconces. Light that dazzled the eyes, shimmering on pearl-encrusted silks and damasks and illuminating the rich jewel-like colours of the banners and wall-tapestries. Light that glowed, dark and sullen, through glass goblets filled to overflowing with ruby-coloured wine.

In a few places the light was muted. As well as the tables and benches, the hall was furnished with several carved wooden screens, placed to create discreetly shadowed corners for the benefit of those guests who wished to conduct their little amours in some privacy. Most of them were too drunk to bother, but lolled in their seats, sporting openly with whomever took their fancy. Those who could still remain upright were dancing in the centre of the hall, circling to the strains

of lute and clavichord, a hazard for anyone with escape
on her mind.

Nell dodged a couple who staggered out of the line
of dancers and wished she could be magically trans-
ported somewhere else. Preferably her bedchamber.
Her feet ached from hours of dancing, her face ached
from the constant smile she had affixed to it, and if the
unceasing cacophony of loud talk and clattering dishes,
interspersed with coarse male laughter and female
shrieks, didn't strike her deaf it would be a miracle of
saintly intervention.

'Not dancing, dear Cousin? Have all your partners
deserted you?'

A titter of spiteful laughter brought her head around
as the dancers swept past in a swirling array of movement and colour. The overblown blonde who had
spoken smiled back over her shoulder, patently false
sweetness on her sharp-featured countenance.

Nell smiled back just as sweetly, and refrained from
replying in kind. A cousinly exchange reminiscent of
spitting cats was more than she could cope with at
present. And besides, she reminded herself, the festiv-
ities were in honour of her imminent departure. This
was the last time she would have to put up with the
way her cousin turned every banquet into a contest to
see who could garner the most compliments or collect
the most partners.

'After tonight you can have the field all to yourself,'
she muttered beneath her breath. Mayhap, then, she
thought, Margaret would not feel obliged to wear a
gown that was disgustingly tight and cut so low that
Nell decided her cousin's plump breasts were about to
burst free of their precarious confinement at any
moment. Judging by the expression of lecherous anticipation on the face of Margaret's partner, whose ener-

getic performance seemed expressly designed to hasten such a scandalous exhibition, she was not alone in holding to that opinion.

Nell giggled, then abruptly sobered as she glanced down at the ermine-trimmed, silver and blue brocade gown she was wearing. Like all her cousin's clothes, its fashionable neckline was so low that it would be enough to make the boldest harlot blush. She gave the bodice a surreptitious tug and wished she had a piece of silk, or even lace, with which to cover the generous expanse of flesh thus exposed. Margaret might not have been so quick with her malicious tongue, Nell reflected, if she had known how little her cousin relished the male attention provoked by the revealing costume. Fortunately, since she was considerably less well-endowed than Margaret, the borrowed gown wasn't quite as shameless as it might have been. In fact, even when added to sore feet, tired eyes and deafened ears, it would not have made her presence at the banquet any more of a distasteful ordeal than usual—had it not been for one other circumstance.

Without moving her head, Nell glanced cautiously towards the screen passage at the far end of the long hall. The stranger was still there, leaning against the wall, a big, dark shadow among the shadows cast by the overhanging minstrels' gallery. She didn't need to see his face clearly to know he was watching her. He'd been watching her since she'd first noticed him standing there a little over an hour ago, tall and powerful and unsmiling.

Despite the heat of the room, an odd little chill tiptoed down Nell's spine. There was something about the man's stillness, about the way he just stood and watched. Something leashed and waiting. Something. . .predatory.

She shivered again, then jumped as a hand came down on her shoulder.

'Sweet Cousin! All alone? Come and dance with me.'

'Oh, Tom, you startled me.' Turning, Nell managed to slip out from under her cousin's hot, sweaty palm. Tom had had plenty to drink by the look of his flushed cheeks and glazed eyes, but he was still capable of movement. Even as she tried to step away he grabbed her about the waist and swung her into the midst of the dancers. Pulled so abruptly off-balance, Nell was fully occupied for several seconds in regaining her footing and rescuing the train of her gown.

'Do we both have to caper about like drunken mummers?' she gasped, catching her breath enough to resist Tom's efforts at a high leap. It wasn't easy. He had her clamped against his side in a position that virtually compelled her to follow him. 'This is your father's hall, not a village maypole.'

Tom roared with laughter, and leered at the gentle swells of flesh visible above her neckline. 'The leaps have a purpose, little prude,' he chuckled. 'God's nails, who'd have thought you'd turn out as frigid as a dried-up old nun.' The thought obviously annoyed him because the laughter vanished from his eyes, to be replaced by an unpleasant mixture of sullen resentment and frustration. 'Look about you, dearest cousin,' he advised sarcastically. 'Your prudish morals are of scant use to you here. 'Twould suit you better to change your manner, otherwise I might taste the honey you guard so closely without the benefit of marriage.'

'What, are you still at that?' she scoffed, not bothering to do as he bade. She had already seen enough to know that her uncle's guests were indulging their senses to the fullest. She only wished she'd managed to escape before Tom had noticed her standing alone.

'My father's intention in summoning me to Hadleigh Castle is to arrange my marriage to someone other than yourself, Cousin,' she reminded him, unsurprised to see his scowl deepen. As her father's only child she was a matrimonial prize that Tom and his parents were loath to see slip out of their grasp. ''Tis about the only useful thing he's ever done for me since he sent me here to live,' she finished, a slight trace of bitterness in her tone.

Tom's already heated face flushed dark red and his arm tightened around her waist, dragging her closer. 'You scornful little jade,' he hissed in a furious undertone. 'Always thinking you're too good for the rest of us. Oh, aye,' he added at her surprised glance, 'did you think I hadn't noticed? I watched you look down your nose at us the minute you climbed out of that litter ten years ago. Pampered little princess. But not for much longer. You're a long way from wed as yet, sweet Cousin, and your scorn will be of poor comfort when you're forced to spread your legs for me.'

'You're drunk,' stated Nell, not bothering to conceal her disgust. Tom's fingers were already digging with bruising force into the side of her breast, but she ignored the pressure and managed to get her elbow between them. A good jab to his ribs had him turning purple and choking.

Nell didn't wait to see if it was in rage or pain. She wrenched herself free and stalked off—straight into the big, dark stranger.

Up close he was huge. The thought flashed through Nell's mind even as her startled senses were bombarded by the feel of large, powerful hands steadying her with a grip that edged on painful, by the rough warmth of a

woollen surcoat against her palms, the lean, hard
strength of the body beneath. Instinctively, her fingers
curled into the solid muscles of his chest in an attempt
to lever herself away.

Merciful saints, she thought faintly. He's immovable.

'Lady Eleanor fitzWarren.'

It wasn't a question, but Nell nodded automatically.
Then shivered slightly as the deep, husky tones flowed
across her nerves. His voice was as overwhelmingly
masculine as the controlled power of his hands and the
sheer size of him. The cool scent of wind and rain still
clung to him, mingling with his own clean male essence
and teasing senses that had had a surfeit of the close
smoky atmosphere of the hall and men who smelled of
stale perfume and wine. Momentarily entranced, forgetting her initial intimidation, Nell leaned closer.

'No doubt you mean to be welcoming, Lady Eleanor,
but I prefer not to be one of a crowd.'

The sarcastic tone was like a pail of cold water
dashed over her. Nell gasped and stepped back, snatching her hands away as she looked up. Sweet Jesu, he
was dangerous. The predator she had imagined. Eyes
the colour of frozen amber, as fierce and intent as a
hawk's, stared back at her from beneath frowning black
brows. His hair was black also, cut unfashionably short
and brushed back from a face of hard contours and
aquiline features, with a firm, sharply chiselled mouth
that only just escaped being brutal by the unexpected
fullness of his lower lip.

Nell couldn't have spoken if her life had depended
on it. Indeed, she could barely recall what the stranger
had said to her. But it was not the compelling strength
of his face or the open contempt she saw in his icy gaze
that had the breath catching in her throat; it was the
scar. Thin and white against his tanned skin, the

unmistakable mark of violence ran down his temple in a straight line from above his left brow to below his eye, where it formed a short curve along his cheek-bone. It wasn't disfiguring, but it made an already hard face look positively menacing.

'Having second thoughts, Lady Eleanor? You surprise me. You bestow your favours so indiscriminately, I wouldn't have thought this——' he touched his scar lightly '—would deter you.'

This time the insult registered. Nell's breath came back with a rush. 'Precisely what favours are you referring to, sir?' she demanded through set teeth.

He shrugged and folded his arms across his chest, causing a ripple of muscle to disturb the fabric of his surcoat. Nell suddenly realised he wasn't dressed for a feast and felt a surge of confidence. He was probably some upper servant belonging to one of the guests. A bodyguard, perhaps—in these dangerous times, few wealthy men travelled without several of the uncouth creatures. She would soon send him about his business.

Then, as her eyes met the stranger's, her certainty wavered. This man looked as if he gave orders, not obeyed them. It was in the arrogant way he stood leaning against the wall, in the dangerous glitter of those golden hawk's eyes and the unrelenting line of his mouth.

'I'll admit you're more subtle than the other ladies,' he drawled, the faint emphasis on the word 'ladies' telling Nell exactly what he thought of the women present. 'You entice with smiles and laughter, Lady Eleanor.' His gaze wandered with slow insolence across the revealing bodice of her gown. 'You let them stare, and occasionally whet their appetites with forbidden embraces in dim corners, before you snatch the prize away. It's been an interesting exercise in tactics to watch. Tell me, how many men do you draw into your web before you make your choice?'

'Why, you——' Nell could scarcely get the words past the tightness in her throat. She felt the most absurd desire to burst into tears, and told herself it was fury. How dared this. . .this. . .uncouth *brute* accuse her of. . .? When most of the women were already. . . When she had struggled so hard to avoid. . .

Her thoughts fragmented into complete turmoil under the impact of her own rage and the faint infuriating smile on the stranger's face. 'You don't even know me,' she burst out at last, unable to think of anything else that came even close to expressing the extent of her outrage.

'I don't have to,' he dismissed. 'Women like you litter the Court like beggars at a feast.'

Her gaze flashed briefly to the white rose insignia embroidered on his sleeve. Memory, sharp and cold, stabbed through her. 'Encouraged by your Yorkist king.'

His brows went up at the fiery scorn in her tone. 'So, despite this being a Yorkist stronghold, you're one of those who would rather have a drooling idiot on the throne. That shouldn't surprise me, since Henry is led around by his wife like a performing bear—in much the same manner as you lead your partners, my lady.'

Nell couldn't believe what she was hearing. 'I don't know who you are, *sir*——' her own emphasis was as biting as his own '—but be assured my uncle will hear of your insults.'

'Rafe Beaudene,' he supplied briefly. 'And I wouldn't bother, if I were you.' He jerked his head sideways. 'Sir Edward appears to be busy.'

Nell made the mistake of following his gesture. Hot colour stained her cheeks as she saw her uncle grab

hold of a passing guest and pour the dregs of an ale-jug
down the front of her gown. The lady shrieked and put
up a mock struggle, which ended with her landing in
his lap and commanding him to clean her up. Laughing
raucously, he bent his head and complied. Not two
places away, Aunt Maud did nothing more than titter
and turn back to the gentleman with whom she was
conversing. They were sipping from the same wine-
cup, Nell noticed.

Conscious of reluctance, knowing what she would
see, Nell searched among the crowd for her cousins.
Tom was nowhere to be seen, but fourteen-year-old
Edmund had cornered a maidservant. The girl's dress
was down around her waist and he was openly pawing
her breasts. Margaret and her partner sat nearby,
indulging in much the same sort of scuffle, except that
her cousin's protests were accompanied by giggles and
not tears. The rest of the company were pursuing
drunken oblivion or amorous adventure with equal
fervour, and Nell knew it would get worse until the
guests fell asleep where they sat.

Miserably, she had to admit that the stranger's
contempt for the company was justified. But *she* had
no reason to be ashamed, she reminded herself. She
wasn't drunk, nor was she allowing some lout to maul
her the way Edmund——

A quick memory of Tom's painfully grasping fingers
pulled her thoughts up short. Some of her other
partners, too, had given her a few unpleasant moments
before she'd managed to have herself whisked off by
the next man waiting to dance with her. Nell blushed
again, this time in embarrassment. Beaudene, or whoever he was, had obviously seen it all and drawn his
own conclusions. And he didn't look like the sort of
man to listen to explanations.

Anger flickered again. She had no need to explain. Who did he think he was to sit in judgement of her, anyway? No! She didn't owe him any explanations! But if there was one thing Nell had learned in the past ten years, it was how to defend an indefensible position. And when your opponent was intensely male, over six feet tall and unlike any man you had ever encountered, you used whatever weapons came to mind. Her chin went up.

'Rafe Beaudene?' she repeated, a languid question in her voice. 'I don't believe I know the name. If you are here as bodyguard to one of the guests, I suggest you rejoin your fellows out in the bailey. I am sure their company will be more to your taste.'

'Since most guards have at least some notion of honour, I'm sure of that, too,' Rafe snapped, cursing the instant response of his body to the blatant feminine challenge in her. It wasn't the first time she'd had that effect on him, and he didn't like it any better now than he had earlier. Anger at his lack of control had him biting off the next words with savage inflexion. 'However, as much as I would like to follow your advice, Lady Eleanor, we're stuck with each other. 'Tis your body I'm here to guard.'

The resurgence of warm colour in her cheeks had his eyes narrowing briefly. It surprised him that the little minx was capable of blushing and yet, for a moment, she seemed genuinely uncomfortable, her eyes holding a mixture of anger, shock and confusion. A trick of the light, he told himself cynically. No one who behaved as she did would be shocked or confused by anything a man chose to say to her.

He thought back over the last couple of hours, and almost laughed aloud at the notion. He'd lost count of the number of times she'd vanished with her partner of the moment into a dimly-lit window embrasure or behind a screen, to emerge several minutes later smoothing a long sleeve, straightening her gown or, on one occasion, refastening the wide belt at her waist. And then she would beckon another victim, with nothing more than a look from her dark hazel eyes, a sweep of long ebony lashes, a turn of one delicate, almost bare shoulder.

And, God damn it, watching her, he'd felt the hot pulsing of his own blood in response to her tricks. The violence of his reaction had stunned him. The slender arch of her throat when she'd laughed up at her partners, the alluring sway of her hips beneath the heavy brocade of her gown, had made him want to drag her under him—never mind where they were— and subdue the subtle movements of her body with the force of his, to watch the laughter in her eyes change to passion.

He'd stamped down on the feelings immediately, of course, but the easy control he'd always taken for granted had been forced. Even telling himself that her passion would likely be as false as her bright smiles of promise hadn't helped.

As for what he'd overheard——

Nell almost reeled beneath the fierce anger that flashed into Beaudene's eyes. It was gone almost immediately, but the dangerous expression, added to several years' experience of unpleasant innuendo and less subtle suggestion, at least convinced her of one thing. He had meant nothing more than the literal truth by the way he'd phrased that last remark.

'I'm not sure I understand——' she began cautiously, only to break off with a startled squeak when he came away from the wall with the speed of a striking adder. Before Nell had time to wonder what was going on,

there was a flash of movement to her right and the
victim of her cousin Edmund's attentions darted past
them, making for the screen passage beyond, and
escape.

Whirling about, she saw that Edmund was right
behind the girl, haring across the hall and whooping as
if he was on a hunt. He was almost level with them
when Beaudene took one step forward and extended
his arm. Edmund hit it at full speed and rebounded as
if he'd run headlong into a stone wall. He sprawled on
his back in the middle of the dancers, nearly taking two
couples down with him and cursing viciously. There
was a roar of drunken laughter from a near by crowd.

Nell didn't bother with Edmund. She glanced back
swiftly at the entrance to the screen passage. The girl
had halted, clutching at her torn dress and staring wide-
eyed at Beaudene. There were traces of tears on her
cheeks and she looked pale. She was a mere twelve
month younger than Nell's own sixteen years, and yet
Nell felt suddenly immeasurably older.

'Go quickly, Alison,' she whispered urgently, waving
her hands for emphasis. 'Sleep with Jacquette and
Lucy, and stay out of Edmund's way until after your
wedding.'

'Aye, mistress.' The maid turned and vanished
before the words were finished.

'A plague on you, Cousin,' roared Edmund, picking
himself up off the floor. He glanced quickly at
Beaudene then advanced on Nell, clearly considering
her the less threatening opponent. 'Father said I could
have the wench before she married. You think sending
her to sleep with a parcel of women is going to stop
me?'

'Probably not,' Beaudene interposed coolly. He had
dropped his arm as soon as Edmund had been sent

flying, but hadn't resumed his lounging position against
the wall. Now he stepped into the boy's path. 'But you
may find it difficult to have her, or any woman, without
the proper equipment.'

'What? Who the hell are you?' Edmund demanded,
his voice soaring to a shrill note that betrayed his
youth.

'Someone who can do you a great deal of damage.'

The words were uttered in a tone of such cold
certainty that Nell shivered. As if he'd seen the small
movement, Beaudene glanced down at her. 'The girl's
to be wed?' he asked shortly.

She nodded. 'Next week. To our steward.'

'Bondman, or free?'

'He's free, but——'

Beaudene turned back to Edmund before she could
finish. 'If you want to function like a man when you
reach the age,' he said with soft menace, 'you'll take
warning, boy. There are enough easy women here
more suited to your purpose than a maid already
promised.'

'We'll see what my father has to say about that,'
Edmund blustered.

'Don't be an idiot, Edmund,' Nell advised, deciding
to enter the fray. 'Who do you think hired this. . .
this. . .?' Her voice faded away as she suddenly
realised she didn't know Beaudene's exact status. His
name and arrogant self-possession hinted that he was
no common man-at-arms, but whether he was knighted
or merely a squire she had no idea.

Temper flashed in Edmund's eyes as he turned on
Nell. 'Well, if I have to settle for a strumpet, I'll start
with you, Cousin. You owe me for letting that puling
little ninny escape, so 'tis you who must pay the forfeit.'

'By the Rood, Edmund!' Thoroughly exasperated,

but too inured to her family's ways to protest at the insult, Nell responded only to the threat. 'As if Thomas's attentions aren't enough. Do you have to emulate everything he does?'

Her cousin's hand whipped out and fastened around her wrist. ''Ware your shrewish tongue, wench, or—— Ow!'

'Let her go,' Beaudene said very softly. He had moved so swiftly to counter Edmund's attack that Nell hadn't seen the hold he had on her cousin's shoulder until she heard his yelp of pain. Eyes fastened in unwilling fascination on Beaudene's hand, she watched his long fingers flex ever so slightly. She was freed at once. 'And whatever favours your brother enjoyed in the past from Lady Eleanor are now at an end,' he finished in the same chillingly soft tone. 'Do I make myself clear?'

Edmund nodded sullenly and was released. Sending Nell a look of dislike, he stumbled off, cautiously feeling his neck and shoulder.

'Come on, Lady Eleanor, we've provided enough entertainment for your uncle's guests to gape at. Let's try something more sedate like the allemande.'

'The allemande?' Nell's gaze travelled in disbelief from Beaudene's mud-splashed, knee-length leather boots to his plain black hose and matching surcoat, unadorned but for the white rose and a wide fur trim. 'If you think I'm going to dance wi——'

She was yanked into the dance with startling velocity.

'Is this what you call guarding my body?' she demanded indignantly, then promptly fell silent when his long fingers slid down the inside of her arm to wrap her hand in an unbreakable grasp.

The first few steps passed in a daze. Somewhere in the distance Nell could still hear the clatter of dishes, the talk and laughter of the guests, even the minstrels' lutes above her, picking out a familiar melody, but they were sounds without meaning, not real; all her senses were focused on Beaudene. For some reason, dancing with him made her feel suddenly, unexpectedly, small and vulnerable.

She had been aware of his height and size from the moment she'd cannoned into him, of course, but now that awareness was almost terrifyingly acute. He seemed to tower over her like a huge black shadow, his strength a threat—leashed, aye, but *there*—and the way her hand was totally enveloped by his was utterly unnerving. It was the only contact between them, and yet her entire body was awash with heat, as though he was touching her all over. She felt chained. . .captive. . .*possessed*. It was all she could do to follow the procession of dancers without faltering.

'What? No sparkling wit? No polite conversation? You disappoint me, my lady.'

'I don't waste my wit on a hired bodyguard,' Nell managed to retort. She winced inwardly at the breathless sound of her voice and hoped he hadn't noticed. What was the matter with her? Why wasn't she depressing his pretensions and making her escape?

'You are labouring under a misapprehension, Lady Eleanor. I am not for hire. Especially not by your uncle.' Rafe glanced down at her just as they passed a flaring sconce-light and felt his blood surge in another rush of desire that completely drowned out her startled, questioning response. The torchlight flickered over her upturned face, casting pools of shadow in those seductive hazel eyes. Eyes like a forest at sunset, green and gold, light and dark, clear and mysterious.

Her other features held the same contradictions, he thought, frowning slightly. Her brows and lashes were dark, but the light captured the warm gleam of chestnut in the hair flowing free from the back of her headdress. Her face was fine-boned, almost fragile, the lines of cheeks, nose and jaw drawn with exquisite clarity, but her mouth was full and soft, just a fraction too wide for the current fashion of pursed lips prevailing at Court. It was a mouth made for passion, for kisses that were long and deep and utterly consuming.

God, what insanity had made him dance with her? Rafe asked himself, forcing his eyes away from that lush mouth in an attempt to subdue the throbbing tension in his body. His gaze dropped to the gently swaying movement of her skirts as she stepped sedately along by his side, and he realised suddenly how small she was, how delicately made. The steeple headdress, from which floated a veil of silver tissue, gave an illusion of height, but without it the top of her head would just reach his shoulder. Her hand felt tiny in his. Warm and soft, it quivered slightly, like a small captured bird.

Rafe's fingers tightened involuntarily. He saw her flinch and knew he was probably hurting her, but he couldn't seem to loosen his grip. The clenched strength of his hold was the only thing preventing him from dragging her into his arms so he could hold all of her, touch all of her.

'My lands lie half a day's ride beyond your father's.' His voice sounded hoarse and he forced himself to concentrate on speaking. It wasn't what he wanted to do, but talking would serve to remind him why he couldn't drag her into the nearest solar and take what she'd been offering every man in sight. 'Since my return from Court coincided with your own journey, he asked that I accompany you.'

'My father?' Nell repeated, frowning. 'But Tom and

several men-at-arms will be escorting me. Why would he ask such a favour of you?' The increasing waves of heat caused by Beaudene's long scrutiny of her face ebbed away beneath another, different sense of unease. Some very odd things had been happening lately. It tended to make a girl wary of anything out of the ordinary.

Instead of answering her question, Beaudene asked one of his own. 'Are you aware of the reason your father has sent for you, Lady Eleanor?'

Nell made a small, dismissing motion with her free hand. 'He intends to arrange my marriage,' she said briefly. 'What of it?'

'You don't appear to be overly interested in the prospect.'

'Why should I be? Whoever my father has in mind will only be marrying me for the wealth and lands I will inherit. Truly, I would rather be a pauper and retain my freedom.'

'Spoken in the sure knowledge that you would not remain a pauper for very long,' he stated sarcastically. 'Easy words, my lady.'

'You don't believe me?' Stung, Nell glared at him. 'Once I'm married my property becomes my husband's. I will own nothing except my marriage portion, a mere third of my inheritance, *if* he honours the law. I will also forfeit the freedom of my own body. Tell me, sir, why would I have any use for marriage?'

'Would you prefer the alternative? A nunnery? Or perhaps you would rather be a man's mistress than his wife?' The supposition was loaded with contempt.

'Why not?' she flung back, tossing her head. ''Twould be less restricting than either marriage or the cloister.'

A qualm shook her the moment the reckless words

were out, but Nell was too angry to take them back.
She glanced around the hall with scornful appraisal
until her gaze rested on a couple half-hidden behind
the back of a tall settle. The man was fondling his
partner with an intimacy that was better suited to the
bed-chamber, and though the woman laughed and
wriggled invitingly as his hand disappeared beneath her
skirts, exposing her plump white thighs, Nell saw her
turn her head away. The expression in her eyes was
one of amused tolerance.

'A perfect example,' she pointed out airily, devoutly
praying that Beaudene hadn't noticed how quickly she
had averted her own face. At past banquets she had
always managed to retire long before her uncle's guests
started making such an exhibition of themselves.
'They're not wedded, so at least she'll be able to seek
the privacy of her own bed once he's finished.'

'Not if she wants to be well-rewarded,' he promptly
returned. 'You see, everything has a price, my lady.
But perhaps 'tis as well you don't wish for marriage.
The price your husband would pay for the pleasures of
your body would be far too high.'

'Beyond your means, that is for certain,' Nell retal-
iated, and had the satisfaction of seeing his eyes
narrow.

'I don't recall making an offer,' he snapped.

'Thank the saints for that,' she retorted. 'Because I
would have no hesitation in refusing it. And if the man
my father has in mind for me is an ill-mannered,
overgrown lout like you, I'll send him packing as well.'

One black brow went up. 'You haven't sent me
packing,' he pointed out in a tone that made her want
to scream. 'In truth, now I come to think about it, you
don't have the authority to send me packing.'

Nell came to a dead stop in the middle of a turn. She

had to unclench her teeth so she could speak. 'I don't have to continue with this ridiculous dance, however,' she declared. 'If you will be so good as to cease breaking my fingers, sir, I wish to retire.'

'That's taking yourself off. Not nearly as satisfying as sending me packing.'

'Ohhh!' Wrenching her hand from Beaudene's grasp, Nell turned on her heel and, for the second time that night, abandoned her partner, Unfortunately, this time she had ended the dance at the far end of the hall and had to negotiate her way through several couples whose progress was erratic to say the least.

By the time she reached the entrance to the screen passage, she had been jostled from side to side, had had the long points of her new shoes trampled on, and had fought off the separate advances of three drunken would-be partners. Fortunately, she hadn't had to fight very hard, and she was just congratulating herself on her easy escape when the reason for it loomed up beside her.

Angry, nervous, and feeling extremely put-upon, Nell turned on him. 'Didn't you hear me? We will be making an early start in the morning. I wish to go to bed.'

'An excellent idea. Which way is your room?'

'*What*?'

'Oh, don't concern yourself. I have no interest in doing more than accompanying you to your door—and then making sure none of your suitors accepts the invitation you've been putting out to follow you through it.'

Nell clamped her lips shut and told herself that slapping his face and screaming like a fishwife would not help. She had to get rid of the man. There was something she had to do before she retired for the night, and she didn't want any company while she did it. Especially his.

A servant walked past carrying a platter of left-over food and inspiration dawned. 'Go and have something to eat, or whatever it is bodyguards do when they're off duty,' she commanded, waving a small, imperious hand. 'I sleep with Margaret and my two younger cousins—*girl* cousins,' she added for emphasis, '*and* their nurse, so you have no need to concern yourself with my virtue.'

Beaudene's reply was to wrap his long fingers about her arm. 'A wasted effort, no doubt, but 'tis why I'm here, nevertheless. Which way?'

Furious but helpless, Nell gestured to the stairway at the end of the screen passage. 'Do you intend to accompany me to the privy as well?' she asked with heavy sarcasm as they reached the upper gallery. 'I really don't need a bodyguard for that, you know. I've been managing on my own for quite some time now.'

'Obviously without being put over someone's knee at an age when it might have done some good,' he said grimly.

Nell jerked her arm out of his hold and marched on ahead. Innate, if silent, honesty compelled her to admit that she had probably deserved that remark, but the knowledge did not soothe her temper one whit. 'This is my chamber,' she managed to enunciate when they reached a door halfway along the gallery. Several chests were stacked against the wall, ready to be loaded into the baggage wagons in the morning. Beaudene stepped around them and, somewhat to her surprise, opened the door. He didn't say anything, just glanced into the room then stood aside for her to pass.

And all at once a curious feeling of reluctance swept over her. Of sudden regret at their unpleasant begin-

ning. Beaudene might be an arrogant boor who had
badly misjudged her, and he had obviously taken her
in dislike, but it was equally obvious that he took his
role as bodyguard seriously. And she had been so alone
here. Surrounded by family and wealth and luxury, but
still alone. Maybe she did need. . .

She looked up.

'Don't try it,' he said, his eyes arctic.

Hot colour surged into Nell's cheeks. Without utter-
ing a single word, she turned, marched into the dimly-
lit room and slammed the door behind her with as
much force as she could muster. 'Ignorant *savage!*' she
stormed. '*Brute! Oaf!* Stupid——'

A sleepy grumble came from one of the beds.

Nell ignored it. Her disordered mind was too busy
wondering how she was going to get through the next
few days. With her cousin Tom and that. . .that. . .
lout. . .as escorts, she was sure it would be the worst
few days of her entire life.

CHAPTER TWO

IT HAD been raining. Nell glanced up at the midnight
sky as clouds like black wraiths scudded across the face
of the moon, and hoped the next downpour would hold
off for a while longer. She hadn't bothered with a
mantle, but at least the night air wasn't too cold for
comfort. She began to pick her way carefully around
the puddles left by the recent shower, keeping to the
shadows as much as possible and skirting the perimeter
of the bailey rather than going straight across the open
space.

Creeping out of the hall had been blessedly easy.
She had half expected to see Beaudene standing guard
outside her door when she'd warily opened it a crack a
few minutes ago, but apparently the hour she'd waited
had been enough to convince him that she was safely
bundled out of the way for the night. Perhaps he'd
taken her advice and gone to chase up some food. He
might even drink himself into a stupor like everyone
else.

The thought of his inevitable discomfort on the
morrow cheered her for a moment, before she dismissed it. He didn't look like a man who relinquished
control of his senses—to anything.

A dog whined nearby and she froze, recalled to her
purpose. Once she reached the stables she would be
out of sight, but first she had to get there without
drawing the attention of the guards at the gatehouse.
Fortunately, they were some distance away, and, judging by the slurred snatches of bawdy song that wafted

towards her, were in much the same state as their master.

Nell gathered up her full skirts and tiptoed onwards. Not that she cared if Margaret's second-best gown trailed in the wet and mud, she thought crossly. It would serve her cousin right for slashing to pieces the gown Nell had intended to wear that evening; a nasty piece of spite that deserved retribution. But, on the other hand, she didn't need the weight of a water-logged hem dragging behind her when she returned to her chamber. One had to be practical, after all.

The stables materialised in front of her and she peered cautiously around the corner. All was still and quiet. Everyone not attending the banquet would be sound asleep by now—the guests' servants in the lodging-hall across the bailey, the grooms and stable-boys in the loft above the wagon-room. No one would hear her, and besides, she wouldn't be out here long. Her hand brushed over the big double doors. They were too heavy for her to open quietly; Nell ignored them and edged along the wall until she reached a smaller door at the end of the building. Easing it open, she slipped inside.

Instantly the smell of horses and hay assailed her, the mingled odours familiar and comforting. Nell felt her heartbeat slow. She hadn't realised how nervous she'd been, but when she groped on the shelf next to the door for the candle and flint she had left there earlier in the day, she noticed that her hands were trembling slightly. Taking a steadying breath, she lit the candle and held it aloft, glancing around as though to reassure herself that the stable was, indeed, the safe haven she had often used during the past years.

The long corridor stretched ahead of her, disappear-ing into darkness beyond the light of the small candle-

flame. Stalls were ranged on either side. Tonight most
were occupied, but only the occasional shuffle or sleepy
whicker disturbed the stillness as Nell glided quietly
down the passage. She passed the big main doors and
stopped at a stall a short distance further on. The little
palfrey within lifted her head and blew gently in
greeting.

Nell searched in the pocket of her gown for the apple
she had brought as a farewell gift. 'Here, Chevette, is
this what you're waiting for?'

At the sound of her voice, large hooves stamped
angrily at the far end of the stable and there was a loud
thud. Nell glanced that way to assure herself that her
uncle's stallion was securely locked up. The horse was
a brute, bad-tempered and dangerous, unusually nervous of open spaces, and possessed of a marked dislike
for the human race, particularly women. It occupied
the only stall fitted with a door, because if it saw
daylight between itself and an object of dislike, it
tended to charge. More than one stableboy had been
savagely attacked by the animal.

'If Tom is planning to ride that seed of Satan
tomorrow, we're going to have a merry time of it,' Nell
muttered, peering uneasily into the shadows. She
couldn't be sure, but the door at the end of the corridor
seemed to shift. As if someone had just closed it and
she had caught the last few inches of movement from
the corner of her eye.

'Idiot,' she told herself bracingly. 'You're imagining
things.' The door led only to the storeroom, the outer
door of which was always kept locked. No one would
be in there at this late hour.

Still mentally chastising herself for her nervousness,
she ducked under the rope across the front of
Chevette's stall while the mare was placidly munching

her apple, and crouched down before the wooden manger. It was the work of seconds to reach under it and run her fingers along the space between the manger and the wall until they slipped into the rough hollow she had slowly and painfully gouged in the wood three years ago.

The crucifix hidden within fell into her hand with an almost soundless whisper of its gold and ruby chain.

With only the briefest glance at the precious object, Nell lifted the hem of her gown, fumbling for the pouch she had tied around her waist. It was awkward with her other hand holding the candle, but she didn't dare set the light down while she was in Chevette's stall. Only when the crucifix was safely out of sight again did she rise and duck back under the rope. Her heart was racing again, but this time with elation. She had done it. Now it wouldn't matter if anyone saw the faint light in the stable—an unlikely event in any case, since the windows were small and high. She could relax and turn her attention to her other reason for being here.

She reached out to stroke Chevette's cream-coloured velvety muzzle and was rewarded with an affectionate shove. 'So, this is farewell, little friend. I wish you could carry me home, but 'twill be a long journey over rough country and you're far too delicate a lady to—'

This time the movement of a door was unmistakable. Nell's breath caught as a ripple of cold air brushed her face and made the candlelight flicker wildly. A small click sounded in the darkness, but not from the direction of the storeroom. She whirled at once to face back the way she had come, cursing the blackness that made it impossible to see more than a few feet beyond her meagre light.

There was absolute silence—but she was being

watched. There was a presence. She could feel it. Her skin prickled all over with the primitive awareness of danger.

'Tom. . .? Edmund. . .? If that is one of you playing some stupid trick, I swear I'll throw this bucket of water over you.'

Keeping her gaze fixed on the shadows, she reached under the rope again, her free hand groping for Chevette's drinking pail. The waiting stillness was nerve-wracking. She didn't know who to expect to emerge from the darkness. Edmund seeking revenge for her earlier interference? Tom intending to force his attentions on her?

Or worse! Nell's stomach clenched as she remembered Tom's words before she'd left him in the middle of their dance. She had assumed his subsequent absence meant he was indulging himself with some other woman, but had he seen her enter the stable? Had he decided to force her into a position where she would have no choice but to marry him? Merciful saints, would be actually rape her? Was he capable of it? The questions raced through Nell's mind, freezing her in her half-crouched position. Tom was capable of the act, aye. But did he have the wit for such rapid planning? Sweet Lord, where was the pail?

'A wasted gesture, my lady. I can split you where you stand before your hand even reaches that useless weapon.'

Nell straightened slowly as a man appeared at the edge of the circle of light cast by her candle. She didn't know him. Another stranger, she thought inconsequentially. But though the man's features were unknown to her, and hazy in the dim light, the dagger in his hand was terrifyingly distinct. Her frightened gaze dropped to the weapon and she took an instinctive step back. 'Who are you?' she whispered. 'What do you want?'

The man only smiled in answer and moved forward a pace. He made a small, sharp gesture with the knife, and light shimmered over the long blade as though caressing it. Nell edged away again. Somewhere in the back of her mind she was aware of movement as the horses in the nearby stalls shifted nervously, sensing something amiss, but she continued to retreat, watching the blade as if mesmerised. The man matched her, step for step, still not speaking.

His silence was more frightening to her than all the rest. There was a cold inevitability about it that was chilling; as though he had no doubt as to the outcome of their slow progression. She had to think! She had to get away somehow. The storeroom! If she could just reach the storeroom. . .hide in the darkness. . .unlock the outer door. . .

A series of angry snorts and the crashing of hooves sounded behind her and Nell glanced back involuntarily. She was almost there. She was going to escape. A shivery sense of anticipation raced through her. The man could surely see what she intended, but he was making no attempt to stop her. Perhaps he was only intent on stealing a horse. A few more steps and she would be able to reach back and——

The stallion's stall was open!

Nell froze, unable to believe that she was seeing dark space where there should have been a solid oak door. A faint glimpse of movement inside the stall convinced her. When had it happened? she wondered dimly, her gaze whipping back to face her attacker. How? Why hadn't the horse bolted out of its stall? Was it waiting for her? Holy Mother of God, she had to stop this. She had to move. But her feet felt as if they were nailed to the floor. . .her legs were shaking. . .she felt sick. . .

'Keep going, my lady.' The man's voice was soft in the silence. He was smiling.

Did he know she was trapped? Where could she go? Forward to certain death at the hands of a thief? Backwards to be trampled beneath the hooves of an enraged stallion? For the horse would surely charge as soon as she drew level with the stall.

'Please, if you'll just go. . . I won't say anything. . . I won't tell anyone. . .'

'Tell them what, my lady?'

'I don't know.' She made a helpless little gesture towards the stallion. 'But. . .'

'You think I came for the horse? You're easier to deal with than that brute. Aye, I know you don't want to pass him but you will, my lady.' He smiled again. 'You will.'

'I don't understand,' she whispered. 'Who. . .? Why. . .?'

He laughed softly, almost as though humouring her, and opened his mouth to speak. Nothing came out. An expression of stunned amazement filled his eyes. They stared into hers a moment longer, glazed and glaring, then he pitched forward to land face-down at her feet. The jewelled hilt of a dagger protruded from his back, straight over the heart.

'Don't move,' said Beaudene quietly from the shadows halfway down the passage. 'And don't make a sound.'

Nell was quite incapable of movement. Or of speech. As one in a daze she watched Beaudene come forward and step over the body, as if it were a bundle of rags that someone had carelessly left lying there. He passed her without even a glance and slowly approached the stallion's stall.

'Easy,' she heard him say, his voice very low. 'Easy, boy.' The murmured words continued until the stallion's snorts and stamping hooves gradually became muffled as the stall door swung closed. Beaudene moved back into the corridor, tucking something into his surcoat.

'Unusual to find a horse who feels more secure in a confined space,' he muttered, as he fastened the latch and strode back to her.

The words seemed to be spoken more to himself than to her, Nell thought, but for some reason she felt compelled to answer. 'Some of the grooms. . .think he may have been attacked out in the open. . .as a colt,' she said faintly. 'Fired upon from a distance, where he couldn't see. . .' Her voice trailed off. Why, in the name of all the saints, was she having this stupid conversation about a horse when she was standing here with a corpse at her feet? Had fear laid waste her wits?

Her rescuer appeared to be totally unmoved by the situation. He stepped past her, took the candle from her limp grasp and went down on one knee beside the body. Nell had to avert her gaze when his hand went to the dagger. She swallowed hard, not daring to ask any questions until she had her stomach under control. When she forced herself to look down again, Beaudene had turned the man over and was staring at his face. His own expression was grim.

'How——?' she began shakily.

'Quiet!'

The curt order succeeded in jolting her out of her shock-induced state. 'What do you me——?'

'Shut up!' Beaudene rose, flashed her one savage look that raked her from head to toe, and grabbed her arm. 'Unless you want to rouse everyone in the place, we'll talk away from that stallion before he kicks his stall to pieces.'

'Oh, pardon me for wanting to know what's going on,' she snapped beneath her breath. 'How very inconsiderate of me.' The anger felt wonderful, Nell discovered. She was actually beginning to feel some warmth creeping back into her body. 'Are you just going to leave that. . .it. . .him. . .there?' she demanded as Beaudene propelled her down the passage. Chevette's head poked over the rope as they passed, her face looking enquiringly after them.

'I'll deal with it later.' Beaudene came to a halt near the door and swung Nell around to face him. He wasn't gentle about it, nor did he relinquish his hold. 'But before I do, you, madam, have some questions to answer. Our friend over there obviously knew you use this place for your assignations, so we'd better get your lover out of the way first. Who did you come here to meet, and where the hell is he?'

Belatedly, Nell realised that her new bodyguard wasn't quite as unmoved as she had thought. He was keeping his voice low from necessity, but it was clear that he was blazingly angry. Instead of offering a few kind words of comfort, he was questioning her as if *she* was the felon. 'How do you know it wasn't him?' she flared, gesturing wildly in the direction of the corpse.

His fingers tightened so painfully that Nell gasped. He released her arm as if she had burned him.

'Don't play your games with me, my lady. You may be wanton, but you're not stupid enough to arrange a tryst with your own murderer.'

'Mur——' The tide of rage washed out of Nell in a rush, leaving her weak and shaking. 'What do you mean? He was trying to steal my uncle's stallion. I must have disturbed him. The stall was open. . .and the storeroom. I saw the door move, but thought I'd imagined it.'

'And then he went to the trouble of letting himself out of the storeroom so he could come back through this door and continue his theft while you were still here? Don't be such an idiot!'

There was one thing to be said for his insults, Nell reflected. They stopped her from falling apart.

'Why would he want to kill me?' she demanded angrily. 'I didn't even know the man. He was probably going to force me into the storeroom and lock me in, but I knew if that stupid horse saw me it would——'

'He knew that too, you little fool! Weren't you listening to him? Sweet Jesu!'

Rafe turned away from the stunned look in her eyes and shoved his free hand through his hair. He knew he shouldn't have said anything, but he'd had to shut her up before she described a picture that was already sickeningly clear in his mind—a picture of soft, fragile woman beneath the hooves of half a ton of enraged stallion. Damn it, he had to stop thinking of her as soft and female and desirable, and figure out what the hell was going on here.

'I don't remember,' she stammered. He looked back at her sharply, hearing real confusion in her voice. 'At first I thought he was——'

'Ah, yes, your lover. How soon can we expect him?'

Her eyes darkened with such fury that for a moment Rafe thought she was going to hit him. He half hoped she would try it so he could have the pleasure of subduing her. Something told him it would go a long way towards relieving his feelings.

'Well?'

'I did not come out here to meet a lover!' Her voice

was shaking with rage, but every word was enunciated
with great precision. 'I came out here to say goodbye
to my *horse*!'

She flung out her hand on the last word, drawing his
gaze down the line of stalls to the palfrey looking back
at them. The little mare's expression was so thoroughly
disapproving and indignant that, despite the rage burning fiercely inside him, Rafe nearly laughed. The
damned horse looked as if she knew exactly what was
being said and that if he knew what was good for him,
he'd better believe it.

'All right,' he allowed, smiling reluctantly. He
wanted to hang on to his anger, damn it. At the
moment it was the least dangerous of the emotions
rampaging through him. 'I suppose I'll have to believe
you, since she's telling the same story.'

'Don't fall into a seizure from the effort,' Nell
muttered, but she was uncomfortably aware that the
retort didn't have quite the force she'd intended.
Beaudene's brief flash of humour had taken her completely by surprise. She hadn't thought him capable of
humour, never mind that his wry smile, fleeting though
it had been, had done something very strange to her
insides. The quietness of the stable seemed to close in
around her suddenly, making her conscious of the
lateness of the hour and how alone they were.

'Well, I suppose. . .' She glanced down the passage,
thankful that the body lay in the shadowy darkness. 'I
suppose we should call the guards. Not that they'll be
particularly surprised.' A small laugh escaped her and
she began edging towards the door, knowing she was
babbling but unable to stop. ''Tis all of a piece with
everything else that's been happening to me lately.'

The humour vanished from Beaudene's face as
though it had never been. His eyes narrowed on her

retreating figure and he put the candle down on the shelf with a care that was ominously deliberate. 'What has been happening to you lately?' he asked, in a tone so dangerously soft that Nell halted in mid-step.

'Nothing important,' she said, sending him a swift, nervous glance. 'Just. . .accidents. Little things. Stupid things, really. I wasn't even hurt.' She slid one foot sideways.

Beaudene reached out, clamped both hands around her shoulders and yanked her back so forcefully that Nell had to put her hands against his chest to stop herself colliding with him. Her startled cry was lost beneath the suppressed rage in his voice.

'Accidents have been happening to you, and you still came out here alone, in the middle of the night, just to say goodbye to your horse? Holy Mother of God! Did I say you weren't stupid? I take it back!'

'I am not stupid,' she protested breathlessly, trying to push herself away. 'How was I to know there would be a thief out here? We've never had one before.' She thought briefly of the hidden pouch hanging from her waist, then shoved the image out of her mind.

'He wasn't a thief, you little idiot!' He shook her hard. 'He was an assassin, God damn it! A hired thug——' she was shaken again '—and you go and make his task a whole lot easier by traipsing around as if 'tis broad daylight, in a costume expressly designed to upset a horse that already hates females!'

'How do you know he hates females?' she asked weakly, and immediately winced at the look of impatience that crossed his face.

'One of the grooms was at great pains to tell me the details when I noticed the animal earlier. Now, shall we see if you're capable of intelligent answers as well as stupid questions? Talk!'

Talk? How could she talk when her head was beginning to spin? Heat swirled around her, heat from his eyes, from his hands, from the closeness of his powerful body. Heat that scorched, and yet lured, as flame lured a moth to its own destruction. Again, Nell tried to free herself. It was impossible; the heat and power of his body simply overwhelmed her, sapping her will, making a mockery of her efforts. 'When you take your hands off me,' she managed, desperate enough to plead.

He released her. 'They're off.'

It didn't help. She could hardly think, let alone talk. One moment she had been feeling almost grateful—after all, he had saved her from injury or worse, even if she hadn't acknowledged it—but now. . . Tiny shivers were racing through her, following each other so rapidly she was sure her trembling must be visible. She had thought she knew every danger a woman faced with a man, but there was a new danger here. Something beyond her knowledge. A threat without name. A threat she had never before encountered.

'Start with the first accident,' he ordered, snapping her out of her daze. 'When did it happen?'

'A. . .a few days after my father's letter arrived,' Nell stammered, forcing her brain to some sort of coherent thought. 'We were hawking, and something startled my horse. She reared and I fell, but 'twas nothing. I wasn't hurt, not even bruised.'

'And then?'

'Then. . . I think. . . Aye, 'twas the pennant in the hall. The standards hanging over the minstrels' gallery. One of the lances came loose and fell on me. Then, the day after that, I was locked in with the mastiffs. They hadn't been fed because my uncle intended to hunt wild boar the next day, but——'

'God's blood! And you didn't suspect anything?'

'Suspect what?' she cried. 'Nothing happened. The mistake was discovered almost immediately and I was freed.'

He ignored that. 'So, 'tis obvious the dogs failed to make a meal of you. Were there any more so-called accidents after that?'

'Well, there was the arrow that just missed me when we were shooting at the butts, and then the broth. And today my gown, but noth——'

'Aye, nothing happened. We'll argue about it later. I hope you've said all your farewells here, my lady, because we're about to leave.'

Nell gaped at him, certain she hadn't heard aright. 'Leave? *Now*?' Her voice soared.

'That's what I said. Which horse were you going to ride tomorrow?'

'Rufus, but——'

'The chestnut next to your palfrey?' His gaze followed the direction of hers. 'Good. He looks strong. Where's your saddle?'

'Where's my——? Have you lost your senses?' she demanded, finally recovering from her stupefaction at this abrupt turn of events. Leave? Ride off into the middle of the night? *With him*? She wasn't that mad. 'You can't expect me to leave just like that,' she spluttered. 'Without telling anyone, without any baggage, without——'

She broke off, realising that Beaudene was taking not the slightest notice of her protests. He stepped into one of the stalls and led out a powerful-looking bay with a black mane and tail. The horse stood quietly while its bridle was fastened and the blanket smoothed into place. Beaudene reached for the heavy saddle resting atop the side wall of the stall, lifting it with easy

strength and laying it lightly across the horse's back.
Two leather bags followed. Not until he had tested the
straps and saddle-girth did he turn back to Nell and
raise an imperative brow.

'Will you listen to me?' Nell commanded, stamping
her foot in frustration. 'This is to act without reason!
What about my baggage? I don't even have a mantle.'
Her voice rose to a note that was perilously close to a
wail.

'Then you'll just have to make do with that gown
you're almost wearing,' he retorted with a distinct lack
of gallantry. 'Unless you can tell me which of those
chests stacked outside your room holds your mantles.'

Nell stared at him in dismay.

'No, of course you can't. You probably didn't even
direct you own packing. Ornamentation and coquetting
is about all you're good for, isn't it, my lady?'

'There's a mantle in my chamber,' Nell said through
her teeth. 'I could fetch that, if you insist on pursuing
this madness.'

'I'm not letting you out of my sight, and if we both
return to your chamber what we'd fetch would be a
heap of trouble. As well ask the town crier to proclaim
our departure.'

'As well depart tomorrow morning, with an escort,
like civilised beings,' Nell shot back. 'There's no reason
to creep away like thieves in the night, and if you
think——'

'There's every reason, you little fool,' he cut in
brutally. 'We're going to be travelling for several days,
and I can't watch you, and your cousin, and a round
dozen of his men, every mile of the way, all day and
night. We'll be safer alone.'

'In your opinion,' she scorned. 'Why should I listen

to you? Tom wants to marry me, not kill me. I'm not much use to him dead.'

'I haven't got time to argue with you,' Beaudene dismissed. 'We're leaving as soon as I stow our friend in the storeroom. By the time he's discovered, we should have several hours' start.'

'Oh, wonderful! You expect my uncle to come after us? That should put him in a festive mood. I'll probably have a beating to look forward to. Well, you might have saved me from injury, Sir Rafe, or whatever your name is, but I don't have to obey your orders. I'm not going as far as the gatehouse with you, let alone——'

The tirade was abruptly cut off when Beaudene took a menacing step forward and captured her face in one large hand. His golden eyes blazed down into hers, fierce and implacable. 'If you want to live, my lady,' he said very softly, 'you'll shut up and do exactly as I say. If I say we're leaving tonight, that's precisely when we leave. If I say ride hard, you'll ride harder than you've ever ridden in your cossetted, useless life. If I say walk, you'll walk. If I say crawl on your hands and knees, you'll damn well crawl on your hands and knees. Do you understand me?'

Nell was trembling by the time he'd finished, but it wasn't in fear of Beaudene. At least, she didn't think it was. His forceful insistence that they flee her family, his arrogant confidence that he was right, shook her more than she cared to admit. What if she was wrong? What if the slashed gown was the only piece of spite Margaret had indulged in, and the other incidents real attempts on her life?

It came down to a simple choice, she told herself. She either travelled with Tom and his henchmen, who would obey any order her cousin saw fit to give them, or she accepted Beaudene's protection—the protection of a man she had known only a matter of hours.

'Let me make the decision easy for you,' he continued, obviously losing patience with her long silence. 'You can co-operate, my lady, or I can knock you senseless, tie you hand and foot, and take you out of here slung over your horse like a slaughtered deer.'

'Is that supposed to reassure me?' Nell muttered. Then cried out as he released her and drew back his fist. 'All right!' She only just managed to stop herself flinching away. 'I'll go with you.'

'Do I have your word on that? You won't try anything stupid? You'll obey my every order?'

'Aye.' She almost flung the word at him. 'You don't have to keep threatening me.'

The fist lowered. Nell's wary gaze followed it. Not until Beaudene's fingers uncurled did she lift her eyes to his face. With the candlelight shining directly below it, his scar stood out in harsh relief, a stark relic of violence.

'You really would have hit me,' she whispered, 'wouldn't you.' It wasn't a question.

'Just remember that whenever you're tempted to try your hand at rebellion,' he said curtly. 'Now, come and help me with this corpse.'

Nell swallowed as the candle was shoved into her hand. 'Can't you just leave him here?'

'For the stableboys to trip over at dawn?' He sent her a withering glance. 'Eventually they'll notice the horses are missing, but we'll need every minute of advantage we can get. Don't look if you're squeamish. And for God's sake, keep your mouth shut when we go past that stallion.'

Turning his back on her, he strode down the corridor and picked up her erstwhile attacker. The effortless way he handled the body of a man almost as big as himself gave Nell a daunting idea of his strength. She gritted her teeth and followed, making a wide detour around the patch of blood-stained straw. She was not going to be sick, she told herself with fierce determination. She would act as if moving corpses was as commonplace to her as it apparently was to Beaudene.

They reached the storeroom door and he jerked his head, indicating that she should open it. Nell obeyed, hating him. He knew what she was feeling when her gown brushed the limp form in passing, but there was not so much as a flicker of sympathy or kindness in those hard amber eyes. He dropped the body behind a large barrel and kicked some straw over it. Then he motioned her to hold the light higher while he examined the harness stored to one side of the room.

'That's not it,' Nell objected, when she saw what he had selected. The saddle in his hands looked large enough to fit three of her. She'd never stay in it. He stalked out of the storeroom without answering, forcing Nell to hurry after him. 'Don't you ever listen to anyone?' she demanded in a furious whisper as he unhooked the rope from Rufus's stall and began murmuring reassuringly to the horse.

'Don't you ever stop complaining?' he countered in the same low, angry tone. 'We're not going on a bloody picnic along the river. For a journey like this a side-saddle is not only uncomfortable but damned dangerous. Now, just for once in your life, you can do something useful and throw some straw over that blood.'

He expected her to refuse. She could see it in the mocking challenge in his eyes, the arrogant tilt to his head. Nell tipped her own chin up and wheeled about. She'd defy him to find even one drop of blood when she was finished, she vowed passionately, kicking furiously at the straw. A nervous grumble from the stallion's stall had her going about the business more quietly.

Males! Human or equine, they were all the same. Dangerous, threatening and violent. Using intimidation to get their own way. Clearly there was no justice in a world where a woman needed one of the brutes to protect her from all the rest.

'Are you done?' Beaudene took the candle from her and cast an all-seeing eye over the straw-covered floor. 'Go and wait by the horses, but stay clear of Samson.'

Don't bother telling me I did a good job, Nell fumed silently, sending a rebellious glare after Beaudene as he replaced the candle on its shelf. She took a few steps after him and found herself trading stares with the huge bay. 'Samson,' she murmured, hoping the animal wouldn't take it into his head to move. One well-aimed kick from those big hooves and she'd be as insensible as even Beaudene could wish.

'You can forget the charm.' The hard words came from somewhere in the shadows. 'You won't find Samson as susceptible as his namesake.'

'Especially if he takes after his master,' Nell muttered beneath her breath. She would have liked to have said the words loud, but didn't quite have the courage. Instead, she looked across at Chevette, still watching the proceedings with interest, and impulsively crossed the passage to put her arms about the mare's neck. At that moment it seemed the little horse was her only ally, her only comfort in a world that was suddenly full of danger. Her throat tightened convulsively on a wave of emotion.

'Farewell, little friend,' she whispered, pressing her

cheek hard against the palfrey's mane to stifle the tears
that sprang into her eyes. 'Be safe.'

Uncomfortably aware of Beaudene's presence, Nell
waited until she was sure all traces of tears had been
blinked away before stepping back. She needn't have
worried. At the same moment the stable was plunged
into total darkness.

'Don't panic,' he said, right beside her. Nell felt his
hands circle her waist. He turned her towards the
horses.

'What are you doing?' she quavered, unnerved all
over again by his closeness in the impenetrable blackness surrounding them. She had thought dancing with
him made her feel small and vulnerable, but this—
standing alone with him in the dark—was ten times
worse. With the loss of sight, every other sense became
almost painfully acute. Her heart thundered in her
ears; with every ragged breath she drew she inhaled
the scents of man and horse, and his hands. . .so hard
and warm and strong. She trembled in his grasp,
wanting to escape that overwhelming strength and yet
fascinated by it, intrigued, wanting——

Horrified, Nell barely heard the small sound of shock
that escaped her dry lips.

'I'm just going to lift you on to your horse.' His
voice, soft and deep, rasped over her taut nerves. 'Can
you reach the reins?'

For a moment Nell didn't think she could move.
Then, slowly, she forced her arms upward, groping for
the reins with one hand and the saddle with the other.
The position made her feel even more defenceless.
When Beaudene spread his fingers wider and tightened
his hold she shivered violently and almost cried out.

'For God's sake, relax,' he snarled in her ear. 'I'm

not going to drop you.' An instant later he lifted her into the air with breathtaking ease.

Nell didn't know if it was instinct or desperation to have his hands off her that had her swinging her leg over the saddle, but, whatever it was, she found herself atop Rufus's back, shaken but secure.

'Are the stirrups all right?' His hand went to her ankle.

She immediately put her weight on her left foot, knowing that, to Beaudene, it would feel firmly in place. 'They're perfect,' she got out, only then realising that she hadn't taken a breath for what seemed like hours. The stirrups were far from perfect, but if he touched her again Nell knew she would probably fall right off the horse.

He moved away and she went limp with relief, grateful now for the lack of light. If he had seen the way she was blushing and trembling, her humiliation would have been complete.

A second later a faint lightening of the gloom told her he'd opened one of the big double doors.

'I'm going to lead the horses out through the postern,' he said barely above a whisper. 'Once we're in the woods we'll be away clear. Until then, not a sound.'

Apparently taking her obedience for granted, he led the horses through the narrow opening, turned back momentarily to close the door, then faded into the shadows against the bailey wall, leading Samson. Rufus followed the other horse instinctively, their hoofbeats muffled in the long grass.

They were going to get away with it, Nell realised, as the postern gate loomed up beside her. It was locked, but that little circumstance presented no problems to Beaudene. And there were no guards posted here. Why would there be when, with the final destruction of Lancastrian hopes, there was no longer any danger of siege? The gate closed behind them as soundlessly as the stable door. A few minutes later, the dark of night gave way to the deeper blackness of the woods.

'We'll keep to the trees for a mile or so than rejoin the road,' Beaudene said quietly as he mounted. 'Stay close by me, Lady Eleanor. 'Tis easy to become lost without moonlight, and if I'm put to the trouble of searching for you, you'll find that saddle damned uncomfortable to sit in for the next few days.'

Nell didn't bother to answer. Maybe she was becoming immune to his threats, she thought broodingly. Or maybe there were too many other things for her to worry about, like deciding whether she was relieved or apprehensive that no one had noticed their escape.

The question was still occupying her mind when the rain started again.

CHAPTER THREE

THREE hours passed in a silence broken only by the sounds of rain and swiftly travelling horses. Rafe told himself he should be grateful that he wasn't having to listen to a barrage of complaints, but some perverse whim made him want to goad his charge out of her sulks. Fortunately, disgust at his own contrariness kept him quiet. She was a duty, an obligation, nothing more.

He grimaced into the darkness. He might be annoyingly perverse where Lady Eleanor fitzWarren was concerned, but he hadn't started lying to himself. He had no obligation to her, and even less to her father. There were other reasons why he was riding along a dark road on a filthy night when he could be in a warm bed catching up on some overdue sleep. And, of course, the scene he'd walked into in the stable could hardly have been ignored, even if the little idiot had brought the danger on herself.

Rafe frowned and cast a glance at his silent companion. She had dropped back a little, but not enough to draw a comment from him. Had she really considered all those incidents she'd described to be genuine accidents? Taken alone, such a conclusion might be excusable, but together? She would have to be a complete innocent, or a simpleton, and he had already decided that Lady Eleanor fitzWarren was neither of those things.

The irony of the situation caused a grim smile to twist his mouth. The fact that she was neither innocent nor simple made everything very straightforward or very complicated, depending on which way you looked at it. And if he had any sense at all, he'd look at it the way he usually faced his problems. Head-on.

He wanted her. Badly. Despite everything else.

Or perhaps as well as everything else.

He hadn't expected it. He most definitely did not like it. But he couldn't ignore the fierce surge of desire she aroused in him whenever they touched. Touched! God, it seemed he only had to be near her.

The memory of the soft fragility of her body between his hands when he'd held her in the darkness of the stable had his fingers clenching on the reins. Only the need to get her away had stopped him sliding his hands higher, until he could close them over the sweetly rounded breasts half-exposed by her gown. A sight that had tormented him since he'd first seen her in the hall, weaving her spells. Definitely no innocent.

And she didn't want marriage.

So why not take her? And, in the process, he could even take what else was owing to him. The perfect revenge, he thought with a cold, silent laugh. Take from the daughter what the father had cheated him out of years ago. Take and give nothing in return, except the payment expected by a courtesan for the use of her body. Set her up in her chosen vocation. A swift, savage grin slashed across his face at the idea. She wanted to be a mistress rather than a wife? Then, why not make it so? And don't think about the rest of it.

Nell didn't want to think at all. Unfortunately, her mind wouldn't co-operate with her inclinations. Strange images kept dancing in her brain, making her wonder if she was becoming delirious from the cold and wet.

Wasn't hell supposed to be a fiery place of torment,

where demons persecuted their victims with pitchforks? After hours of hard riding, Nell knew better. Hell was a dark, endless tunnel through a forest of moaning, rustling spectres, whose weapons were stinging needles of rain. It was chafed, aching thighs whose cramped muscles had to grip the saddle with no respite because the stirrups were too low to support some of her weight. And it was a confused, frightened mind that was beginning to question the wisdom of trusting Beaudene.

What sort of bodyguard forced a lady to travel in these appalling conditions, just because *he* said she was in danger? Why was she supposed to take *his* word for everything? What would he say if she accused *him* of trying to kill her, rather than Tom? Because at this rate she would be dead of lung fever before her supposedly murderous cousin crawled from his warm, comfortable bed in the morning.

Nell shivered violently as a sudden gust of wind whipped at an overhanging branch, spraying water all over her. Not that it mattered. She was already soaked to the skin. Her full skirts, with their ermine edging, felt like dead weights hanging from her waist, the same fur trim around her bodice was plastered to her chilled flesh, her headdress dragged at its pins, making her head throb, and the pretty silver tissue veil was a sodden rag that slapped against her neck with every movement of her horse.

Even if she survived this hideous nightmare, what was she supposed to change into when the rain stopped? If it ever did. She had nothing but what she stood up in. No clothes. No maid. No——

Her maid! Mother of God, why hadn't she thought of that before? She wouldn't have been alone with Tom and his men. Lucy would have travelled with her and they'd intended to sleep at religious hostels or respectable inns along the way. Instead, she was completely at the mercy of a man who was bigger than her, stronger than her, who had already threatened her with violence, who had killed a man without a single question or qualm, who—

The list stopped abruptly as Nell's heart jolted sickeningly in her chest. Other pictures flashed through her mind. Pictures that chilled the blood in her veins even as the rain chilled her flesh. She had seen no one speak to Beaudene in the hall before she'd collided with him. She had not seen her aunt or uncle acknowledge him. He had simply appeared. She knew nothing about him—except that he was arrogant, ruthless, that he killed without any sign of emotion, and considered her a loose woman.

And, God have mercy on her, she only had Beaudene's word that he had come from her father!

That last frightening realisation had Nell tugging frantically on the reins. She was not going another inch until she got some answers. And if she didn't like those answers, she would run. Away from the road where the darkness would hide her. Even a night in the forest would be preferable to stepping into the terrifying pit of danger yawning at her feet.

As if he knew the instant she stopped and why, Beaudene reined in and wheeled his horse about in the same motion. His voice was a whiplash, cracking with command. 'We ride until I say stop, my lady, and that isn't here or now.'

Nell leaned forward over the saddle, trying to ease her aching thighs. 'Please,' she whispered, her cold lips scarcely able to form the words, 'I need to alter the stirrups.'

She didn't care that he would know she'd been lying

earlier. She didn't care if she begged. She had to get off the horse.

After an almost imperceptible pause, Beaudene nodded and dismounted. 'A few minutes, no more,' he said.

Nell didn't wait for him to offer any assistance. Letting herself fall against Rufus's neck, she forced her leg over the saddle and slid to the ground. Her legs almost gave way under her when she landed.

Tears of pain and weariness burned her eyes. How was she going to run away? She could barely stand. Her legs ached and quivered with strain, and the soft flesh of her inner thighs was sore and burning from contact with the hard leather of her saddle. She let her weight rest against Rufus for a moment, trying to gather enough strength to move, but the wind snatched at her veil, slapping it against the horse's flank. Rufus snorted and shied away in alarm, nearly pulling her off her feet.

'For God's sake!' Beaudene grabbed the horse's bridle with one hand and Nell with the other, while she made a futile attempt to control the veil, which had now wrapped itself soggily around her throat. 'Get rid of the bloody thing, unless you want to travel the rest of the way on foot.'

'Rufus isn't nervous,' Nell muttered. 'It just startled him for a moment. He's used to more elaborate headdresses than this.'

'Nobody could get used to such a piece of useless idiocy,' Beaudene growled, tying the reins to a tree. He came back to Nell and started pulling pins out of her hair. In the fitful moonlight that had emerged to chase the clouds across the sky, she could see the narrowed glitter of his eyes and the hard, set line of his mouth. The combination was enough to keep her from protesting, until he ripped the veil from its moorings and tossed the limp remains of her headdress into a pile of leaves.

'What do you think you're doing?' she demanded, lifting her hands to stop her hair from tumbling over her shoulders. 'I can't ride with my hair blowing every which way.'

'Turn around.'

'Not until I know——'

'*Turn around*!'

Nell turned. She felt Beaudene's hands wring some of the wetness out of her hair, then he gathered the heavy tresses into a thick fall and used the length of silver tissue to tie it at the nape of her neck. Nell tried not to feel grateful. The relief to her aching head was wonderful, but that was no reason to trust him. An action prompted more by practicality than kindness didn't furnish any proof of Beaudene's story.

'What's amiss with your stirrups?' he asked curtly as he stepped away.

'They need to be raised a notch.' Nell stayed where she was, keeping some distance between them. Now, she told herself. Ask your questions now. But she wasn't quite sure where to start. With her father? With Beaudene's arrival? With his insistence that she was in danger from the relatives who had housed, fed and clothed her for ten years? Perhaps she should just vanish into the darkness without worrying about questions to which she might or might not receive truthful answers.

'You'll get chilled standing there,' he said over his shoulder, before she could decide. 'Walk around a bit. Keep warm.'

'I wasn't warm to start with,' she retorted. But she began walking up and down, stumbling at first when her stiff muscles protested at the exercise. Unfortunately her brain wasn't recovering as easily. All she seemed able to think about was how cold and wet and miserable she was.

'You'll live,' was Beaudene's unsympathetic response. ''Tis September. You're not likely to freeze to death because of a few drops of rain.'

Nell stopped her pacing and glared at him. 'It's been raining for hours,' she pointed out, ignoring the fact that the rain had now stopped. 'That's more than a few drops.'

Beaudene walked around to Rufus's other side. 'Well, if we reach the place I have in mind before dawn, we'll be able to light a fire. I've a mantle in my pack you can wear while your gown is drying.'

The deeper implications in this statement went right over Nell's head for the moment. 'You mean you've had a mantle in your pack all this time, and you made me ride through that downpour until I was wet to the skin?' she cried in outrage. 'How could you?'

'It was amazingly easy,' he purred, coming around Rufus to stalk towards her. There was so much menace in his slow advance that Nell started to retreat. 'I decided you'd prefer to have something dry to wear when you have to strip off that gown, but if you'd rather run around stark naked, my lady, I can——'

'I wouldn't,' said Nell hurriedly. She backed into a tree and had to stop.

Beaudene didn't even hesitate. He kept walking until he was looming right over her, crowding her against the tree and forcing her to tip her head right back so she could still glare at him.

'You're trying to frighten me,' she accused. *Trying*! He was succeeding. She could hardly breathe with the way her heart was beating in her throat, but she would die before she humiliated herself by letting Beaudene know the effect his nearness was having on her. 'But it won't work. I don't frighten easily.'

His teeth gleamed in a brief, dangerous smile. 'You don't back down, either. I'll say that for you, my lady. Not even when you were facing that knife.'

'Backing down wouldn't have saved me then, any more than it will now.'

He leaned one hand against the tree beside her head and his voice lowered to a lazy growl. 'Now? Judging by the way you're walking, I'd say you've been punished already for lying to me about those stirrups. What more do you think I'm going to do to you?'

Nell shivered. 'How can I answer that? I don't know anything about you.'

'That's true, but 'tis no cause for alarm. You'll have plenty of time to learn.' His free hand lifted to brush back a damp tendril of hair that had escaped his earlier ministrations. 'I think we'll both learn something over the next few days.'

'What I want to know will only take the next few minutes,' she choked out through suddenly dry lips. She had the strangest feeling they were having two separate conversations, one of which was somewhere beyond her comprehension.

'Minutes? Have all the men in your life rushed you, little temptress? Do you tease and tantalise until they're so wild to have you, they care nothing for your pleasure? Is that how you control them?'

'What has that to do with anything?' Nell cried, thoroughly confused. She forced the next words out in a breathless rush before she lost her courage. 'All I know is that you appeared in the stables at a very opportune time, killed a man without bothering to ask him why he was there, and dragged me away from my family. And I want to know why.'

Beaudene drew back a little. In the intermittent moonlight Nell could see that the faintly mocking smile on his face had been replaced by a frown. 'You know why.'

'No, I don't,' she denied heatedly. 'You said you came from my father, but how do I know that? And that man. . . You *killed* him! You just killed him as if it meant nothing.'

'Would you rather he'd killed you, while I stood there debating the issue with my conscience?'

'That isn't what I. . . How can you be so sure he was a hired assassin? How—?'

'Because I knew him, damn it!'

Nell went very, very still. 'You knew him?'

'God's blood! We don't have time for this.' His long fingers closed around her arm. 'You can trust me or not, as you please, Lady Eleanor, but you're getting back on that horse.'

'Or what? You'll knock me senseless?' Nell heard the rising note of hysteria shatter the night-time quiet, but couldn't control it. Every nerve was screaming a warning at her. She was in danger from this man. If she knew nothing else, that fact was absolutely certain. 'How do I know that's not what you intend doing at some other time? How do I know you didn't plan all this. . .that you. . .that you didn't hire that man yourself so you could frighten me into going with you?'

The annoyance in his eyes exploded into searing rage. 'My God, if I hadn't promised the King I'd see you safe home, I'd damn well leave you to your cousin's mercies.'

'The King?' she stammered. 'What——?'

'Shut up, or, by God, I *will* knock you senseless.

Now, move!' He jerked her away from the tree as he spoke.

Nell screamed as pain shot across the back of her head. The sound pulled Beaudene up short.

'What the——?'

'My hair,' she whimpered, not caring about the tears that rushed to her eyes. At that moment nothing else mattered except freeing herself. ''Tis caught. . .on the bark.'

'God Almighty!'

''Tis not my fault,' she said faintly, reviving the instant he pushed her back and the pressure eased.

'Just keep still, and that goes for your damned reckless tongue as well.'

The warning was unnecessary. The instant Beaudene's grip left her arm, Nell forgot about talking. He stepped to the side, the better to release her hair from its entanglement. She tensed, expecting pain, but his fingers moved with surprising gentleness against her damp scalp, sending tingling ripples of warmth down her neck, across her shoulders. . . She almost arched her back like a cat waiting to be stroked.

She went rigid with shock, struggling to push the alarmingly delicious sensations aside. They were part of the danger, part of the reason why she had to escape. And she could run. . .*now*. . .while it was still dark and she was only a few hours from home. There might not be another chance. God knew where Beaudene might take her, and she would have to follow blindly, not knowing where she was, not knowing what he intended. He had mentioned the King. Nell remembered her only encounter with the tall, handsome victor of the fight between York and Lancaster. The memory was three years old, but still she shuddered. That was when she had vowed never to become any man's possession.

'Turn your head a little.' The command came, disturbingly soft and husky, out of the darkness.

Nell obeyed. She was almost free. She could feel it. Another second and——

She ran. Strands of hair caught. . .tore free. . . making her eyes water and momentarily blinding her, but she ran, unheeding of the smarting pain. And, almost immediately, she knew it was futile. Her clothes, heavy with dampness, weighed her down. The ground, made treacherous with wet leaves and hidden roots, caused her to stumble before she had taken more than a dozen steps. Fear, wild and desperate, forced her on, but it was already too late.

Beaudene closed the distance between them as if it was nothing, his arms catching her about the waist as he took them both to the ground in a low tackle. He turned as they fell, cushioning Nell from the worst of the impact. Then, before she could recover, before she could even catch her breath, he rolled, pinning her beneath the suffocating weight of his body.

Nell fought back with every ounce of energy left in her. She twisted frantically, tried to get her legs free, tried to lash out with her hands, but he was too big, too strong. He spread his legs, clamping hers between them. His hands snapped around her wrists like manacles, forcing her hands down to the ground on either side of her head. His weight settled more deeply into her lower body in a ruthless demonstration of sheer masculine dominance.

A scream of pure helplessness tore through Nell, only to emerge as a choked cry that was barely audible. Her breasts heaved as she struggled to drag more air into her lungs. The hidden crucifix, displaced by her writhing, dug painfully into her back.

'You can't win, so stop fighting me,' Beaudene ordered, glaring down at her.

He wasn't even breathing hard, she noticed, almost sobbing as her own breath came back in ragged gasps. 'Let. . .me. . .go!'

'When I think you've regained what little sense you had.'

'How can I?' she cried. 'When you're. . .you're——' She broke off, paralysed with shock, as a cascade of piercing awareness poured through her from her head to her toes. He was covering her everywhere, his powerful shoulders blocking out the moonlight, his long limbs rigid bands of muscle controlling her without effort. She couldn't move so much as an inch. His size and strength were terrifying, and yet—he wasn't hurting her. He was warm and heavy and——

Shuddering, shaken to the depths of her being, Nell stared up at the hard face above her. 'Please,' she whispered.

For a nerve-stretching minute she felt as though even her heart had ceased beating. Then, very slowly, his eyes never leaving hers, Beaudene released her wrists, flattened his hands on the ground and lifted himself away, hunkering back on his heels beside her.

'Just where,' he began, much too quietly, 'did you think you were going?'

Nell slithered back a few inches before pushing herself up on one elbow. She was trying to think of something to say that wouldn't enrage him further when she saw his eyes lower, and become suddenly, fiercely, intent.

Startled, she glanced down and felt her breathing stop. The low-cut bodice of her gown had been wrenched from the wide belt at her waist during her struggle with Beaudene, and now hung loosely from her shoulders, exposing one pale, rose-tipped breast. Unable to move, terrified of what she would see, Nell looked back at him.

In the moonlight his face was a primitive mask of desire, his eyes narrowed to glittering slits as he stared at her. Tension was an almost palpable force, vibrating in the air between them. His? Hers? She didn't know, could only feel. When he reached out a hand towards her, Nell shrank, a thin, high sound of fear escaping her lips. The sound of a trapped creature in the presence of the hunter; motionless, waiting, hovering on the edge of panic.

She saw his gaze lift to her face, the golden eyes burning into hers before they widened suddenly, becoming arrested. He frowned, the intensity in him changing as he registered her panic-stricken expression.

'Be easy,' he said, very low. 'I'm not going to hurt you.'

She didn't believe him. 'If you lay one finger on me, I'll kill you,' she whispered. 'I swear, somehow, some day, I'll kill you.'

He was still for a moment, watching her, then he moved. His hand flashed out with the same lethal speed she had seen in the hall, capturing her free arm and immobilising her. Nell went rigid, bracing herself to resist the shove that would put her flat on the ground again. He raised his other hand, his gaze lowering once more to her breast, and very gently, very carefully, pulled her bodice back into place over her shoulder. His knuckles lingered, brushing her skin in a feather-light caress before withdrawing.

'Like I said,' he drawled softly, 'you don't back down, my lady.' He got to his feet with a quick lithe movement and reached down to pull her upright. 'Shall we go?'

Nell nodded mutely. At that moment she was so stunned, she would have agreed to anything. She allowed herself to be led over to the horses and was again lifted into the saddle. Beaudene checked both stirrups before mounting Samson.

'This time,' he said, reaching for Rufus's bridle to bring her horse alongside his, 'if you want to be able to walk when we stop, push your skirts between your backside and the saddle.'

The night crawled with increasing reluctance towards dawn. Beaudene kept the horses to a steady pace that ate up the miles without exhausting the animals. Occasionally, when a small hamlet or manor loomed up ahead, he would detour into the forest. Once he dismounted to lead the horses separately over a footbridge spanning a narrow river, keeping to the grassy verge so any wakeful inhabitants of the nearby village would hear nothing.

Nell scarcely noticed their route. Indeed, so stiff and weary was she that they could have ridden through London itself without arousing a flicker of interest in her. And she had long since ceased trying to fathom the reasons for Beaudene's actions, apart from dispelling any illusions that her threat to kill him had had an effect. It was a wonder he hadn't laughed in her face.

She stared numbly at the straight figure riding easily in front of her and decided the most obvious answer was the correct one. Right now he didn't have time for dalliance. And, right now, she was simply too tired to worry about later. Her head drooped, she was chilled to the bone, and every muscle ached. Wistful visions of a cosy inn and a warm bed began to flit tantalisingly

through her mind. All in all, it had been an exhausting
night.

'Ahh.'

The short, satisfied exclamation brought Nell's head
up. They were deep in the forest. Somewhere along
the way, Beaudene must have led them away from the
road again, for here the trees were so dense the
moonlight scarcely penetrated the branches overhead.
Rufus slithered down a steep bank of earth, following
Samson, and Nell had to grab hold of the saddle to
keep her seat. When they reached the bottom,
Beaudene had already dismounted, and was leading
Samson along the base of the embankment. He stopped
when they'd gone about a hundred yards and began
carefully moving branches aside.

Nell peered about her. Halfway up the embankment
the exposed roots of an ancient beech, which had been
blasted by lightning during some long-forgotten storm
and now lay on its side, jutted out over a pile of rocks,
hiding the entrance to what looked like a deep
depression in the earth. Nell wasn't quite sure if she
was looking at a hollow or a cave, but she was sure of
one thing. It wasn't an inn. Suddenly, Beaudene's
earlier remark about lighting a fire returned with
ominous clarity.

'Why are we stopping here?' she queried, her voice
husky with weariness.

'Because I haven't had any sleep in three days and
there won't be much of it in the next three. A few
hours now, before the hue and cry starts, may be all
we'll get.'

'You expect me to sleep *here*? What's wrong with an
inn? Not even a peasant would——'

She stopped abruptly when he strode over to her.
'For the last time, Lady Eleanor, this is not a pleasant

jaunt around the countryside. Unless you want to leave a trail that a blind beggar could follow, you'll forget about inns, soft beds and warm food for the duration of this entire journey. Now, get yourself off that horse and gather something for a fire while I go back and wipe out the tracks we made when we left the road.'

He was gone before Nell could gather enough breath to protest at the abrupt order, melting into the silent darkness of the wood.

She sighed and managed to slither off Rufus in an even less graceful fashion than before. 'Well, 'tis just you and me,' she muttered to the horse, clinging to his neck while she waited for her legs to take her weight. The circulation returned slowly and painfully. A few yards away, Samson snorted softly.

'Aye, and that great brute, too,' she added. 'What am I supposed to do with the pair of you? Brush you down? Water you? Did he think of you when he decided we're going to live like animals in a cave? Gather firewood, he says. How am I supposed to gather firewood when I can't see?'

Moving gingerly, she crouched down to run her hands over the ground. The light covering of leaves was slightly damp, but the sheltering trees had prevented the worst of the rain from reaching any twigs and small branches underneath. Still muttering, Nell began to build a small pile near the black entrance to their sleeping place.

'He needn't think I'm going in there on my own. I'd rather sleep in the open. How does he know there isn't a whole pack of wolves waiting to——?'

'Because I've used this place before.'

The soft, faintly menacing tone came from right behind her. Nell shrieked and leapt to her feet, spinning around so fast she nearly lost her balance.

'What do you think you're doing, sneaking up on me like that?' she yelled. 'You frightened me out of my wits.'

'What wits?' Beaudene retorted. 'With the noise you were making, both the Yorkist and Lancastrian armies could have marched past without you noticing. What's all this stuff?' His booted toe pushed at her collection of bracken and twigs.

Nell opened her mouth to argue further and then decided it wasn't worth it. The possibility of warmth was too alluring. ''Tis for the fire you wanted.'

'God's teeth, woman, what kind of fire is that going to make? Couldn't you have found something bigger?'

She gritted her own teeth. 'We aren't all used to creeping around in the dark and living in caves. If you can do better, go ahead. And while we're on the subject, what about the horses? They're wet, too, you know.'

There was an odd little silence. Nell could feel him watching her, although how he could see anything of her except a vague shadow, she had no idea.

'The horses will be all right once I've rubbed them down,' he said at last. 'Go inside. You can't tell in the dark, but there's plenty of room and 'tis dry. Just put your left hand on the wall, walk straight ahead about twenty paces and wait for me.'

'To be attacked by rats or spiders? I'd rather step off the edge of the world.'

'And I just might give you a helping——' He bit off the rest with a muttered oath. 'Listen very carefully, your ladyship. I can't take care of the horses, and find enough dry wood to give us a decent fire so we can dry our clothes, if I have to play nursemaid to a whining, useless, pampered little princess. Now, move!'

Nell obeyed, vowing silent vengeance every step of

the way. The words 'pampered little princess' stung,
more so than when Tom had used the same phrase
earlier that night. She had *not* been whining. And how
dared Beaudene call her useless and pampered just
because she hadn't gathered the right materials for a
fire? If he was so fussy, he should have given her a list.
As for the horses——

Her toe struck something hard and she made a
startled sound, cursing as she remembered that she was
supposed to be counting her steps.

'What is it?' Beaudene asked at her shoulder.

Nell's heart jumped into her throat before she
realised he must have followed her in. She clamped her
lips shut on another frightened gasp and made a second
vow. Before this was over she was going to put a stop
to his habit of creeping up behind her if it was the last
thing she did. 'I don't know,' she bit out.

She felt him pass her in the darkness, then heard the
sound of flint striking stone. A tiny flame appeared,
illuminating a small circular fireplace at her feet.
Beaudene hunkered down beside it and scooped a pile
of cold ashes into his palm. He opened his hand, letting
the stuff sift through his fingers.

'Is something amiss?' Shivering, Nell wrapped her
arms around herself, momentarily forgetting her griev-
ances as she saw him frown slightly.

'Someone has been here,' he answered, but absently.

'Well, I suppose if you know of it, others will also,'
she said reasonably, not understanding his abstraction.

He shook his head. 'Once the entrance is covered
the keenest-eyed hunter of the King's deer couldn't
find it. Even in daylight. There is only one other man
who knows of this shelter.'

She considered that. 'A friend?'

This time Beaudene nodded. 'Once. But I haven't

seen him for. . .a long time.' Abruptly shaking off his odd mood, he bent to the task of preparing a fire. ''Tis not important.'

Nell was too cold and tired to pursue the matter, but, curious now, she looked around, blinking a little as the light grew stronger.

It wasn't a cave, she saw, but a small square chamber at the end of the narrow corridor they had traversed. Rocks had been piled atop each other around the perimeter of the room to form surprisingly even walls, and the floor was of beaten earth. The air was still and musty but not unpleasant, what little smoke there was from the fire drifting upwards to vanish into the darkness above her. 'What is this place?' she asked wonderingly.

Beaudene glanced up from the fire and shrugged. 'Some sort of ancient burial mound, I think, judging by the bones in the side chambers. Roman, maybe. Who knows?'

'Bones?' Nell peered into the shadows beyond the fire and hurriedly crossed herself. 'Sweet Jesu, we can't sleep with a whole lot of corpses. 'Tis. . .'tis. . . indecent.'

''Tis also damn wet outside, but suit yourself.' He stood up and went back to the entrance where the horses waited.

Obviously he couldn't care less where she spent the rest of the night, Nell thought indignantly. She decided not to complain any further about the bones, however. She had far too many other things on her mind. And besides, if they were Roman bones perhaps it wasn't quite so bad. They'd been pagans, hadn't they?

Stifling a groan as her muscles protested, she sat down by the small fire, rubbing some feeling back into her cold hands. When Beaudene returned with their saddles and his packs, some of the chill had left her flesh, and the fur across her breasts was beginning to dry in small, matted peaks. She watched in weary silence as he placed the saddles on the other side of the fire and tossed the leather bags down beside them.

'Don't just sit there waiting for me to turn into a tiring-woman,' he grated, throwing her an impatient glance. 'Get out of those wet clothes.'

Nell got slowly to her feet, somehow dredging up enough energy to demand a little privacy. 'When you have the courtesy to wait outside.'

'Not a chance, your ladyship. In case it's escaped your notice, I'm as wet as you are, and the fire's in here.' He undid his belt as he spoke, dropped it to the ground, then stripped off his surcoat to reveal an unexpectedly fine linen undershirt beneath. The shirt wasn't as wet as the surcoat, but it was still damp enough to cling to an intimidating expanse of chest, revealing the hard muscles of his shoulders and a disturbingly primitive-looking pelt of dark hair.

Nell's mouth went dry.

'Besides, 'tis a little late for modesty, isn't it?' he added, slanting a mocking glance up at her as he pulled off a water-logged boot. 'I've already seen your charms.' He grinned suddenly. 'Well, one of them.'

A tide of heat swept over Nell's face to her hairline. 'A remark typical of an uncouth bodyguard,' she flashed, telling herself that the fluttering in her stomach was due to embarrassment and not that unexpectedly wicked, very male grin. 'And you wonder why I'm not willing to throw off my gown while you stand there mocking me!'

The second boot hit the ground. 'You'll not only throw off your gown, princess, but everything else as well,' he stated, turning away to pick up one of the packs. 'If you sicken on this journey because you were stubborn enough to sleep in wet clothes, you'll be nothing but a damned nuisance. Now strip, or I'll do it for you.'

'When men fly!'

Beaudene's head whipped around. His face was in shadow, but when he straightened slowly and set the pack down implacable determination was evident in every line of his body. Then he took a few steps forward to pin her gaze across the firelight, and Nell wondered how eyes the colour of amber could look so frigidly cold.

'I intend to get some sleep,' he began very softly. 'If you have a tithe the sense God gave you, you'll do the same. 'Twill be easier on you if you're warm and dry, and 'twill be easier on me if I don't have to worry about you running off. There's only one way to ensure that, little princess, and I'm big enough and mean enough to enforce it.' His tone became even softer, as dark and still as the night. 'Take off your clothes.'

CHAPTER FOUR

THE musty air in the chamber seemed to thicken, to
catch in her throat, making it difficult to breathe.
Across the fire Beaudene waited—the hunter, big and
powerful, his eyes intent on hers. He meant every
word, Nell realised. He had given her a direct order
and he intended to be obeyed.

She stepped back a pace, shaking her head. 'I'll take
off my gown to dry it,' she said huskily. 'But nothing
else. I'm not here for your amusement—and you know
that.'

One eyebrow quirked. 'I'm supposed to know that
because you panicked when you weren't in control
earlier? The trouble with you, Lady Eleanor, is that
the men in your life have been blinded by lust, slaves
to their desire and therefore slaves to you, obedient to
your hand on the reins.'

'And you're not, I take it?' The reckless challenge
was out before Nell could put a guard on her unruly
tongue. But she couldn't stay silent under the lash of
his scorn. It hurt. It hurt her more than she cared to
admit, and instinct bade her strike back, blindly, before
she weighed the risks.

'I won't be your slave,' he agreed softly. His eyes
glinted in a sudden flare of sparks from the fire, and
Nell shivered at what had been left unsaid.

'You won't be my anything,' she retorted. Unable to
hold his gaze, she turned away under the pretence of
unlacing her belt, striving for a show of unconcern.
'Fortunately, that is one of the advantages of being

69

one's own mistress instead of some man's wife,' she tossed back over her shoulder. 'A lady may choose her lovers, and I don't take mine from the ranks of bodyguards.'

Holy Mother of God, had she really said that? She who had never had a lover in her life was speaking as if they were legion.

'And if a would-be lover does not abide by your choice, my lady? If he decides to take you, regardless? What then?'

Nell's fingers stilled on her laces. Laugh it off, she ordered herself desperately. Laugh it off, before he sees the fear in your face, hears it in your voice. He's only a man. A man like all the others you've known.

But—sweet Lord—why was it so hard to dismiss what he said? Why was it so difficult to treat him with the carefully calculated evasiveness she had used with men since that dreadful night three years ago. Beaudene was right. They had been easy to dismiss, easy to control; each one left with the impression that, for the moment at least, she belonged to another and they would have to wait their turn.

It had been an act that had become almost second nature to her, and so well did she play the game of manipulation that only her cousin Tom, who had lived in the same house for years, had guessed the truth. Guessed, and kept her secret, because he wanted her for himself, wanted to be the first.

And wanted her inheritance, Nell thought cynically. And as long as her game remained just that, as long as her suitors had been kept at a distance, unsure of the identity of her lover but convinced there was one, she had been safe.

Until now. Until that moment in the hall when, instead of dismissing Beaudene's insults with a careless shrug and a laugh, and then forgetting him, she had responded instinctively—as herself.

Nell looked down at her hands and saw them clenched, white-knuckled, clutching her bodice. Very deliberately she relaxed them before she turned to meet the intent, watchful eyes of the one man who had changed the rules of the game on her.

'Do you speak of yourself, sir?' she asked with feigned nonchalance. 'I think not. No matter who employed you, 'twould impugn your honour to force me.'

He was silent for a moment, then a slow smile of amused appreciation curved his mouth and the waiting tension seemed to leave his body. 'You, my Lady Eleanor, are a worthy opponent,' he informed her. 'You're right. If I come from a concerned father, 'twould be an act of the most foul to betray his trust, and if I don't——' He paused and the smile turned rueful. 'Well, you've just put your own trust in my honour, little princess. Only a conscienceless villain, or a fool, would use force against you in those circumstances.'

'And you're no fool?' She watched him warily as he retrieved the abandoned pack and loosened its cords. He extracted a long woollen mantle of a blue so dark that it was almost black, and walked around the fire to look down at her. There were barely two paces between them.

'No,' he agreed. 'Nor am I conscienceless. But remember, my lady, there is more than one alternative to force, and villainy must be redressed.'

'You speak in riddles,' she said with a light laugh. 'Are you threatening to seduce me? Surely not. You prefer not to be one of a crowd, as I recall.'

'The crowd no longer surrounds you, Lady Eleanor. You stand alone. With me.'

A cold ripple of dread uncurled in the pit of Nell's stomach. That Beaudene was so aware of her utter vulnerability to him made it worse, somehow. But what had she expected? she asked herself wildly. That he wouldn't notice how completely she was at his mercy? That the only weapon she could pit against his male strength was her woman's wiles?

'That makes little difference,' she said, almost whispering. The effort of maintaining her cool demeanour was stripping her nerves raw, but if wit was her only defence she had to use it. Think! Reason! The men she had known hadn't cared how many lovers a woman had taken, but she thought this man would. The game was the same, she assured herself. Only the rules had changed. The realisation lent more strength to her voice.

'The crowd still exists,' she pointed out. 'Whether now, or in the past. As for the future, well, in sooth, bodyguards are not to my taste. That being so, instead of trying to scare me with meaningless threats, you would do better to give me that mantle so I may obey your command to remove this wet gown.'

His eyes narrowed. 'Why don't you just breathe in?' he demanded. 'And let the damn thing remove itself. Another inch should do it.'

Nell's overwrought nerves snapped. 'Why don't you stop baiting me?' she cried, forgetting games and strategy as temper and weariness got the better of her. 'And stop leaping to conclusions while you're at it. Margaret slashed my own gown to ribbons in a fit of spite while I was bathing, and the rest were already packed away, so I had to borrow this one. And if you had the least notion of colour and fashion, Sir Rafe, instead of being an ignorant clod, you'd have known this gown was made for a blonde and not for me.'

The instant those last furious words left her mouth, Nell was wishing them unsaid. Beaudene's eyes focused on her body like a hawk sighting prey, bathing her in golden fire. She felt as if he was stripping her, as if the heat of his gaze could peel the clothes from her body one by one, leaving her naked and defenceless.

'Men don't care what colour the gown is, princess. They only see the body inside it——' the searing fire stroked across her breasts '—or mostly out of it, in this case. And before we go any further, 'tis Lord Beaudene.'

'Is it? Well, I'll call you "my lord", if you stop calling me horrible names.' Her voice wobbled desperately and the words sounded childish in the extreme, but Nell was beyond caring. She had never felt so strange. Hot and shivering at one and the same time, her breasts flushed and heavy, her nipples tingling and unbearably sensitive against the cool fabric of her gown. Not only was Beaudene playing games with her mind, he was manipulating her body as well. Without touching her!

Even when his gaze lifted to her face, the strange sensations didn't abate. She wondered how much longer her trembling legs would support her!

'You don't like "princess"? How about "temptress", then? "Seductress"? "Siren"? "Delilah"? They suit you better than prim and proper Lady Eleanor, but——'

'Nell,' she got out, unable to say more.

The single syllable had a wholly unexpected effect. The sardonic curve of his mouth softened and he tilted his head slightly, as though considering. 'Nell,' he repeated slowly.

As if he was tasting her name on his tongue, she thought dazedly. And another ripple of sensation feathered across her over-heated flesh at the sound of her name spoken in that dark, gravelly voice.

Then he raised a brow, mocking again. 'So, what colour was the gown you were going to wear, my lady Nell? Scarlet?'

'Heaven save me. A man of humour,' she muttered. 'No doubt you'll be astonished to hear 'twas green and gold.' And one of her favourites. Tiredness washed over her suddenly, wave after wave of fatigue breaking over her, as the events of the last day and night took their toll. She was simply too weary to fight him any more. Too weary to care what he said.

'What does it matter?' she asked bitterly, almost of herself. 'Think what you like of me. You speak of honour so glibly, *Lord* Beaudene, but, bodyguard or baron, you're no better than——'

'*Don't say it!*' The snarled words slashed through the air towards her, shattering Nell's apathy. The sudden impact of emotion was stunning. Sheer unadulterated rage blazed from his eyes. For one fleeting, heart-stopping second, Nell thought Beaudene might actually strike her. Violence seemed to fill the small chamber, reaching for her, beating at her with invisible, rushing wings. She almost cried out from the fierceness of it.

Then the threat was gone. As abruptly as it had flared, the savagery in his eyes went from molten gold to frozen amber in seconds, and his taut muscles unlocked. He gave a short laugh, lifted the mantle in a mock salute and tossed it to her.

'You can trust me not to use force against you in one respect,' he growled softly. 'But don't push me too far, princess.'

He turned away, snatched up his boots, and strode towards the dark corridor without looking back. 'You've got three minutes.'

Nell stayed absolutely still, clutching the cloak to her as she would a shield. Trust him? How could she trust him? He had not struck her—in truth his control seemed formidable—but that hardly reassured her. He had killed a man before her very eyes while remaining totally in control. Somehow the memory of that cool, contained violence was more frightening than an outburst of rage. And, having seen Beaudene rein in both desire and anger, how could she help but wonder just what it would take to make him unleash the full force of his emotions? And what would happen if he ever did?

She shivered at the thought. Trust him? She had once trusted another man, a man whose word should have been inviolate, and she had discovered just how much force men were prepared to use against women to have their way. Trust was for fools.

And yet. . .

Beaudene had held her helpless beneath him on the road and had not so much as touched her intimately. On the contrary, he had covered her nakedness with a care that had left her speechless and shaken. And, earlier, he had gone out of his way to defend a serving-girl who meant nothing to him.

A log on the fire crackled, sending sparks flying upward, and Nell jumped, suddenly aware that she was wasting precious time. There was one thing she could count on, she thought. If Beaudene had said she had three minutes, that was precisely what he meant. And she needed to rest. Even if she couldn't sleep she still needed to rest before she could cope any further with a bodyguard who made veiled threats of seduction or worse.

And if sleep eluded her, then she would feign slumber if she had to act as she had never acted before.

But an act wasn't necessary. Even as she curled up in Beaudene's mantle, her hand closing protectively around the crucifix still hidden in its pouch, even as the feel of the jewel reminded her of the other, secret purpose of her journey, exhaustion claimed her. The black curtain of sleep fell over her like a second mantle, closing her eyes, stilling her mind. She didn't hear Beaudene return. Didn't know he stood over her, watching her sleep.

Which was not surprising, Rafe thought, because the three minutes had stretched to ten, during which time he had wondered, with growing irritation, if ten *hours* would have been enough to restore his control where this girl was concerned.

Why had he felt that wild surge of fury when she'd been about to question his honour? It shouldn't matter. She was simply a pawn, a means to an end, by whatever method he used. Seduction, or——

What? he asked himself silently, looking down at her. The more honourable course of marriage? Take a wanton to wife? Which she surely was. If he'd had any doubts on that score after her fear on the road, they'd been thoroughly allayed in the last hour. By the Rood, she couldn't have been more open about her lovers short of giving him a list of names!

And yet, lying here sleeping, the mysterious, seductive depths of her eyes hidden, she looked. . . bruised. . .fragile. . .unutterably innocent.

The other side of sin, he mused. Innocence.

And he was all kinds of fool for even thinking of innocence in connection with Lady Eleanor fitzWarren. That look of fragility was more likely caused by exhaustion.

Rafe went down on one knee beside her and noted the faint mauve shadows beneath her closed lashes, the pale translucence of her skin against the dark sable lining of his mantle. He'd pushed her hard tonight, wanting to put as many miles as possible between themselves and pursuit, so they could snatch this respite before an even harder day of riding. But she'd kept up—without complaint.

The thought drew his brows together. She had also given as good as he'd verbally served up, until that moment when she'd turned even paler and had seemed to droop right before his eyes.

'You have courage, princess,' he murmured beneath his breath. 'Even if you are spoiled and wanton, and damn near useless as a wife. And is it any cause for wonder, coming from that household?'

Annoyed with himself for the statement, Rafe got to his feet and yanked off his boots. God above, was he now making excuses for the wench? He strode around to the other side of the fire, dumped his boots, and was reaching for his open pack when he stopped cold.

There, lined up in a neat row between Nell and his baggage, were a pair of dainty leather shoes, a pair of silken hose, two gold ribbon garters, the sadly stained and muddied silver and blue gown, and a shift of the sheerest gossamer gauze.

His gaze flashed to Nell. She had wrapped herself so tightly that all he could see from his half-crouched position was a glimpse of chestnut hair, but——She was lying completely naked within the enfolding warmth of his mantle.

Desire ripped through him so savagely it nearly sent him to his knees. Slowly, as though drawn against his will, he reached out a hand and lifted the shift, letting the filmy garment drift over his fingers and back to the ground. The delicate fabric was wet and totally transparent.

A stifled sound, half-groan, half-curse, escaped him. Telling himself that she had merely followed his orders and had sensibly removed all her wet clothes did nothing to alleviate the pulsing heaviness in his loins. He wanted her so badly he ached all over.

With an effort that pulled every muscle in his body tight, he turned his back on Nell and reached into his pack for some dry clothes. God, if she could do this to him just by sleeping naked in his mantle, what would happen if——?

He snapped off the thought—before it had a chance to turn into the suspicion that his control was balanced precariously on the edge of something he'd never experienced. Something new. More than lust. More than desire.

Need?

Another stifled curse sounded, this time one of anger and self-disgust. Anyone would think she'd cast a spell on him. Need! He didn't need anyone, least of all a woman. In that direction lay weakness and the destruction of a man's will. Who knew that better than he? The only need he wanted to satisfy was physical. He'd never taken more from a woman, never wanted more. And, by God, it would be no different with Lady Eleanor fitzWarren.

Rafe tossed his wet garments aside, changed quickly and stretched out by the fire. No different at all, he told himself, closing his eyes with grim determination. And in that instant, coldly and deliberately, he decided he would have her. On his terms. The way he'd always taken a woman. Pleasure given and received, but a part of him always distant, always contained. He'd have to plan it. She was angry now, and disliked him, but that didn't worry him. Like all women, her anger and dislike would melt like snow in a spring thaw when the right incentive was dangled in front of her. They all had their price and he had the time to find hers. They would be alone for several days. It would be easy. He would have her.

And then—maybe—he'd decide whether her seduction fitted in with his other plans.

Nell woke to muted light and the knowledge that she was alone.

Completely alone, she saw, sitting up with a startled exclamation. Not only was Beaudene missing, but so were the saddles and his packs. The fire had died down to a pile of brightly glowing embers and, apart from her clothes and the confused trails of footprints crossing each other to and from the corridor, there was no sign that the chamber had ever been occupied.

Heart thumping much too fast, Nell struggled to her feet, hampered by the length of Beaudene's mantle. She grabbed up as much as she could of the heavy garment and hurried outside, speeding past the dark rectangles that led to the other chambers. Bright sunlight hit her eyes when she emerged from beneath the uprooted tree, bringing her to an abrupt halt.

The horses had gone.

For a minute Nell couldn't even think. She stared blankly at the spot where the horses had been tethered, as if their disappearance was a trick of the light and they would surely reappear at any moment. She couldn't believe Beaudene had left her. He wouldn't do that.

'He just wouldn't,' she whispered, and wondered what in Christendom made her so certain of that. What gallantry had he shown her? What had he done except snap orders at her in between bouts of biting sarcasm and unnervingly enigmatic remarks?

All the questions she had shoved aside earlier in the interests of sleep now began to clamour for attention. And the only answer she had was that Beaudene had removed her from her family, taking advantage of the situation she had found herself in last night, for reasons which she suspected had more to do with his own purposes than in protecting her. This morning he could just as easily have decided she was too much trouble and left her here for Tom to find.

The sudden rush of tears to her eyes appalled her. What was she doing, crying over a rough, ill-mannered——?

'What the hell are you doing out here dressed like that?'

Nell cried out and jerked around to the side as Beaudene emerged from the trees, looking more than a little annoyed. His sudden appearance sent her heart into an even faster rhythm. And it was her own fault this time, she told herself despairingly. She had been so busy trying to conjure up horses that weren't there, she'd forgotten about his habit of creeping up on her. Unfortunately, the combination of shattered nerves and overwhelming relief did nothing for her temper.

'You're the only danger I have to worry about,' she retorted. 'No one else knows I'm na——' She bit her tongue, almost choking on the rest.

'Naked under that cloak,' he finished, coming up to her.

Nell met him look for look, but she was trembling inside. How could she have forgotten how big he was in only a few hours? How fierce the glittering amber of his eyes; how unyielding the grim set of his hard mouth and the taut line of his jaw. His scar was clearly visible in the daylight—the mark of a warrior. He looked tough. Big and tough and dangerous.

And she had an utterly insane impulse to reach up and touch the scar with her fingertips, somehow to heal the hurt.

'I. . . I thought you'd gone,' she stammered, thoroughly flustered.

The annoyance left his eyes, to be replaced by a quizzical gleam that was devastatingly attractive. 'That gives me a very poor opinion of the men you seem to admire, princess. Have they always let you down?'

He wasn't being sarcastic, Nell decided, blinking in surprise. He sounded as if he really wanted to know. 'Those strutting popinjays!' she scorned, before she could think of the wisdom of such a reply. 'They probably would have run from that thief last night, let alone abandoned me in this forest. All they care about is whether or not to have their sleeves slashed, or the colour of their hose.'

His black brows shot up. 'Indeed? And here I thought my lack of—uh—an appreciation of fashion was an annoyance to you.'

The answer had its predictable result. Nell glared at him, effectively silenced.

His mouth relaxed into a smile that echoed the wicked amusement in his eyes. 'As much as I would like to continue this interesting comparison of bodyguards and popinjays, my lady, I think 'tis time you dressed.' When she didn't move, he added softly, 'Because if you let that mantle fall any lower, I might assume you've changed your mind about taking a bodyguard for your next lover.'

'*What*?' Nell gasped and looked down. She had been so enthralled by the fact that Beaudene was actually teasing her that the precarious hold she had on his cloak had loosened rather drastically. Both her shoulders were bare, and only her fingers clenched

around a fold of wool between her breasts kept her
decently covered—just.

Nell made a grab for the rest of the garment and her
wits. Her next lover? *Him*?

'Every man at Court will repent and become a monk
before I let you lay a finger on me,' she spluttered,
finally retrieving her voice. Whirling, she stalked back
into the corridor, uncomfortably aware that her outraged departure was consideraby hampered by the
unravelling length of cloak trailing behind her, baring
more of her back with every step.

'Mannerless brute! Overgrown. . .*bodyguard*! How
dare he mock me so?' Muttering furiously, conscious
that she was as angry with herself as she was with
Beaudene, Nell sent a fulminating glance back over
her shoulder to make sure he hadn't followed her
before discarding his mantle and yanking her shift over
her head. She debated for a moment about whether to
wear the crucifix around her neck, then decided against
it. Beaudene might notice its sudden appearance and
wonder why she hadn't been wearing it before. She
fastened the cords of the pouch around her waist. Her
gown followed. It was still damp around the skirts but
she scarcely noticed the slight discomfort.

'Next lover! Fish will walk on land first.' She pulled
on her white hose, grimacing at the muddy stains that
all but obscured the dainty gold stars embroidered on
the silk. Her shoes, which had not been fashioned with
exposure to inclement weather in mind, were in no
better condition. As well as being scratched and dirty,
the long points had curled up and inwards and stiffened, making them difficult to put on. 'This is all his
fault,' she ground out, teeth clenched as she balanced
on one foot and tugged at the recalcitrant leather.

'Next lover! What a jest! If he was the last man left on this earth he wouldn't be my next lover.'

'If I was the last man left on this earth, you wouldn't have a choice.'

A startled squeak echoed through the chamber as Nell lost both her shoe and her balance. She teetered for a moment, then fell forward against the fireplace. Her outflung hand ploughed straight into the pile of hot ashes, sending sparks flying.

Beaudene was across the small chamber in seconds, cursing savagely as he scooped her away from the fire and up into his arms. Nell barely had time to feel the pain of her burns before they were outside and she was being carried swiftly through the trees.

Even then pain was only a vague sensation. She had never been carried in a man's arms in her life. The sudden feeling of helplessness was frightening. She wanted to struggle, to fight her way free, but at the same time she wanted to cling, to nestle into his strength. The conflicting sensations swirled around her, colliding with a dizzying awareness of the heat of his body and the coiled power of the arms that held her.

Dazed, desperately praying that he couldn't feel the way she was trembling, she scarcely noticed when they emerged into a small glade dissected by a stream. The horses were grazing nearby, already saddled.

Beaudene lowered her to the ground and grasped her left hand. 'Sweet suffering saints,' he ground out, examining her reddened palm before pressing her down on to the grassy bank and kneeling beside her.

Still more shaken from being carried than by her injuries, Nell peered over his arm. ''Tis not so bad,' she murmured. 'A few blisters. I doubt the saints will take much notice.'

He sent her a look that could have raised blisters

without the help of any fire, and shoved her hand unceremoniously into the stream. Nell gasped as her burned flesh reacted painfully. She would have snatched her hand back, but Beaudene's fingers tightened around her wrist, holding her still.

'I know it hurts,' he said, his voice surprisingly gruff. 'Try to relax. It will stop stinging in a minute.'

'You must have a lot of success against enemies with that trick,' Nell muttered after a moment, gradually unclenching her teeth as the cool water began to take the sting away from the small wounds.

'What trick?'

'Sneaking up on people.'

He looked at her, amusement flickering in his eyes. 'My enemies don't spend a lot of time talking to themselves, princess. They're too busy listening for me.'

'I'll remember that,' she retorted as he turned away again, but she couldn't wholly suppress the answering smile that tugged at her lips. He looked so much younger when that wicked gleam replaced the coldness in his eyes and——

He *was* much younger than she had first supposed, Nell realised with a sudden, startled little intake of air. And handsome. Why hadn't she seen that? Her smile faded as she took in the broad, high cheekbones, the straight blade of his nose, the firm line of his jaw. Against the backdrop of sunlit trees his profile had a stern masculine beauty that yet was faintly softened by the intriguing lines fanning out from the corners of his eyes. Lines that hinted at humour. While his mouth. . .

Nell's gaze lowered and a deep, very feminine frisson of awareness shimmered through her. He was hard and dangerous, aye, but in the passionate curve of his full lower lip she saw something that might once have been gentleness.

For the first time she found herself wondering how he'd got his scar.

'Nell?' The husky sound of her name brought her gaze slowly upwards. One dark brow was raised in amused patience. 'Your hand,' he said, clearly repeating the question, 'does it feel better?'

'Hand? Oh. . .oh. . .aye. 'Tis no longer stinging,' she stammered, flushing hotly. What was wrong with her? She had been in Beaudene's company for hours now. Why was she suddenly blushing and stuttering like a fool just because he smiled at her? Why did she feel as if she was seeing him for the first time? As if she was only just now *noticing* him?

Noticing him? Had her wits gone a-begging? He hadn't exactly been invisible before! And what of all the questions she had put aside last night? she berated herself, ruthlessly dragging her wayward thoughts back to the here and now. Never mind about his scar and who had given it to him. Probably some other unfortunate female he had tormented beyond bearing. Was she to join the ranks of the addle-brained just because of a smile?

Summoning all the resolution that had seen her through the last three years unscathed, Nell forced herself to meet those disturbing eyes with their lurking smile. And, quite suddenly, in the clear light of morning, she knew exactly where to start.

'What does the King have to do with all this?' she demanded. And watched his face go still.

CHAPTER FIVE

'NOTHING.'

For a minute Nell couldn't believe that that one brief word was the only answer she was going to get. Then, with an abrupt movement that made her start nervously, Beaudene released her wrist and rose to his feet. 'Keep your hand in the water a while longer,' he said curtly. 'I'm going back for your shoes and to cover the entrance.'

'But. . . Wait!' she cried, slewing around, still on her knees, as she realised he was walking away.

He had already reached the trees. He paused, glancing back, and his gaze was so hard, so cold, that a primitive awareness of a force more powerful than any she had ever encountered swept over her. So might the hawk look upon the earth from its unassailable eyrie, she thought, shivering. Proud and aloof. Invincible. And she expected to pit her will against his? 'What about. . .what about. . .breakfast?' she asked weakly.

Just as he turned away, his mouth twisted into the more familiar sardonic smile. 'You're soaking your hand in it.'

Nell glared at the cheerfully bubbling stream washing over her hand, and didn't know whether to curse Beaudene or herself for the ease with which he had just intimidated her. Of course, if she hadn't been so shaken by his changed manner this morning, it might never have happened. Not to mention the shock of being carried off in his arms.

No! Better not to think of that. Even the memory of

86

it caused a most unsettling sensation of weakness to flow through her limbs. And she would *not* be weak! She would have the truth. 'I *will*!' she whispered, determination firming the set of her mouth. After all, she was no stranger to men who used charm—and when that didn't work, intimidation or force—to have their own way. Surely she was strong enough to stop Beaudene deciding her fate without so much as a whimper of protest or question from her? There had been secrets in that cool, distant gaze, and, by the saints, she would have them out.

And what of your own secrets? demanded an intrusive little voice inside her head.

Nell frowned and withdrew her hand from the water, examining her palm before gingerly patting it dry on her gown. The movement shifted the hidden crucifix slightly. If Beaudene had his secrets, then so did she. Even more. If he expected her uncle to follow them, he would take the most direct route to her home, for their only hope of reaching it safely lay in outrunning their pursuers. How was she to persuade him to make a detour to the cathedral at Wells without revealing a truth he might not believe? Especially when there was already a barrier of suspicion between them.

A barrier that would not be removed by blunt demands for information, she mused, as Beaudene reappeared. He moved through the trees with the purposeful stride of the hunter who knew that his prey was within easy reach. It was better not to watch that swift, almost silent approach, Nell decided. The urge to run was far too acute. And the most frightening part was that, this time, she wasn't at all sure she would run *from* him.

The unnerving thought had her quickly bending down to the stream. If water was the only sustenance

available, she might as well use it as an excuse not to
look at him. In truth, it would be a good idea to take a
drink, if she could only stop her hand from shaking.

'Here.'

The curt word brought Nell's head around, water
dripping forgotten from her fingers. Beaudene's long
legs, clad in dark burgundy hose and knee-length
boots, filled her vision. Her shoes dangled from his
hand, held by one finger hooked under the misshapen
points. Not daring to glance upwards, Nell reached for
them.

'Not so fast,' he said, coming down on his haunches
beside her. One forearm rested across the taut muscles
of his thigh. 'How do you expect to get your feet into
the stirrups wearing these?' he asked, swinging the
shoes back and forth in front of her wary gaze. 'More
to the point, how do you expect to get them out again?'

Nell tried to quell a feeling of defensiveness. She
would not let him intimidate her again. 'I wouldn't
have to wear them at all if you hadn't kidnapped me
last night,' she pointed out. 'Those shoes are fashioned
for indoor use, not for riding in pouring rain.'

'Ah.' His mouth twitched. 'My ignorance of fashion
again. I cry pardon, my lady. But the problem still
remains, unless. . .'

'Unless what?' Nell frowned intently at her maligned
footwear and tried to think of a solution. It was difficult
when her wretched brain kept thinking instead of the
way Beaudene's eyes held that hint of a smile again.
Why couldn't he remain arrogant and sarcastic and
cold? Then *she* could remain angry. 'I knew you should
have let me go back——' she began in a praiseworthy
attempt to whip up some righteous outrage. It was cut
off abruptly when Beaudene drew his dagger.

Without so much as a single word of warning, he

placed the shoes on the grass, held them steady with his free hand, and brought his dagger slashing through the air in a swift downward arc that was so fast Nell could have sworn the very air between them had quivered and been rent asunder. The curled-up points of her shoes lay on the ground, sliced through as cleanly as if he'd wielded an executioner's axe.

In the ensuing silence the gurgling stream and early-morning birdsong filling the glade sounded unnaturally loud. Nell picked up her shoes and examined them. 'You're very. . .quick. . .with that knife,' she observed faintly.

The smile that slashed across his face was predatory in the extreme. 'In this world, princess, 'tis the quick or the dead. And no one has succeeded in killing me yet.'

Only by a fierce effort of will did Nell prevent her gaze going to the scar that gave his handsome face its hard look of danger. 'Well,' she managed, then had to take a deep breath before she could get the rest out, 'my toes will probably freeze, but at least I won't be dragged behind my horse should I lose my seat.' She bent to put on the shoes. 'Thank you.'

'No.' He made a quick survey of the glade. 'I'll do it. The leather is stiff and you only have the use of one hand. We need to be on our way again without delay.'

Something in the way he'd scanned their surroundings had Nell proffering one small silk-clad foot, then the other, without argument. As her shoes were slipped on, her own gaze followed the path Beaudene's had taken. She could not see far into the trees, but all seemed quiet.

'Would I be missed already?' she asked. 'So early?'

''Tis not of your family I'm thinking,' he told her, his hand lingering on her shoe. 'After last night they're

likely to be still abed, nursing sore heads. Even if they
find that body, we should have another hour or two
start on them.'

'Then, what?'

He shrugged, as though not greatly concerned, but
the look he sent her brought all Nell's senses alert.
'There are other dangers to be encountered on the
road, my lady. But I wouldn't expect you to know of
them.'

'I haven't been locked away in a convent for the past
ten years,' she retorted, incensed. 'I do know something of the world.'

'Aye. The desire of men and how to use it.' The
words were angry, but a second later his voice lowered
and went soft, and the hand still resting on her foot slid
upwards until his long fingers closed in a warm, gentle
vice around her ankle. 'But what of your own desires,
princess?'

Nell amost lifted straight off the ground in shock.
Tingling needles of fire raced straight up the inside of
her leg to the very centre of her being. She couldn't
breathe, couldn't speak. And even as her brain commanded her to move, to kick free, to break his hold,
the feeling of being held captive once again swept over
her.

'What are you doing?' she squeaked, forcing the
words out.

Torturing myself, Rafe thought, clenching his teeth
against a wave of raw need. Her immediate, unfeigned
response to his touch had his blood pulsing so fiercely,
so instantly, that he was almost grateful for the warn-
ings of danger his instincts had been sending him since
he'd woken. Otherwise he wasn't sure he'd be able to
keep from stripping them both right now, lying Nell
back on the grass and covering her with his body.

Taking her, claiming her—mating like creatures of the forest, with the sun beating down on their naked flesh until its heat was lost in the hotter fires of passion. And pursuit be damned.

But even as he forced the tormenting images out of his mind, he could no more stop his fingers sliding upwards than he could stop his next breath. Under the soft silk of her hose her flesh was warm; he had to know if it would feel as soft.

'My lord?' Nell's voice, trembling and confused, pierced the fog of desire threatening to swamp his sanity. He dragged his gaze from the slender limbs exposed as her gown gave way before the slow advance of his hand, and went still when he saw her eyes.

Desire was there, soft and helpless, but overtaking it was confusion and the beginnings of fear.

Rafe's eyes narrowed. Was she playing some deep game? Did she think to hold him at arm's length by feigning maidenly nervousness? It wouldn't work when he could see the rapid pulse beating in her throat, hear the way her breath caught on each tiny gasp of air. His nostrils flared as the faint scent of her perfume came to him, betraying how warm her skin had become. Desire raked across his nerves like tiny claws, and he cursed silently as he remembered that this wasn't the time or the place to seduce her. But it would come. Oh, aye. It would come. Of that he was very sure.

His mouth curved in a smile. 'You know something, princess? I think I just found a price you've never thought to demand of a man. And I'm going to be more than willing to pay it.'

'Price?' Nell's mind reeled. She couldn't make sense of his words. What was he doing to her? His fingers still encircled her leg, lightly stroking the back of her knee, but it was only a touch. A tiny caress. Barely felt. How could she feel so. . .so. . .chained to the ground, so unable to move? The sensation was frightening, but underlying it was a shivery excitement that rippled through every nerve in her body until she wasn't sure which emotion was dominant.

Then, with one last lingering caress, his touch was gone, and she could breathe again.

'You forgot your garters,' he said, as calmly as if touching her had not affected him at all.

Hot colour flooded Nell's cheeks as she realised that was probably all too true. He didn't like her, and there was no reason to think his unsettling behaviour this morning meant any change in that regard. She stared blindly at the hand that reached into his surcoat to draw out two lengths of gold ribbon. Breathing was one thing. Rational thought still seemed beyond her. But when his hand went to her knee again and pushed her skirts higher, desperation jolted her brain and tongue into action.

'No! They tie below the knee.'

Golden eyes, glittering and intent, gazed straight into hers, and their expression was anything but calm. 'I don't think so.'

'Then let me. I can. . .'

But she couldn't. If she even tried to take over the small task Beaudene would see how badly she was trembling. All she could do was watch helplessly as he smoothed her hose up her legs and tied the garters in place. His long fingers brushed over the delicate flesh of her inner thighs and Nell had to bite her lip to stop the tiny whimper that demanded escape from her tight throat. Dear God, it was worse than before. Her heart was pounding so hard she was almost jolted by each beat, and she wanted. . .saints have mercy. . .she wanted to lie down, to feel his hands——

'There.'

The purr of satisfaction in his voice cut through her whirling senses. A satisfaction, she noticed uneasily, that was reflected in the brief smile he gave her.

Completely unnerved, Nell wondered what had gone so disastrously wrong with her plan to keep Beaudene at a distance. What had happened to his distaste for being one of a crowd? What had happened to *her* distaste at a man's touch?

Before an answer presented itself to her stunned mind, Beaudene stood, reached down for her hand and pulled her upright in one easy movement. She stiffened her knees just in time to stop herself sinking right back down again.

'Time to go, princess.'

'Aye,' she whispered, and closed her ears to the unmistakable note of panic shaking her voice.

'Tell me about those accidents that befell you.'

The command came as Beaudene slowed the horses to a gentler gait after several miles at the gallop. The pace had been dangerous, given the density of the trees still in full leaf, but Nell hadn't questioned it. She had been grateful for the concentration needed to follow Beaudene along a path that seemed visible only to him. She hadn't wanted to think about the meaning of the burning look he had given her before tying her garters. Even less had she wanted to think about the way she had all but melted at his touch.

Now, as they left the shelter of the trees and rejoined the road—more a wide path cut through the forest than a proper thoroughfare—she cast a quick, sidelong glance at him, wondering how much to say. He didn't seem to be in any hurry for her answer, she thought. His keen gaze scanned the woods on both sides of the road, constantly alert, and though he sat his horse with the ease of a man used to long hours in the saddle, she sensed a waiting tension in him, as though he was ready to meet an attack head-on.

What would he say if she told him that she knew what it was to live like that? Always watching, always waiting, constantly aware of danger. The sudden feeling of affinity, almost of recognition, made her uneasy, and yet curiosity stirred. Who was he, this man who could flay her with his scorn last night and tease her this morning? Who could tend her hurts one moment, then become as remote as the moon in the space of a breath? Who could kill with cold, silent efficiency, but who had touched her with a gentleness that had made her forget everything the past had taught her?

'You said something startled your horse a few days after your father's letter arrived summoning you to Hadleigh? Was anyone near you at the time?'

Nell started slightly, her cheeks warming when she realised that Beaudene's hawk-like gaze had shifted from the forest to her face. She fought back the betraying heat, hoping he hadn't been aware of the way she'd been staring at him for so long. The faint upward curve of his mouth told her that he had.

'No one was near me. I wasn't hurt. And, despite what you think, it *was* an accident. Now, tell me about the King.'

His brows shot up so fast that for the first time in hours Nell felt like smiling herself—in undisguised triumph. 'Did you think I would be satisfied with "nothing" for an answer?' she asked, miraculously restored to composure at the knowledge that, for once, she had managed to take her formidable bodyguard completely by surprise. Even the narrow-eyed stare that accompanied his next question didn't shake her.

'Do you know Edward?'

She met his look coolly. 'We've met.'

'Indeed? It must have been a memorable meeting for the King to concern himself so closely with your safety.'

'Wrong, my lord.' Her chin lifted another notch. 'Edward of York concerns himself rarely with the safety or honour of women. I doubt his memories of me are pleasant ones.'

'Oh? What did you do? Demand favours that were beyond his power to bestow?'

The suddenly biting tone flicked Nell like a whip, but she kept her expression frozen. 'Something like that.'

Something like that? Rage tore through Rafe with a speed and violence that shocked him. So what if Edward had been before him? He'd known he wouldn't be the first. God's teeth, she could have lain with all condition of men, from the King to the humblest spit-boy, and it wouldn't change the only use he had for her. Why did he feel this anger, this fury, this insane urge to seek out the King and throttle the truth out of him? Like almost every other man in the kingdom he had always regarded Edward's incessant wenching with a kind of amused indulgence. Men made jest of the fact that no woman was sacred. Wives or daughters, married or virgin, all were meat to his insatiable palate, but Nell——

Had the King been her first lover? Had his friend of ten years used his legendary looks and charm to seduce the niece of a potential supporter, leaving her wanton? For, once a maidenhead was lost, it mattered not how many others came after.

He looked at her, riding proud and silent by his side, and the question gnawed at him like a cankerous growth. *Had* she gone to Edward's bed? By the fiend, *had* she known the King as well?

'Something like that,' he repeated, controlling his voice with an effort. Anger would not serve him now. Anger, unleashed, destroyed rather than served. He had learned that lesson well—at the same time that he had learned never to trust a woman. 'By your tone 'twas not a happy occasion. Do your sympathies lie with Lancaster, then, my lady, as did your father's? Dangerous politics in these times.'

'My sympathies lie with neither,' Nell stated. 'Unless it be with their unfortunate wives.'

The statement surprised him, but only for a moment. 'Don't waste your pity,' he advised. 'One is a termagant, and the other so cold 'tis a wonder Edward doesn't freeze every time he climbs into bed with her.'

Nell glared at him. 'What else should he expect when he threatened to take Mistress Woodville at knifepoint because she withstood his blandishments rather than compromise her virtue?'

'Aye.' A short humourless laugh escaped him. 'Elizabeth knew what she was about; that is for certain. From a penniless widow with two sons to Queen of England in a matter of months, and never mind that an important French alliance founders in the process.'

'Just like a man to blame the woman in the case,' Nell retorted hotly. 'The truth is that your king thinks every woman was put on this earth for his amusement, and he couldn't bear to be bested by one. He could have left Mistress Woodville alone, he could have helped——'

She stopped dead, only to hurry into speech again when Beaudene turned an intent probing stare on her. 'Henry of Lancaster might be weak—— Very well, simple-minded,' she amended when one black brow went up. 'But at least he's not a whoremonger.'

'Mayhap we have something in common then, my lady,' he drawled. 'You have little time for the King, and I have none at all for the Queen. On the other hand, at least cold ambition is preferable to Margaret of Anjou's viciousness. While Henry sank into the witless state he seems to prefer, she and her paramours damn near-ruined the country. As for the atrocities of her army——'

'It sounds to me as though you have little time for any woman,' Nell interrupted without ceremony. 'Margaret is a mother, remember? Perhaps she fights for Henry's son?'

This produced a snort of derision. 'Henry's son? Aye, and I'm the Pope. If Henry himself can wonder at the boy's begetting, what are the rest of us to think?'

'A truly fascinating question,' Nell observed, refusing to be dragged into an argument over the paternity of the boy whose mother stubbornly persisted in calling the Prince of Wales. 'But it does not tell me what the King has to do with this journey, and why you would need to make a promise to him regarding my safety.'

He threw her an exasperated glance. 'If it sets your mind at rest, madam persistence, your father is wooing the King, hoping to be confirmed in his lands by renouncing his allegiance to Lancaster. Edward merely asked me to assure your safe journey as a sign of good faith while he considers the matter.'

'But the Court is presently at Reading, and Hadleigh Castle and your own lands in Somerset.' She frowned, remembering that he had evaded a very similar question last night when they'd been dancing. 'Do you ask me to belive that the King and my father both expected you to travel all the way to Langley when I already had escort aplenty?'

He shrugged. 'Believe what you like. As it happens, I also have a petition awaiting Edward's attention. To travel a day or so out of my way seemed a small price to place on account towards a favourable outcome.'

'Indeed? And has your gallant escort been so rewarded?'

'Only time will tell,' he said enigmatically. 'Now, can we move on to more pressing concerns? You said something about the standards in the hall.'

'Holy saints! And you call *me* persistent!' When he narrowed his eyes at her, Nell capitulated. She wasn't entirely satisfied with Beaudene's explanation, but without knowing precisely *why* she felt she had missed something important, it was difficult to know what questions to ask. She heaved an exaggerated sigh. ''Twas merely one of those unchancy things. I was standing in the hall and one of the lances jutting out from the minstrels' gallery must have come loose, or perhaps 'twas never securely fastened. In any event, it fell and struck my shoulder—not with the point, fortunately.'

'Fortuitous, indeed. Was anyone up there?'

'Saints above, how should I know? The stupid thing was so heavy it knocked me to my knees, and I was buried under the banner for a full minute.'

'You couldn't have been alone in the hall. Didn't anyone see anything?'

'No one was looking up,' Nell said drily. 'They were too busy exclaiming and wringing their hands, or trying to free me.'

He smiled slightly in rueful acknowledgement. 'So you weren't hurt at all?'

'Well——' Nell paused and an irrepressible little

gurgle of laughter escaped her at the memory '—I
sneezed a lot. That accursed banner was full of dust.
Hadn't been washed in years.'

Beaudene's answering shout of laughter sent an
inquisitive rabbit fleeing back into the forest and took
Nell completely by surprise. Glancing sideways at him,
she saw that he was still smiling, his tawny eyes alight
with amusement. A little bubble of warmth burst
somewhere inside her. She felt happy all at once, as
though in making him laugh she had accomplished
something special. The sense of recognition, tentative
and fleeting, rippled through her again. Suddenly
tongue-tied, she smiled shyly back at him.

'You thought 'twas your cousin Margaret indulging
her spite, didn't you?' he said almost gently.

Nell hesitated, then nodded. 'I still do,' she murmured, hoping her insistence wouldn't shatter the
fragile mood between them. 'I *know* she slashed my
gown, and as for the other things—'twould be just like
her to slip a physic in my broth, or lock me in with the
dogs, or claim she misfired at the butts. She never liked
me. Nor did my aunt. Not that I was broken-hearted
about it, but. . .' Memories flitted through her mind
and she pushed them away with a little shiver. 'The
younger girls were all right, but Thomas and
Edmund—well, you saw them.'

'Aye.' He looked at her thoughtfully. 'Tom wants to
marry you. Then your uncle must expect to gain a
papal dispensation without any trouble.'

'Oh, Tom is not really my cousin.' Nell grimaced.
'Thank the Lord. My uncle was a widower with Tom a
babe when he married Aunt Maud. 'Tis Margaret,
Edmund and the rest who are true kin.'

'Don't be in such a hurry to thank your maker,'
Beaudene advised. 'If there's no need for a dispensa-

tion, any plans they have to marry you to Tom may proceed apace.'

'Not any longer,' she pointed out.

'As you say.' He smiled slightly, then stared abstractedly ahead between his horse's ears. 'If something happens to you, my lady, who inherits your father's property?'

Nell frowned. 'I'm not sure. There's no one on my father's side. I suppose Uncle Edward could claim it by right of my aunt.'

'Your mother's sister?'

When she nodded, he went on. 'And since your aunt is presently hand in glove with the Queen their way would be clear. 'Twould then pass straight to Tom, or even the younger boy.'

'Nothing,' stated Nell with loathing, 'would induce me to marry Edmund! Or Thomas, for that matter.'

'You forget. We're talking about what would happen in the event of your death.'

'What a cheery subject,' she muttered. 'Do you think we could change it?'

'Blinding yourself to the facts won't change anything. I agree that marriage would be the easiest way of obtaining your inheritance, but if you've been holding firm in refusing I wouldn't give a groat for your life. And your father may have suspected as much,' he added slowly.

'My father!' Nell's bubble of happiness vanished. 'I haven't seen nor heard from my father in more than ten years. When it became clear that my mother would bear no more children, he set up a separate household for us in Wells so he could continue a way of life that did not take account of a wife and child. He never visited, never sent to know how we fared. I grew up listening to my mother's tears. She died when I was six, and even then he had no time for his daughter, but had servants escort me to my aunt's house. 'Tis only now that I may be useful in gaining him more wealth, or a powerful alliance, that he remembers me. Well, I am not my mother! I will not meekly obey and then spend my days weeping. *I* will be mistress of my fate!'

Her outburst was followed by a taut silence. Somewhat uneasily, Nell wondered what Beaudene was thinking, but he still seemed intent on her inheritance. She didn't know whether to be relieved or incensed that he had ignored her diatribe.

'Whatever your father's motives, he apparently does not wish to see his property fall into Langley hands, my lady. And if he made that plain in his letter to your aunt, those accidents you so blithely dismiss as spite could well have been aimed at delaying your departure with a view to forcing your hand. 'Tis not so easy to resist when you're injured or sick.'

Nell sniffed. 'No one forces me to anything.'

Beaudene turned to look at her, eyebrows raised.

'If you are thinking of last night,' she retorted, flushing, ''twas because you confused me so that I let you kidnap me. If it hadn't been for that thief——'

With a muttered imprecation, Beaudene reached over and pulled both horses to an abrupt halt.

'What do you think you're doing?' Nell gasped, her defiance crumbling with unnerving speed.

He reached back, extracted a length of rope from one of his packs and thrust it at her. 'Stripping the blindfold from your eyes,' he grated savagely. 'Look well at that, my lady, and then tell me your assailant was a thief. This rope came from around the neck of your uncle's stallion, and has been cut through but for a few threads. *Cut*, Nell, not frayed. If that damned horse had charged, the rope would have snapped, and your fond relatives would have thrown up their hands in horror and blamed some hapless stable lad for using a frayed tether. *Look at it!*'

Nell stared at the evidence literally right under her nose. Denial was impossible. The rope clenched in Beaudene's fist had indeed been neatly sliced through, so that only a few strands remained. One good tug would have been all that was needed for the stallion to break free. Even a horse of Chevette's size and placid temperament could have done it. She could have done it herself. She looked up into Beaudene's grim face and said the first thing that came into her mind.

'Why were *you* in the stable at that hour?'

He withdrew his hand and shoved the rope back out of sight, seemingly unconcerned by the blunt question. 'To collect these,' he said, indicating his packs. 'As I crossed the bailey I saw someone outside the stable and wondered at it. Had I known 'twas Rouget I would have moved faster.'

'Oh.' Nell mulled this over. 'Well, you were in time. 'Tis all that matters in the end.'

'I commend your equanimity, my lady.'

'I don't believe in gnashing my teeth over something that's done with and past,' she retorted, detecting sarcasm. 'At least. . . Will trouble follow you for killing that man? You said he knew about the stallion. He must have been told. . .' She let the words trail off. Even with the evidence of the cut rope, it was still hard to admit aloud that her own family had conspired to injure or kill her because she wouldn't fall in with their plans.

Beaudene shrugged. 'There'll be no hue and cry over his death. Rouget had a reputation. He was a good soldier once, but, of late, whenever he was around, people who were an inconvenience to someone would suddenly turn up conveniently dead. I doubt your uncle will confess to admitting such a man to his house. He'll probably spin the same tale of attempted thievery that you were so anxious to believe.'

'But won't they know. . .? I mean, won't they know that *we* know. . .? That is to say—— Oh, dear.'

Beaudene laughed and leaned over to smack Rufus on the rump. He nudged Samson into a fast trot at the same time. 'Don't tie your tongue in a knot. I know what you mean. But whatever your uncle suspects we know, he or your cousin will still come after us.'

At her quick look of surprise, he added drily, ''Tis the only way they can cover their backs, princess. I warrant you they've already put it about that you've been kidnapped, or, more likely, run off with me.'

'Run off with you! I only met you last night!' Indignation brought an angry flush to her face.

'So?' His eyes were suddenly narrowed and glittering. 'Was every gallant you were cosying up to at that banquet a lifelong acquaintance?'

The question was flung at her so savagely, his amusement gone so quickly, that Nell scarcely had time to comprehend the sudden change of mood, let alone marshal any defence. Shaken, dismayed at how badly she wanted to defend herself, she could only let the storm break over her head.

'Of course they were not. Nor did it seem to matter to you. My God, I even overheard wagers running as to how long it would take a man to get you or Lady Margaret alone in a dim corner, or whether that was the night fortune would smile on one of them because you might feel like a change of lover.' And, with that, Samson bounded forward under the sudden command of a booted foot.

Neither spoke again for the next several miles. Nell

stared stonily ahead and told herself that she didn't want to rail at Beaudene for believing ill of her. She didn't want to explain. She didn't want to scream that he was wrong, that she had pretended to be just like her dissolute family in order to protect herself, that the most likely reason she had let him carry her off last night was because the strain of juggling men and lies and pretence, while clinging desperately to her own truth, had brought her almost to breaking-point. He'd never believe her. And besides, hadn't she deliberately fostered his low opinion of her? It was supposed to be her protection. Wasn't it?

She shook her head in despair at her confused thoughts. The problem was becoming too complicated to solve on an empty stomach. In fact, now she came to think on it, hunger was probably the cause of the hollow emptiness that had been gripping her insides since Beaudene had called her princess again, and had then flung those disgusting wagers in her face as if she had entered wholeheartedly into the business.

A cry of protest rose in her throat. Nell tried to stifle the betraying sound, but Beaudene clearly had the hearing as well as the eyes of a hawk, because he glanced around, his gaze narrowed and hard.

'Don't fall back any further, princess. We have to put a few more miles behind us before we stop to rest the horses.'

'I wasn't aware that I was lagging,' Nell retorted through her teeth. 'But far be it from me to gainsay one who, I have no doubt, can travel for days without rest or sustenance other than a few hurried mouthfuls of water.'

'Stop complaining,' he ordered, but quite mildly. 'I have no intention of starving you. You'd probably swoon and we'd be forever having to stop to let you recover.'

'Oh, a thousand pardons, my lord. I need food occasionally. How truly heedless. How imprudent. The shame of it! How will I ever hold up my head again?'

Rafe's lips twitched. The little shrew had a trick of disarming him with humour when he least expected it. And, for some strange reason that had nothing to do with physical desire, he was letting her get away with it. He reined Samson back until Nell came alongside, then slowed to a walk. 'I'll strike a bargain with you, my lady. I won't mention your past again if you put a guard on that saucy tongue.'

Nell was surprised to find herself hesitating. His words were uttered in a half-jesting tone, but surely he was proposing a truce of sorts. It would be madness to refuse and spend the next few days snapping and snarling at each other. She craved peace, not arguments, and Beaudene had the power to make this journey easy or hard on her; yet she was dithering like a witless fool because their bargain would be based on a lie.

'Of course, if you think that feat beyond your capabilities——'

'I accept,' she interrupted hurriedly. Then, unable to resist the amused smile playing about his mouth, added, 'What would you have done had I refused?'

His smile was suddenly very wicked and very male. 'Put your tongue to better use, princess, what else?'

Nell promptly blushed a brilliant rosy hue, and the only reason she saw the faintly puzzled frown appear in Beaudene's eyes when she did so was because she was fighting to keep her gaze away from his mouth. The image evoked by his words was already far too vivid for comfort. She could almost feel the brush of his lips against hers.

'Could our bargain include you ceasing to call me "princess"?' she managed, scarcely hearing the words over the pounding of her heart.

'But you are like a princess,' he objected softly, the frown disappearing. 'Beautiful, proud, wilful—recklessly so at times.' The aside was tacked on somewhat drily. 'Of course, you also want your own way, have never learned to follow orders without arguing, and complain about minor inconveniences, but—'

'Don't let yourself get carried away,' Nell muttered, recovering from her stupefaction in a hurry. For one insane moment there she had actually thought Beaudene was praising her. Hunger was obviously making her light-headed. Pride and wilfulness were not exactly praiseworthy qualities, and she couldn't possibly look beautiful after last night's various adventures. She blushed again when she remembered the way her lips had tingled at the imagined pressure of his mouth. As if he would want to kiss someone who looked as if she'd been dragged behind her horse, rolled in the mud, and whose only comb was her fingers.

Merciful saints, what was she thinking? She didn't want him to kiss her. She *didn't*!

Fortunately for her beleaguered mind, a diversion presented itself. With a suddenness that took Nell by surprise they emerged from the forest into a sunlit green vista. At their back and curving around to the right the trees stood dark and mysterious, but ahead and on their left lay undulating hills and meadows, covered as far as the eye could see with a carpet of long grass that rippled in the breeze, swaying and springing back as though an unseen hand brushed over it again and again. The stream that had followed them through the forest, sometimes glimpsed, sometimes veering away from their path, meandered lazily across the land to spill into a small pond before disappearing around a slight incline. Beside the pond, the branches of a solitary oak, left behind when the forest had been cleared, hung low over the water, as though gazing at its own reflection.

'Oh! I know this place!' The exclamation burst from Nell's lips as memory stirred within her.

Beaudene reined in when they were halfway across the first meadow. His gaze, narrowed and intent, surveyed the scene as if he was inspecting every separate blade of grass. His dark brows were drawn together, but Nell was too excited to pay much heed to the small warning sign.

'We stopped here to eat on our way to my aunt's house ten years ago, and one of the servants allowed me to paddle in the stream. Why, that means——' she turned a delighted face to him '—that means the road to Wells is a mere mile or so to the west, beyond those trees.'

'That doesn't concern us,' Beaudene answered, not taking his eyes from the scene in front of them.

Nell grabbed hold of her courage with both hands and told herself to tread carefully. 'Well, I didn't mention this before, because we left in something of a hurry, but. . . I have to stop at Wells before I go on to Hadleigh.'

That got his attention. 'You have to stop at Wells before you go on to Hadleigh?' He didn't sound at all receptive to the idea. In fact he sounded downright incredulous.

'Aye.' She dared a fleeting glance upward. 'I have to visit my mother's tomb. 'Tis in the cathedral.'

There was a long minute of silence, during which

time Nell refused to look at Beaudene again. When he spoke his voice was as smooth and as cold as water gliding over stone. 'Have you forgotten, my lady, that several of your male relatives are probably galloping after us right this minute? This is not the time for a detour so you can say a few sentimental prayers over your mother's grave.'

Nell forgot about caution. 'But I have to——'

'The only thing you have to do is obey my orders. Something you seem to have a great deal of trouble with.'

'But I promised——'

'We are *not* going to Wells. Is that clear enough for you?'

'You don't underst——'

'*Quiet!*'

The angrily whispered command was accompanied by a bone-crushing grip on her wrist. Startled into obeying, Nell saw that Beaudene had gone very still, his gaze searching the forest behind them.

'What is it?' she breathed, and never even questioned why she was whispering too.

'We've been followed for the past mile or two,' he said, so calmly that for a moment the import of the words went right over her head. A second later they sank in.

'Followed!' The word emerged as a muffled squeak. 'Then why are we chatting here instead of fleeing for our lives?'

'Because whoever has been pacing us is mounted and I don't know how fresh his horse is, whereas yours is tired and can be outrun. So far, our shadow seems merely curious, but if we take off as if the devil was at our heels he might be tempted to find out why. Our best defence is to act as if we're not worth robbing.'

His rapier-sharp gaze flicked her up and down. 'Fortunately, you look the part.'

Nell didn't know whether she'd just been insulted or not. She knew she wasn't looking her best, but Beaudene could have been improved by a bath and a shave himself.

Then an idea of such brilliance occurred to her that insults and outrage alike were forgotten. She looked hurriedly away, afraid her expression would betray her.

''Tis just as well we have to cross these open fields for a while,' he said in a voice that carried only to her ears. He released her wrist and nudged the horses forward again. 'Outlaws prefer the shelter of the forest. But stay close, my lady.'

Outlaws! For a second Nell quailed inwardly at what she was about to do. Then she reminded herself that she had made a promise ten years ago that came before any consideration for a bodyguard of recent acquaintance who wouldn't even listen to her. Beaudene could look after himself, and if he objected to being left behind to cope with outlaws, then perhaps it would teach him to be a little less obdurate about side-trips to Wells.

She cast a quick glance to her right, trying to estimate the distance she would have to gallop before she was out of sight. Light and shadow chased each other across the grassy hills as clouds drifted past the face of the sun and she shivered slightly. It had best be now, she thought. Before she lost her nerve.

Without giving herself more time to brood over ill omens, Nell wheeled her horse to the right and clapped her heels to his flanks. Rufus leapt forward as if he'd just left his stable, his stride lengthening into a headlong gallop within the first few paces. A fleeting prayer of thanks that Beaudene had insisted she ride astride flashed through her mind and was gone. Behind her, she heard him curse and start in pursuit, then there was nothing but her racing heart, echoing the pounding of Rufus's hooves against the ground, and a litany of scarcely coherent thoughts.

Let him be right. Let him be right that whoever followed us will give chase. Let me be right in thinking he'll turn and fight rather than risk me being captured by outlaws. Let me escape. Keep him——

The prayer for Beaudene's safety was never finished. At the edge of the forest, directly in her path, two hooded figures rose from the grass, blood-curdling yells issuing from their throats, longbows drawn and ready.

Nell screamed and hauled on the reins so sharply that Rufus reared and nearly went over backwards. Before she could turn him to flee back the way she had come, the figures rushed forward until they were mere yards away. Both arrows were aimed, unwavering, at her heart.

Terrified, she turned to look for Beaudene. At the same moment a flash of darkness streaked past her. Snorting and skidding back on his hocks, Samson was pulled around in a sliding halt that put him between Nell and danger. But the action was only a temporary measure, she saw. Their shadow had indeed given chase. As Beaudene reached for her bridle to pull Rufus closer, another man was reining his horse in beside them.

'A chivalrous gesture, my lord,' the rider drawled in a surprisingly cultured voice. His dark eyes went to Beaudene's scar and lingered. 'But don't try anything else heroic. We have no wish to kill your lady. At least, not unless our leader orders it.' He laughed softly.

Beaudene did not so much as glance at him. His golden eyes were fixed on Nell's face with such ferocity that she would have fled from him as well, given the choice. 'Are you now content?' he snarled.

CHAPTER SIX

'IT WOULD have happened like that anyway.'

Nell huddled on a corner of the wide pallet that, apart from a crudely-fashioned table, was the only piece of furniture in the hut where she and Beaudene had been taken, and tried to sound defiant rather than defensive. It wasn't easy when her bodyguard was prowling around their quarters like a caged wolf.

He halted in front the open doorway of the hut and stared out. 'No, it damn well would not have happened like that,' he grated. 'There was only one man lying in wait in the direction we were supposed to be going. Man!' He snorted and shook his head. 'More like a boy. We could have ridden straight over him.'

Nell glared at his back. 'Aye, and then been shot by the others.'

'A toothless old man and a girl?'

'They knew what they were doing.'

'And they had a deal of assistance from you, didn't they, *princess*?' He swung around to impale her on the knife-edged rage in his eyes.

'Don't call me that!' Nell jumped up from the bed. 'You're blaming me for everything, and if you don't stop I'll——'

'You'll do *nothing*.' As quick as a hawk striking, Beaudene took one stride towards her, wrapped a powerful hand around her arm and pushed her unceremoniously back again. He towered over her, large and menacing. 'You will sit there, my lady, and you will say and do nothing while I try to fathom what's going on here.'

Nell set her lips in a mutinous line. Apparently convinced that he had intimidated her into silence for the moment, Beaudene returned to the doorway and propped one broad shoulder against the wooden frame. He stuck his thumbs in his belt and his fingers curled into fists. By the hard set of his profile, his thoughts were not pleasant. Beyond the doorway, Nell could see a boy sitting propped against a similar rough dwelling, watching them. A small crossbow lay across his knees, its arrow nocked. She looked away, feeling slightly sick.

The open door and one small window were the only sources of light and air in the hut, but with Beaudene filling the doorway very little of either was admitted. Nell doubted that his absence would have made much difference. Fear was the reason why she couldn't seem to breathe easily, why her stomach was knotted with tension. She should have been feeling guilty for leading them into an ambush, but somehow, despite Beaudene's anger at her recklessness, she had the frightening feeling that their capture had been a little too easy. She cast a glance at him from the protection of her shadowy corner. Against the light he looked huge, his back and shoulders broad and hard with muscle, tapering to lean hips and long, powerful legs.

How had an old man, a girl, a boy younger than herself and a cripple managed to disarm him?

Of course, he hadn't known precisely who or what their captors were until it was too late. Guilt stabbed through her at last as she realised that Beaudene's first thought must have been to protect her. It wasn't a comforting realisation, but it was better than the fearful suspicions that had been tormenting her mind for the past hour; better than remembering that the only explanations she'd been given for everything had come from him alone.

But just as she felt her tense muscles relax a little, she caught sight of Beaudene's packs just inside the door. Fear hummed along her nerves again. Their horses had been tethered somewhere, and Beaudene's sword and dagger taken, but everything else was still intact. Nell swallowed and surreptitiously touched the hidden crucifix, as though she needed proof that they hadn't been searched for money or jewels. Her throat felt as if cold fingers were wrapped around it.

'We could try to escape,' she suggested huskily, hardly daring to take a breath in case her voice wavered. She wasn't even sure if Beaudene knew where they were. After an hour of being led through the forest in what had seemed to be innumerable circles, her own sense of direction had been hopelessly lost.

He shot her a quick, lowering glance, then jerked his head towards the boy. 'Do you expect me to kill our watchdog?' he bit out. 'He's a child. Have you ever seen anyone kill a child with his bare hands, my lady?'

Another æon of silence dragged past.

'Why. . .why do you suppose they haven't robbed us?' She tried again, unable to bear the sound of her erratic heartbeat any longer. ''Tis almost as if we're. . . guests.'

'You'd better pray that's truer than you think.'

'What do you mean?'

He shrugged. 'Just an idea. But if I'm wrong, we're in a pother of trouble, thanks——'

'To me,' she finished for him. When he turned to face her she wished she'd stayed silent.

'Enlighten me,' he growled far too softly. Something

leashed but violent glittered in his eyes. 'Just how far did you think you would get alone?'

The tightly coiled tension in Nell snapped without warning. 'All the way to Wells,' she cried, leaping to her feet. 'And, what's more, I still intend to go——'

The words were cut off abruptly by Beaudene's mouth coming down hard over hers.

It was anger, pure and simple. Nell could only stand there while the storm raged around her, her mouth crushed and bruised beneath the force of his, her senses stunned. She couldn't even *feel*. Her body had gone numb with shock.

When he lifted his head, only the relentless grip he had on her arms prevented her from dropping straight to the floor. Nor did he give her time to recover.

'Do you know how close you came to being killed today? *Do you*?' He shook her hard, his words battering at her senses even as his kiss had done. 'God damn it, Nell, if you ever——'

'But I promised!' The desperate cry came from her heart. 'You don't un——'

'Stop it!' he said thickly. 'Just shut up!' The hot pressure of his mouth returned, as furious, as overwhelming as before.

Nell heard herself make a small muffled sound of protest, and then she was weightless, helpless, her body locked to his by arms that felt like steel bands around her.

'Oh! Your pardon, my lord, my lady.'

Beaudene jerked his head up and whipped around, releasing Nell so abruptly that she staggered back, hit the bed and collapsed on to it. She lifted trembling fingers to her lips and felt them part, soft and quivering, as she tried to draw air into her starved lungs. Her vision, strangely blurred, began to clear enough for her to recognise the girl standing in the doorway as one of their captors. She held a dagger in one hand and was balancing a trencher of food on her hip. Nell had never been so glad to see anyone in her life.

'I brought you something to eat,' the girl said, entering and laying the trencher on the table. She straightened and cast a quick, wary glance at Beaudene, her gaze lingering for a moment on his scar. She would have been pretty, Nell thought, with her copper-coloured braids and clear blue eyes, if her face had not been so thin and tired-looking.

'If you wish you may walk outside, within the camp,' the girl continued, gesturing with her free hand. 'You are not. . .prisoners here.'

'Really? What would you call us?' Beaudene's sardonic tone was so like his usual self that Nell could only wonder at how quickly he had regained his control. *She* felt as if she had just discovered what it was like to be struck by lightning.

'We mean you no harm,' their captor insisted.

'I suppose that is why you carry a knife, and your children go about armed with crossbows?'

The girl's expression stilled. 'Desperate times make for desperate measures, my lord. But, whether or not Dickon relieves you of whatever wealth you carry, you will keep your lives.'

'And when is this Dickon supposed to show himself?'

'A day or two, perhaps.' The girl shrugged. 'We cannot be sure.'

She seemed about to say more, but a voice outside the hut shouted, 'Bess! You're needed.' With a quick gesture towards the trencher, she hurried from the hut.

As soon as she was gone, Nell pounced on the food, placing the trencher on the bed beside her. It was simple fare—a loaf of coarse, dark bread and some slices of cold roasted venison, accompanied by two mugs of ale—but she wouldn't have cared if the meal had consisted of a bowl of slops so long as she could use the excuse of eating to avoid meeting Beaudene's eyes. She felt him watching her, and concentrated on tearing a chunk of bread from the loaf.

'Not quite what you're used to?' he asked, reaching down to help himself to some venison.

Nell shrugged and kept her eyes lowered.

'On the other hand, if today was a goodly example, you've probably driven any number of men to that particular act of retribution.'

Sweet Jesu! He hadn't meant the food. The morsel of bread in her mouth suddenly tasted like dried chaff. It went down with difficulty. Defiantly, Nell took another bite. 'If you are talking about the way you just assaulted me, my lord, I don't wish to discuss it,' she announced with slightly muffled dignity.

'Far be it from me to spoil your repast, princess. Just don't expect an apology.' When she didn't rise to that bait, he picked up one of the ale cups and handed it to her. 'Here, try this. 'Twill make swallowing easier.'

Nell buried her heated face in the wooden beaker and tried to pretend that Beaudene wasn't standing over her, fully aware of her discomfort. She only wished *she* could remain in happy ignorance of her own humiliation. To think that earlier she had been imagining his kiss as a gentle brush of lips, a tender caress, when the reality had been a punishing onslaught that had all but paralysed her. The memory made her cringe inside. She'd been a fool! A witless, wanton fool!

'I think you're right, princess.'

Nell promptly choked on a mouthful of ale. 'What?' she croaked when she could speak again. Holy Saints, now he was adding mind-reading to his other diabolical traits.

'We'll have to escape. Two or more days is too long for us to kick our heels in this place. We'd better leave tonight.'

Overwhelming relief nearly caused Nell to drop her cup. He couldn't read minds. No, of course he couldn't. And if he was planning an escape he could have had nothing to do with their capture, she scolded herself, feeling more foolish than ever. She took another bolstering sip of ale. 'Leave. Aye. Tonight. Um. . . how?'

Beaudene pushed the trencher aside, sat down on the pallet and leaned back against the wall. He propped one arm on his upraised knee and stared thoughtfully through the doorway. 'That ill-assorted rabble out there might have captured us, but holding us is another matter. There seem to be very few people in the camp, given the number of huts, which means most of them are with this Dickon fellow, probably off poaching the King's deer or robbing people blind, so escape shouldn't be too difficult.' He turned a piercing stare on her, golden eyes narrowed and intent. 'Especially as, this time, you'll be on my side. Won't you, my lady?'

Nell finished her drink and set the cup back on the trencher. 'Of course,' she said, and, taking a deep breath, forced herself to meet that compelling gaze.

The slow smile he gave her made the bed rock. Which was impossible. She wondered if she'd just imbibed too much ale.

'Good, because I'm going to need your help. That girl—Bess—said we had the freedom of the camp. They'll follow me if I set foot outside, but you won't look like a threat to them. I want you to wander about, talk to people, show Bess a friendly face. And, if you can, find out how many men are in the camp, where the horses are kept, and if anyone guards them—although I think it unlikely when they have only a babe watching us. Do you think you can do that without arousing suspicion?'

'I'm not a complete idiot,' Nell muttered. Only where you're concerned. She rose quickly, not wholly convinced that she hadn't said that last part aloud. Beaudene was still smiling slightly, and the expression made her very nervous.

'Off you go, then. And while you're at it——' He waited until she paused in the doorway and glanced back. 'Tell our watchdog out there to put the bow down whenever he feels like nodding off, or he'll shoot himself in the foot.'

The watchdog did not take kindly to the advice. In fact he denied any desire for sleep so loudly that Bess emerged from a nearby hut, drawn by the noise.

'Hush, Jemmie,' she scolded. 'You'll wake your mam.' She put a hand to the boy's brow and seemed relieved at the feel of his skin. 'Does your shoulder still pain you?'

Jemmie scowled and shook his head.

'The child should be abed at this hour,' Nell said absently, noticing that the shadows of evening were beginning to encroach on the settlement. The air had grown cooler with the setting of the sun, and a fine mist hovered above the ground, wrapping delicate ribbon-like tendrils around the trees encircling the clearing.

At the mild comment, Bess lifted her chin, her lips parting, and Nell turned to her in quick apology. 'But

'tis difficult to get them hence while daylight prevails,'
she added, smiling.

The girl hesitated, then an answering smile lightened
her pale, weary face for a moment. 'It is that, my lady.
I'm Bess, by the way. Is there something. . .? Were
you wanting——?'

'Just a little fresh air,' Nell assured her. 'And please
call me Nell. "My lady" is far too old and dignified,
and we are much of an age, I warrant.'

Bess flushed slightly and was about to reply, when a
low sound came from the hut she had vacated. She
turned swiftly, but Nell stayed her with a hand on her
arm.

'Send the child to bed,' she insisted, too low for
Jemmie to overhear. 'We are without weapons or
horses, so surely do not need guarding, and my lord is
concerned for the boy's safety.'

An inspired statement, she thought, rather pleased
with herself. One less pair of eyes watching them
should please Beaudene also. Which would make for a
nice change.

'I will, my lady, as soon as——'

The sound came again, followed by a harsh, racking
cough. Bess's face tightened. She whirled around and
vanished into the hut without another word, leaving
Nell staring frowningly after her.

It was very quiet.

Too quiet.

Where was everyone? she wondered, glancing about.
Where were the women and children? There was Bess,
and Jemmie apparently had a mother, but surely——?

She let her gaze wander slowly around the shadowy
clearing. The settlement consisted of a dozen huts or
more, placed in a haphazard U-formation, and as many
cooking fires. Only the two nearest her were burning,

she noticed, heating cauldrons of some sort. She could see no sign of the horses; if they were tethered nearby they were well-hidden. Nor were there any guards posted, not even another child.

Of course, Jem and his mother could be the only family in the camp, but Nell didn't think so. Despite the fact that no lights had been kindled in the huts against the onset of night, the place had all the appearance of a reasonably prosperous village, even if it was in the middle of the forest. A few hens scratched about, and there were a couple of goats in a pen behind the cottages. She caught a glimpse of the old man who had taken part in their ambush. He glanced up briefly from milking one of the goats, then returned to his task as though her presence was no cause for alarm.

And yet alarm skittered at the corners of her mind, nudging her forward, pulling at her reluctant feet, until she stood at the lower end of the U and could see inside the dwellings there. At close quarters the reason for their dark air of abandonment was shockingly clear. They had been ravaged by fire, and recently.

Feeling a chill that had nothing to do with the mist that now swirled about her skirts, Nell retraced her steps to the hut Bess had entered. She halted, looking across the clearing towards Beaudene. He was watching her, standing in the shadows to one side of the doorway. She thought he nodded once, in encouragement or command. Hesitating only a second longer, she turned on her heel and stepped into the cottage.

The unmistakable odours of sickness assaulted her instantly. She paused just inside the entrance, waiting for her eyes to adjust to the dimness. When they did she saw Bess sitting on a low stool beside a pallet, her head bowed. The blanket on the pallet had been drawn up so that it covered the figure beneath from head to toe.

The chill in her veins was suddenly ice-cold. 'Holy Mother of God,' she whispered, crossing herself. 'Is it the plague?'

Bess raised her head. It was a measure of the girl's weariness, Nell realised vaguely, that she showed no surprise at her presence. 'Naught but the plague of war, my lady,' she answered, her voice low. 'Men fighting and killing each other whether they be kings or outlaws.'

'Outlaws did this? Oh. We thought——'

A soft humourless laugh came through the dimness. 'Did you think we were the only band of outlaws living in the forest? There are many such as we. But we were strong. We were prospering!' Her voice strengthened suddenly and her gaze sharpened, as though focusing on Nell for the first time. ''Twas greed and envy that did this, my lady. Men who thought robbing us would be easier than waylaying wealthy travellers. They attacked at dawn five days ago—burning, raping, killing.'

'But. . . Surely *all* your warriors were not killed?'

'Not all, no. We drove them off. And now Dickon has taken the men who can still fight and gone after them. A show of strength, he said, so they won't come back. Who knows if our own men will come back? And how many will still be here to see it, when the wounded are dying for lack of proper care?'

Nell glanced involuntarily at the shrouded figure on the bed.

'Aye.' Bess followed her gaze. 'An arrow pierced her lung.'

'*Her*?' Nell's breath caught. 'Not Jemmie's mother?'

'No. Not yet.'

'Dear God in Heaven, is she wounded, too? Did they deliberately loose their arrows on the women and. . .?' She thought of the empty, quiet clearing outside, the burned huts, and couldn't finish the question. The evidence of a massacre was all too clear.

Quick sympathy had her reaching out to touch Bess's shoulder. 'You poor girl,' she murmured. 'How many are left? Have you been nursing them alone all this time?'

'Since old Meg died three days ago.' Bess nodded. 'Simpkin has been helping me, and 'tis not so many, but— Oh, my lady, even if I had the proper herbs and such, 'twould be useless. Meg was a wise-woman, she knew how to make poultices and salves, and draughts to ease their pain. She was teaching me, too, but our stocks were already poor, and are now gone as she is.'

'Well, then, we shall just have to gather more, and *I* will show you how 'tis done. Did your Meg have a garden?'

For a moment Bess stared up at her, as if turned to stone. When she finally spoke her voice was trembling with undisguised hope, and tears welled in her eyes. 'No. We were going to buy them. . . There's a fair. . . crowded. . . We go every year. . .no one notices us. . .'

'Hush. . .wait.' Nell pressed her hand harder to Bess's shoulder to calm the girl. 'This has to be thought on. But first—' she gestured to the shrouded figure on the pallet '—this poor soul must be given Christian burial.'

'Aye.' Bess took a deep breath and lifted a hand to squeeze Nell's briefly. 'Your pardon, lady, I forgot myself.' She rose, bent to touch the still form in a gentle farewell, then gestured for Nell to precede her from the hut. ''Twill be more fitting to talk in my cottage, if you do not mind waiting until I see to the others. As to Nan here, Simpkin and Luke are preparing her grave. It does not take long,' she finished with faint bitterness. 'Christian burial is not for we who live secretly, hidden away from towns and churches.'

There was not a lot she could say to that, Nell reflected. And it would be cruel to remind Bess of the fate of those who died unshriven when there was nothing to be done about it. 'When we get to Wells I'll buy masses for their souls,' she decided, not realising she had spoken aloud until she saw the tired smile again light Bess's face briefly.

'Be sure I will tell Dickon of your kindness, my lady. Now, will you wait with your lord until I may come to you?'

Nell suddenly noticed where Bess was taking her. 'Holy Mother save us! We can't talk in there!' she exclaimed in a frantic whisper, grabbing Bess's arm and making a sharp left turn. She pulled her new friend into the nearest hut, barely remembering to keep her voice down when she saw two pallets against the side walls. The occupants appeared to be asleep. 'And he's not my lord. Let me stay with you. He won't think anything is amiss. After all, he asked me to——' She bit her tongue on the rest.

Bess gave her a curious look.

'It matters not,' said Nell hurriedly. 'But 'twill be better if he doesn't know what we have planned.'

'We haven't got anything planned.'

'Not yet,' Nell admitted. 'But how much planning does it take to go to a fair and buy some herbs and cordials? How did you and Meg manage it?'

'Two or three men would go with us, my lady. They would wait in the woods while we purchased what we needed. Not only herbs, but candles, spices, wool for clothing. Why, you may buy anything you need, and when the stalls are crowded no one thinks to look closely at two women. That is. . .' She paused and peered doubtfully through the gloom at Nell's gown.

'Aye, you'll have to find me some clothes. No country maid would wear this, even filthy and covered in mud.'

''Tis a shame,' Bess murmured, reaching out to touch the rich brocade. 'Such a pretty gown to be so treated.'

'Trying telling that to his lordship,' retorted Nell with great feeling. 'Not that I have any fondness for the wretched thing.' She contemplated the rapt look on Bess's face for a moment, before asking impulsively, 'Would you like to have it?'

'*Me*, my lady? Me wear such a garment? 'Twould not be. . . That is. . . Oh, I would look as fine as the Queen herself,' she finished, so wistfully that Nell found herself laughing.

'Then 'tis yours,' she said. 'So long as you have something to replace it.'

'Oh, aye, my lady. But surely you cannot mean to wear simple homespun? Although there is a velvet surcoat trimmed with miniver somewhere. . .'

The words tripped over each other so quickly that Nell laughed again. 'The very thing. After we see to your patients, you shall show it to me. Then all that remains is to plan how we may slip away tomorrow.'

'But we'll need money, and Dickon keeps it hidden.' Her face, so recently hopeful, fell back into its weary lines. ''Tis only he and Simpkin who know where it is, and Simpkin will never let us go alone.'

'Then I shall have to steal some coins from Lord Beaudene.'

Bess's eyes went wide and startled. 'Steal from your lord?'

'He's not my lord,' Nell repeated absently. 'He's my bodyguard.'

'While you are in this camp, my lady, he had best be your lord,' Bess stated, accepting this brief explanation with a praiseworthy lack of curiosity. 'I'm sorry if you think it unseemly to share my cottage with him, but you'll be safer when the men return, and I'll be sleeping there also. 'Tis not as if you'll be alone with him.'

Nell refrained from telling her that she had already spent one night alone with Beaudene. There were more important things to worry about. Somehow she had to get her supposed husband out of their hut so she could search his packs. And if Beaudene kept his money on his person—— Nell shuddered. She didn't want to think about how she might have to overcome that.

'Bess? Is that you?'

The faint voice from the shadows made both girls jump guiltily. Nell recovered first. 'We'll need light,' she said briskly, turning her mind to the more immediate task demanding her attention. 'And whatever supplies you have, even if 'tis only water and clean linen.'

But water and clean linen could only do so much. By the time full darkness had fallen, Nell had learned just how much devastation had been visited upon the small settlement. In every hut that hadn't been burned lay the sick and injured: two men, both feverish and weak from badly infected wounds, and women and children in a like state from cuts and burns.

The children tore at Nell's heart, especially as she was helpless to ease their pain, but what brought angry, pitying tears to her eyes was the girl lying alone in the hut beside Bess's cottage.

'She can't be more than thirteen,' she whispered when she had examined the girl's injuries and had coaxed her to swallow some water. 'How *could* they? No. Don't answer that,' she added with soft bitterness. 'I know only too well what men are like when they see something they want. The last thing they consider is youth or innocence.'

'She hasn't spoken since Luke found her after the fight,' Bess murmured in the same low tone, although the girl had turned her head away and seemed deaf and blind to their presence. 'Her wounds are not so bad, as you see—bruises, mainly. 'Tis the shock, and the shame of it. Although, Lord knows, none of us would have her feel dishonoured. I'm here myself because my master forced me, then cast me aside when his wife discovered us. But who knows what such a one as she understands?'

When Nell looked a question at her, Bess touched her forehead. 'Simple,' she mouthed. Then whispered, 'What if she should quicken with child, my lady? She would lose what mind she has, for certain. If it didn't kill her.'

Nell gazed down at the still girl. ''Twould take any woman to the brink of madness to bear a babe in such circumstances, let alone a child like this.'

'Meg would have known what to do,' Bess sighed as she bent to draw the blanket up further. 'All the rest of us can do is pray.'

But would that be enough? Nell wondered rather grimly as she followed Bess from the hut. She also knew what to do. She had grown up knowing. Had often heard her aunt's friends discussing their visits to a certain apothecary to rid themselves of possible reminders of their indiscretions. And though the discussions had been conducted in whispers, though the

Church condemned such a practice as a hideous abom-
ination, a crime deserving of eternal damnation, surely,
here, the circumstances were very different? Surely,
here, her knowledge could do only good?

'Look.' Bess touched her arm, distracting her from
her uneasy questions and drawing her attention to the
group of men around one of the fires. 'Simpkin and
Luke are back. And your lord is with them. They'll be
wanting their supper.'

Nell glanced up. By the light of the fire she could see
Beaudene hunkered down on his heels, talking to the
other men. He looked up briefly, the light reflecting in
his amber eyes as he stared at her across the flames.
Half-formed plans raced through her mind like clouds
before the wind. All were dangerous. All risked
Beaudene's wrath. And one in particular might risk
her very soul—if she had the courage to carry it out.

'See if you can keep them there for a while,' she said
softly. 'Long enough for me to find some money, if
there's any to be found.'

'A wise man keeps his purse close, my lady. You
may take it from me. But I'll do my best.'

Bess had been right. There was no money in the packs.

Nell had just discovered that fact for herself when
the door was pushed open and Beaudene strode into
the hut. He pulled up short at the sight of her crouched
over his belongings, candle in hand. For what seemed
like an eternity, Nell could only stare up at him, frozen
with dismay, before she managed to force herself to
her feet.

He reached out and pushed the door closed without
taking his eyes off her, leaving his hand braced against
the wooden panels. 'Find what you were searching

for?' he enquired, in a soft tone that sent a chill down her spine.

Nell's gaze went from his face to the door and back again. Why did she have to choose this particular moment to notice how big his hands were? she wondered a little wildly. To remember the power in those long fingers when they had gripped her arms, the equally powerful restraint when he had captured her ankle.

'I. . . I thought to dry this,' she stammered, snatching desperately at the excuse when she realised his black surcoat was clutched in her own hand. ''Tis still damp.'

His eyes narrowed. 'Interesting.'

'Wh. . .what?'

'You don't lie very well.'

Dear God, if he only knew. The last three years had been a lie. Something deep inside her shuddered once, uncontrollably. She was suddenly afraid. Stricken with a fear that had nothing to do with the decision she had made.

'What were you looking for, princess?'

That name! He was using it again, deliberately to——

'Money,' she declared boldly. And immediately, quailed inside. Had she run mad? But she must not show her fear. She must not give him that advantage. He respected strength and——

'Money?' Beaudene's brows went up. 'You're looking for payment before you deliver?'

Nell frowned. Had she just missed something while rallying her courage? 'I don't expect payment for finding out about these people. Besides, I have little enough to tell you, probably less than you gathered for yourself.'

There was an odd little silence. Before she could make out the expression in Beaudene's eyes, he removed his hand from the door and took a step towards her. His voice was softer than ever. 'Why money, then, princess? Were you thinking of buying your way out of here?'

'No, of course not,' she said, more puzzled than ever. ''Tis not for me. And we can't leave tonight, anyway.'

'This grows even more interesting.' He took another step forward. 'Let me guess. You've decided to give your cousin a sporting chance at catching you.'

'What in Christendom are you talking about?' Nell demanded, now totally confused. She remembered her light-headedness earlier. Surely the cool night air had banished any effects of the ale. Had *he* been imbibing too much? She suddenly noticed how close he was and took a step back. 'You've been outside. . .spoken to those men. 'Tis surely obvious why we can't leave. There are people dying here for lack of proper care. They need help.'

'From *you*?' His tone had her spine stiffening, as if someone had laid a whip across her back. 'Good God, woman, you can't even get dressed without injuring yourself.'

'I fell over this morning because of your sneaky habit of creeping up on me,' she retorted through gritted teeth. 'Strange though it may seem to *you*, my lord, I am not entirely useless. I have promised to help Bess nurse the sick and wounded, and that is precisely what I intend to do!'

He stared at her frowningly for a moment, then reached out and plucked his surcoat out of her hand. 'Forget it, princess.' He tossed the garment on to his pack with a dismissive action that spoke more surely

than any words. 'You can play the ministering lady of
the manor some other time. Outlaws take care of their
own.'

'Not when they lack medicines and the knowledge of
how to administer them. You don't know what it's like.
The children. . . You haven't seen. . .' Oh, how could
she make him listen? She whirled and dumped the
candle on the table. '*You* go, then, if you fear my
cousin's pursuit,' she told him, plunking both hands on
her hips. 'But I'm staying here! This is not last night,
my lord. You can threaten to knock me senseless all
you like, but if you make one move to take me away,
I'll scream loud enough to be heard in London.'

She had gone too far. Nell knew it the instant
Beaudene's eyes went a fierce, glittering gold. He took
one stride forward, his expression so savage that she
backed against the table with enough force to set the
candle rocking perilously. He shoved it aside with an
impatient curse and loomed over her.

'Stop!' she cried, struggling to keep some distance
between them without touching him. It was well-nigh
impossible. She would have to push him away—an
impossibility in itself—or lean back on her hands,
leaving her lower body vulnerable to the pressure of
his. Panic fluttered in her throat. 'You're trying to
frighten me again, and——'

'I'm trying not to strangle you!' he snarled, planting
both hands on either side of her hips as if his grip on
the edge of the table was the only thing stopping him
from wrapping them around her throat. 'God's blood!
If a man had accused me of fearing that cup-shotten
cousin of yours, he'd be choking on his own tongue!'

'I didn't mean——'

'Oh, aye, you damn well did!'

'No! I was only trying to. . .' Her breath caught and

she faltered, gazing up at him in unconscious appeal. 'I know you're not afraid for yourself,' she finally managed with simple honesty.

To her relief some of the fierceness went out of his eyes and he moved back a little. 'So you know that much, do you?'

'Aye.' Nell took a cautious breath. ''Tis your duty to me that you're thinking of, I know, but don't you see? If we tarry here for a few days, Thomas will go right past us. Why——' She stopped, and a second later a radiant smile suddenly spread across her face. Her panic and Beaudene's rage had just been entirely overtaken by a wondrous realisation. 'Why, we can even go to Wells and——'

'Stop right there.'

'But it couldn't be simpler!' Carried away with her plan, ruthlessly quelling a little voice in her head that was trying to remind her of the disastrous consequences of her last brilliant idea, Nell swept on. 'Just think! While we're in Wells, Thomas will discover I haven't arrived at Hadleigh Castle, and *he'll* hie himself off to Wells because that's where he was to escort me first. And then, while he's searching for me there, we can take a different route home.' A ripple of delighted laughter bubbled over as she thought about it. ''Tis the perfect reckoning. He'll be chasing us around in circles and he won't even know it.'

Beaudene did not seem inclined to share her gleeful triumph. 'And if he goes first to Wells, as you intended?'

She couldn't resist. The temptation was too much. 'Why would he do that?' she asked, widening her eyes with guileless innocence. 'He'll expect us to run straight for Hadleigh. Who would be foolish enough to make a detour to Wells when they're being pursued?'

Beaudene was suddenly very, very close again. 'Who, indeed?' he purred with a smile as dangerous as his tone.

Nell had the grace to blush, even though she continued to watch him with unabashed hope. She was rewarded by the genuine, albeit reluctant smile that tugged at his mouth.

'I hate to admit it, princess, but that strategy is rather sound, up to a point.' Before she could ask what point, he fixed her with a narrow-eyed stare that held a good deal of scepticism. 'Do you have knowledge of medicines, in truth?'

'Aye.' She nodded vigorously. 'Our nurse at Langley taught me.' Seeing the sceptical gleam still lingering, she added softly, 'I was interested.'

'Hmm. Damned inquisitive, more like.' After another minute of intense scrutiny, he added, 'So, how do you intend to obtain what you need, my lady?'

'Well, I——' Just in time Nell remembered his opinion of her lying ability. 'Bess is arranging it,' she amended hastily. Which was nothing less than the truth. 'And she will repay you when their leader returns. He's. . . Did those men tell you what happened?'

'Aye, but little else.' He straightened to his full height and looked down at her. 'I didn't expect a wealth of information. This is an outlaw camp. People come and go, and no one asks questions. Or if they're foolish enough to do so they find their answers at the point of a dagger.'

'Bess told me enough,' Nell said, sobering quickly as she remembered what she had seen. 'You call these people outlaws, and I suppose they do rob to survive, but would we be any different had we been abused by a master like my uncle for instance? He mistreated his people—family, servants, minstrels, it made no difference. And animals. We had a performing dog once, and a monkey. Uncle Edward bought them for my cousins' pleasure. I set them free.'

'And were punished for it?'

Nell shrugged. 'A beating. I would do it again.'

'Aye. I verily believe you would.' He reached out to tilt her chin up with the edge of his hand. 'Very well, my lady, you can have one day.'

'One day? But——'

His thumb lifted to press on her lower lip, silencing her. Nell went completely still.

'One day. No longer. I'll admit to some curiosity about our absent host, which accords with our staying here, but if he hasn't returned by this time tomorrow, we leave.' His gaze dropped to her mouth and he moved his thumb in a slow, stroking caress across her lips before lowering his hand. 'Make sure Bess knows whatever she needs to by then, because after that she'll be on her own.'

Nell nodded. She couldn't speak. Mainly because she had stopped breathing again. Beaudene was still so close that she could feel the heat from his body. It seemed to wrap her around, holding her motionless until he chose to release her. Her lips throbbed where his thumb had touched and she felt strange—on edge, nervous, as though waiting. . .

Her gaze lifted, to find him watching her, his golden eyes shadowed by half lowered lashes, but oddly intent.

'I. . . There's still. . .' With an effort that took an incredible amount of willpower, she tore her gaze from his to glance at his packs.

'The money. I know. But first. . .' Still speaking, he grasped her about the waist and lifted her to sit on the table.

Before Nell could do more than gasp at this unexpected development, he placed his hands on her knees, pushed her legs slightly apart and stepped between them.

She cried out in sheer panic and tried to scramble backwards, but his hand flashed out and cupped the nape of her neck. Holding her gently captive, supporting her weight without effort, he exerted the lightest pressure to draw her close and upright again.

'No!' Her hands flew up to push frantically at his shoulders. Beneath the soft wool of his surcoat, the unyielding power of his body was terrifying. Driven by blind instinct, she swung her foot and kicked him.

He laughed, a low husky sound that made her hands cling tighter, even as she trembled with the knowledge of her own helplessness.

'A flea wouldn't have felt that,' he chuckled. 'Relax, princess. I'm too close for you to do any damage.'

'Let me go,' she ordered, in a voice somewhere between a whimper and a squeak. The aforementioned flea would have doubled over laughing, she thought hysterically. Merciful saints, she had to stop this. She had to pull herself together.

'That's better,' he murmured, as she went still and struggled to think of a way out of this new predicament. The task seemed beyond her. His gentle, reassuring tone, combined with the far from reassuring vulnerability of her position, rendered her totally witless.

'You don't want to develop a kink in your neck from looking up at me,' he continued softly. 'Now we can talk in comfort.'

'T-talk? What about?'

He smiled straight into her eyes. 'Well, it seems to me that I've made most of the concessions here.'

Somewhere in the whirling confusion of her mind,

honesty compelled her to admit that he was right. Wariness kept her silent on the subject.

'That being so, I think a little recompense is in order.'

'Rec—— But I'm not. . . You can't. . .'

'That's the way it works, princess,' he said softly. 'Surely you know that? If you would be mistress of your fate you'll have to learn the ways of bargaining.'

Bargaining? Nell stiffened, realising only then how limp she'd gone. The knowledge added to her sudden outrage, sending a healthy surge of temper through her. Bargaining! He was playing with her. Punishing her for getting them into this situation.

But just as she opened her mouth to tell him she was not so easily defeated his hand moved, stroking her beneath her hair, and she was helpless again. Weak and shivering. What was he doing to her that she couldn't fight, couldn't seem to do anything except feel? All her senses were focused on his hand—the hard strength of his fingers, the gentleness of his touch. The contrast between the two held her enthralled. And the longer he held her the more she became aware of other contrasts. How small she felt so close to his powerful body, how soft to his hardness, how utterly female to his male.

The last awareness was so strong, so *primitive*, it was frightening. Never had she been so conscious of a man, no matter how close they had been. Not even this morning, when Beaudene had been teasing her, had she been so aware of him, so aware of her own femininity.

She looked up at him, words of protest, of fear, of confusion, trembling on her tongue, and forgot every one of them. His mouth was only inches away, his lips slightly parted. Her own mouth felt suddenly soft and pliant and warm. Shaking, she forced her gaze higher, and nearly cried out at the burning intensity of his eyes. They held her, helpless, for a second longer, and then there was something. . .something almost puzzled. . .something searching.

'Strange,' he murmured, so softly that she wasn't sure if he was talking to her or to himself. 'You can't lie convincingly, and yet you look. . .'

He fell silent, then shook his head very slightly. 'Perhaps 'twas because I startled you.' His gaze lowered to her mouth and he bent closer. 'Let's see what happens when I startle you like this, little one.'

CHAPTER SEVEN

His mouth touched hers, gently, softly, and withdrew.

Braced for another assault, Nell was stunned by his tenderness. She went still, scarcely breathing, as his lips returned to stroke hers with a light, brushing movement, tantalising, tempting her with the promise of warmth, of closeness, of a gentleness she'd never expected from a man. But wanted. Oh, sweet. She wanted it, but. . .

Half-frightened by the unfamiliar longing that was increasing with each caress of his mouth, she tried to draw back, only to find that his hold was far too secure. Between the gentle but inexorable hand at her nape and the solid barrier of his body she was trapped. How could that be? she wondered hazily, scarcely noticing that her mouth had begun to follow his, instinctively seeking a firmer touch. She could understand helplessness when he had overwhelmed her earlier, but *this*? She trembled, and a tiny sound of mingled need and doubt caught in her throat.

'Shhh.' he murmured. His warm breath fanned her lips with a different kind of caress, sending yet another cascade of shimmering sensations through her. 'Don't be afraid, little one. This won't be like before. I was. . . angry.' His lips feathered over hers again. 'Open your mouth,' he whispered. 'Let me taste you.'

'No, I——'

He stole the words as he took her mouth, in a slow possession that had her shivering uncontrollably. But not with fear this time. Had she even dreamed of a kiss like this? He left no part of her mouth untouched, claiming it with a gentle aggression that sent lightning strokes of pleasure through her with every gliding caress of his tongue against hers. Pleasure and a sweet, hot weakness that had her clinging, melting, yearning for the hardness of his body against hers. She whimpered again, the sound lost in his mouth, and felt the powerful muscles in his arms tense as though he would pull her closer.

Then, slowly, with hot, lingering touches of his tongue to her lips, he ended the kiss. His hands shifted to her wrists, unlocking her arms from about his neck, and he put her away from him, stepping back with a care that spoke of rigid control.

Nell forced her eyes open. Her lids were heavy, but her body felt light, and quivered inside with a strange heated restlessness. Dazed, she stared at Beaudene. At the powerful hands that had caged her so carefully, at the hard, sharply chiselled mouth that had kissed her with such shattering intimacy, at the eyes that——

Reality crashed back into her consciousness like a blast of cold air. And the chill went straight to her soul. His eyes were a darker gold than usual, but he watched her with an expression that held more frowning assessment than heated desire.

In painful detail she remembered the way her arms had been clinging about his neck—she hadn't even known how they'd got there—while he had held her with nothing more than one casual hand supporting her head, the other braced on the table beside her. The chill was replaced by a wave of embarrassed heat that started at her toes and swept upwards so fast that she felt sick. She couldn't go on looking at him.

And he, it seemed, had looked his fill at her. Without a word he turned on his heel and strode to the door.

As he yanked it open, he reached into his surcoat, withdrew a few coins and tossed them on to the bed. They landed with a musical tinkle that sounded to Nell like the clash of discordant cymbals.

'Your money, my lady,' he said, his voice as cold as the night air coming in through the doorway. The draught was abruptly cut off when the door snapped shut behind him.

For several minutes Nell could only sit there looking at the coins glinting faintly in the dim candlelight. The heat and restlessness had faded. Now she just felt cold. She knew the money was to pay for the herbs she needed. Why, then, did she have the terrible feeling that she had just been paid for that kiss? As if she was. . . As if he thought. . .

Tears filled her eyes, turning the coins into a shimmering silver and copper blur. She swiped at her face, blinking rapidly to force them back. It was no use crying because she had been stupid enough to let herself by seduced by gentleness into a kiss. And that was all it was, she told herself stubbornly. Just a kiss. It meant nothing.

She jumped down from the table, thankful to find that her legs, so weak and trembling only minutes ago, now supported her. 'See, you've already recovered from it,' she muttered, taking some small encouragement from the fact that she could walk over to the bed and scoop up the coins. If there was more than a little bravado in the way she shoved them into the pouch holding her crucifix, Nell ignored it.

She was tired. That was the cause of her tears. Any woman would feel a trifle fragile when she'd been riding for the better part of a night and day with little food and only a few hours' sleep between. She would feel much better tomorrow. She would go to the fair with Bess and enjoy herself. It would be a morning out of time for her. A chance to relax, to be herself, away from danger and pursuit and a man who confused her more with every moment she spent with him.

Confused and frightened her, she amended, going very still as she remembered that moment earlier when she had felt something tremble deep inside herself. As if she held some secret knowledge deep within, and had shuddered away from it, retreating into the safety of ignorance.

Fanciful nonsense, she scolded herself. If she had to stand here in a pother over some man, it had better be the unknown husband chosen by her father who had ignored her for years. What was she going to do about *that*?

Nell shuddered and sat down on the bed. The thought of marriage to a stranger was suddenly more abhorrent than ever. Perhaps she should only think as far ahead as changing her clothes. A more modest gown might even stop Beaudene treating her as if she was some kind of——

No! She scowled at the door of the hut, as if he was standing immediately in front of it. She would not think of that kiss again. He had punished her—in typical male fashion, Nell reminded herself sternly—for getting her way in staying to help Bess. He'd extracted a price.

But he had given in.

Her angry scowl faded. And in its place came a wistful contemplation, a gentle, feminine wistfulness so long suppressed that she was only vaguely aware of it. What had made him so hard? Angry one moment, mocking the next. He had deliberately frightened her more than once. He seemed to despise her. And yet today. . .tonight. . .through it all, she had sensed. . .

What? Nell asked herself, sighing. Was she deluding herself that there was more to Beaudene than ruthlessness and an implacable will, because of the occasional glimpse of tenderness or humour? But she couldn't deny that those qualities existed. She had seen them. Felt them.

She shied away from *that* memory immediately, lying down on her side and curling up, as though protecting herself from some unseen threat. But even as she ordered herself to forget the unexpected tenderness of Beaudene's kiss, to ignore silly, girlish dreams, to banish him entirely from her thoughts until she was rested and more rational, another question hovered tantalisingly at the edges of her mind.

She thought of the scar he bore, and wondered. Had he, like her, buried the gentler side of his nature in order to survive?

How the devil had survival come down to sitting out here by the fire, trying to leash instincts that threatened to destroy years of waiting and planning? Had he been bewitched? Was he taking leave of his senses?

Rafe shifted restlessly on the hard ground and glared at the door of the hut, as if he could see through it to the little temptress on the other side. She'd been one surprise after another today—her humour, even when she'd been complaining, her endurance, her courage, even that stupidly reckless dash across the meadow had provoked more than a twinge of reluctant respect for her determination and quick-wittedness once he'd calmed down—but that kiss! That had taken him so by surprise that he was still shaken by it more than an hour later.

His hands clenched as the memory of Nell's mouth beneath his sent a violent rush of heat straight to his loins. He gritted his teeth against the ensuing ache and willed the memory away, but for the first time in his life his vaunted self-control seemed to have deserted him. He couldn't forget how she'd tasted. Sweet and soft and unexpectedly shy. He couldn't forget the sensations aroused by his possession of that innocent, untutored mouth. Aye, untutored, damn it. She'd yielded, she hadn't responded. He was too experienced not to know the difference.

And as if that wasn't enough to raise several questions, he was beginning to recall too many other instances where she'd seemed puzzled, even totally uncomprehending, over some of the things he'd said. By the Rood, if he didn't know any better——

Rafe's eyes narrowed and he cursed softly. He did know better. Why did he forget that whenever he held her, touched her, looked into those luminous hazel eyes that held the mysteries of the forest in their depths? Her innocence was an act. It had to be. But, if that was so, why suddenly assume it now, after practically shoving the knowledge of her former lovers down his throat? And how had he known the instant she'd lied to him? Could anyone, even a woman, act so well that she could use feigned guilt to cover an equally false innocence, which in turn covered real guilt?

God! Rafe dropped his head between his hands and stifled a snarl of sheer exasperation. His thoughts were chasing themselves around in circles within circles. Any more and he'd go out of his mind.

The image brought another scowl to his face. He raised his head and glared at the hut again. That little witch in there was more dangerous than he'd realised. In all of this he'd almost forgotten the purpose of his journey. He'd almost forgotten the burning desire for justice that had——

'Rafe?'

The soft voice came, totally unexpected, from the woods behind him. Before the single word had faded into the night, Rafe was on his feet and turning, his hand reaching for his dagger in the same swift, smooth movement. He cursed again when he remembered the dagger had been taken.

'No need for weapons, unless you've taken to killing old friends,' said the voice, sounding amused. 'Of course, you've still got your fists. As I recall, they were lethal enough on their own.'

Rafe straightened slowly from the fighting crouch he'd assumed. The man standing in the shadows at the edge of the clearing could have been his brother. He was the same height, possessed the same lean, muscular build and his hair was as black as the night. Only his eyes were different, Rafe knew. They were a clear pale grey. His own gaze narrowed for an instant, then turned quizzical. 'Dickon?' he queried, brows lifting in gentle irony.

A rueful laugh sounded. 'Rather less threatening, I thought.'

A brief smile flashed across Rafe's face then vanished. 'Richard, what in God's name do you think you're doing living like an outlaw and leading a bloody band of cut-throats?'

The man who had once been Sir Richard Peverel stepped forward into the circle of firelight. 'Better that than having my head and shoulders part company. I *am* an outlaw, remember?'

Rafe's mouth thinned. 'Don't stand there babbling such folly at me. Now that Edward's firmly on the throne, do you think he'd rather see you dead because you fought for an annointed king than pardoned and giving freely of your allegiance? Mark me, he would not.'

Richard made a non-committal sound and gestured with his hand. Other men emerged from the trees. With only the occasional curious glance at Rafe they dispersed, some into huts, others to gather around the second fire.

They numbered a half-dozen or so, Rafe estimated, and more than a few looked to be the cut-throats he'd called them. Simpkin came last, a faintly amused expression on his face as he limped towards them.

'So I was right to go looking for you,' he said to Richard. 'This is the friend you once spoke of. The man who bears the mark of a knife on his face.'

'You were right,' Richard confirmed drily. 'But did you have to kidnap him and his lady?'

Simpkin shrugged. 'You have need of him.'

Rafe followed this exchange with grim attention. 'You mean I have this to thank for keeping Nell and myself alive?' he demanded, indicating his scar. 'Many thanks. I suppose, had it been otherwise, we would have died in the forest when you first saw us.'

'What! Me, a cripple, take on a warrior of your size? Not likely, my lord.'

Richard laughed. 'Is Simpkin the reason why you weren't surprised to see me just now? Apart from not hearing me, that is.'

'I must be more tired than I thought when a great ox like you can take me unawares,' Rafe retorted instantly. 'But, aye, I recognised your hand in the way we were ambushed. Or rather, I hoped 'twas you. You've trained this rabble the way you once trained soldiers.'

'We rabble got the task done, my lord,' Simpkin reminded him rather tartly. He turned to Richard. 'Sit.

Bess is abed, but I'll bring meat and ale when I've checked the wounded.'

'Ahh.' His leader stretched and motioned Rafe back towards the fire. 'A happy thought. I could eat the ox this overgrown barbarian called me.'

The comment drew a smile from Rafe, but he sobered almost immediately. As they sat down, he fixed his friend with an interrogatory stare and demanded an explanation.

'I'd rather know what you're doing running around the countryside with a wife at your heels,' Richard answered, yawning. 'God's bones, I'm tired. But we got the job done.'

'My congratulations.'

The sarcastic tone had Richard's brows lifting, but he waited, not speaking.

'She's not my wife,' Rafe said impatiently, but he kept his voice low and glanced warningly at the men sitting several yards distant. 'I'm escorting her home.'

'Well, who knows better than I that the roads are not safe for travellers? But escorting her on your own? Isn't that a little unusual?'

'The entire circumstances are damned unusual, but enough of that. What *I* want to know is how you came to this. And then I'll know how best to help you out of it,' he added grimly.

Richard's soft laugh held a note of bitterness. 'I'm just at the point where I might accept, my friend. Or would you rather I did not call you that?'

'Don't be a fool, Richard. You know why I chose to back Edward. The Duke of York took me into his service when I had nothing. Edward and I have been friends for years, as were you and I. Because you chose Henry of Lancaster doesn't make you my enemy now. You made your choice and honoured it to the end.

There's no shame in that.' He paused and stared into the fire for a moment. 'God knows, in battles between kings 'tis hard to say who has the right of it and who has not.'

'A pity my lord of Warwick does not hold the same view. 'Twas he who was baying for my head after Towton—I swear merely because I unhorsed him. The man was ever a pompous braggart.'

Rafe glanced up again, amused. 'A shrewd, pompous braggart comes closer to the mark, but I doubt he'll bother you now. He and Edward have fallen out over the Woodville alliance. Warwick has retired to sulk in his stronghold, and with good reason, I have to own. Not only was he made to look a fool at the French Court—arranging a match for Edward while the King was secretly marrying Mistress Woodville—but the Queen's relatives have overrun the Court like a plague of rats, all scurrying for their share of the pickings.'

'Aye. A more ill-considered match I can't imagine.' Richard grinned suddenly. 'And damned inconvenient as well. If you hadn't come along, I was going to send the prettiest wench here to petition the King on my behalf. But if the gossip is true, marriage has Edward running in harness.'

'Only until he gets tired of a constant diet of ice. Now, can we have a sober discussion here? What happened to you after Towton?'

'You have lost your sense of humour, Rafe. This escort business must not be much fun.'

'I'm sure Nell would agree with you. Talk!'

'There's not much to tell,' Richard said, capitulating with a careless shrug. 'After Towton there was a price on my head. Hell's fiends, there was a price on a lot of heads, but I didn't fancy having mine adorn the archway of some city gate, so I made for that hole we know of.'

'I thought so. We stayed there last night and I knew someone had been before us. 'Twas another reason why I didn't slaughter that ambitious crew of kidnappers this afternoon.'

Richard chuckled. 'I'll tell Simpkin to be properly grateful. Well, as you guessed, I stayed there until the hue and cry died down. It took long enough, God knows. Warwick is nothing if not tenacious. Then a little more than a year ago I fell in with these fellows. Most of them are good men, believe it or not, and the rest are controlled by the odd robbery. 'Tis not a bad life for some. Drifters from the army, runaway serfs, your true criminal—we have them all. And if a man's name is not the one he was born with, no one questions him about it.'

'I daresay, but 'tis no way for you to live, Richard. Let me intercede with Edward for you.'

'And live on what? A place in his hall, grateful for a few crumbs but expecting little else because I once backed a rival king? No, I thank you.'

'Not at Court.' Rafe hesitated, glancing at the hut before speaking again. 'I may be in a position to grant you some land for your oath of fealty. You're no fool, Richard. Once you're pardoned, you can build from that.'

For the first time there was a flicker of genuine interest in the grey eyes watching him. Then Richard's gaze narrowed and he said softly, 'You're going to reclaim Hadleigh Beaudene. After all these years? How?'

Rafe shrugged. 'Through the King, mayhap. But if not, there are other ways.'

'Hmm. Do those other ways have anything to do with the girl you were hell-bent on protecting today?'

'Hell-bent? Good God! What tale did Simpkin spin you?'

'Nought but the truth,' said Simpkin, coming up to them with a platter laden with chunks of venison and a brimming jug of ale. He also carried Rafe's sword and dagger, which he handed over. 'You would have taken an arrow for her had we fired.'

'Tis my duty,' said Rafe drily, returning his dagger to its sheath and laying the sword beside him. He turned the question on Richard before anyone could comment on that remark. 'Does the fact that you're tempted to accept my offer have anything to do with the little redhead sharing my lady's hut?'

A grin that he could only describe as sheepish spread across Richard's face.

Simpkin laughed. 'Accept on behalf of us all,' he advised his leader with the familiarity of a trusted servant. 'I, for one, grow too old for another winter spent in these woods.'

'An unusual man,' murmured Rafe, watching Simpkin as he returned to his place with the others. 'You would have been pleased with the way he planned that ambush. I knew we were being followed, but not by more than one, nor that Simpkin had sent young Luke off to warn the others and have them waiting. And, by his speech, I'd say he's had some learning.'

'Aye.' Richard nodded around a mouthful of venison. 'He was once a lord's fool. Was even taught his letters and how to figure. An easy life for a peasant born with a twisted foot and withered leg, one would think, but apparently the man abused him whenever the mood was upon him, so Simpkin ran away and ended up here.'

He ate for a few minutes in silence, then looked directly at Rafe over his ale-cup, all traces of careless unconcern gone from his expression. 'He'd probably make a good steward. And there are some others who may wish to follow me. How does that sit with you?'

Rafe smiled. 'Better to end up in honest employment—even as a fool—than wind up at the end of a rope.'

'Then it looks as if you've just gained yourself a fool,' Richard answered quietly. He put the mug down and held out his hand. 'And an oath of fealty, my friend.'

The open field outside the small market town was teeming with people and animals, and alive with the scents and sounds of the fair. Wealthy merchants garbed in their finest gowns rubbed shoulders with sharp-eyed pedlars in simple homespun. Craftsmen hammered and sewed. Townswomen in brightly-hued wools and velvets compared prices with soberly-clad farmers' wives while their husbands eyed the brilliant, cloudless sky and debated how long the unusually fine autumn weather would last.

Everyone for miles around, it seemed to Nell, had chosen that morning to attend the fair.

And there was aplenty to see and wonder at. From the goldsmiths' and jewellers' precious goods, displayed in sturdy wooden booths, to trestle tables piled high with fine English wool and Flemish cloth, furs from the North and spices and sweetmeats from the far-away East. Even the spaces between the stalls and tables were occupied by people hoping to turn a profit: barbers, jongleurs, travelling players, quacks declaiming the dubious properties of whatever potion or elixir they were selling. Pie-vendors wandered through the crowd, adding their voices to the din; children and dogs abounded, darting between stalls and wagons and legs with equally reckless abandon.

And, overlooking all, the castle that held licence for the fair stood apart on its wooded rise above the town in grimly-fortified patronage.

'Do you know who lives there?' Bess asked, seeing Nell's gaze go from the grey-walled turrets above them to the uniformed men-at-arms mingling with the crowd.

'No, and even if I did, I doubt they'd recognise me like this.' Nell glanced down at herself and tried to quell a growing feeling of nervousness. It hadn't been so bad at first. The unaccustomed freedom to wander at will among the stalls and booths had delighted her, as had the lavish way she had been dispersing Beaudene's money on various neccessities for their outlaw hosts.

There was, in truth, nothing to be nervous about. She looked no different from any other fair-goer. Her long hair was braided and coiled into a plain crespinette and the dusky-rose woollen gown Bess had found for her was modestly cut and worn beneath a sleeveless, fitted surcoat of moss-green velvet, neatly trimmed with miniver. She could, in fact, have passed for a respectable tradesman's daughter. Neither the soldiers in the crowd, nor the group of apprentices who had been following her and Bess around the fair, snickering and nudging each other but not venturing nearer, would suspect she was a lady abroad without male protection.

And that was the real problem, Nell admitted silently, as she waited for Bess to purchase a supply of candles. She wasn't afraid of the risk of exposure. She missed Beaudene's presence beside her.

So much for enjoying herself away from him, she

thought gloomily. Somehow, in their brief time together, she had grown accustomed to his protection. After years of constant guardedness, of having to protect herself, there was something very reassuring in the knowledge that his solid strength stood between her and possible danger. He might be infuriating and intimidating, and much too complex for her peace of mind, but she could not think of one other man of her acquaintance whom she would trust with her safety, with her very life.

And that despite her suspicions that he knew more about their capture than he was willing to tell her.

Nell shivered suddenly as an insidious little question crept, unbidden, into her mind. If she trusted Beaudene with her life, did that mean she could trust him in other ways? With the secret she had guarded for years?

With her heart?

A strange stillness seemed to settle around her. The sounds and bustle of the fair faded into a dim, misty background, and all she could see was a series of images. Beaudene leaning against the wall in her uncle's hall, watching her with the golden eyes of a hawk; standing, tall and powerful, across a fire, waiting for her capitulation; blazing-eyed and furious because she had risked danger to have her way.

And, against all that, she had only one kiss. One brief moment, that for all its sweetness had left her bewildered and angry and strangely vulnerable. Why would she trust her heart to a man who had such a very unsettling effect on her? Why had the thought so much as entered her mind?

Oh, aye, he had protected her, but it was merely duty. She would do well to remember that. She might amuse him occasionally, he might be completely unlike the other men she had known all her life, but he was just her bodyguard. She was in his charge. Nothing more.

'My lady? I mean. . . Nell, are you all right?'

Bess's anxious countenance swam before her eyes. Nell blinked, coming back to her surroundings with a jolt. Noise and movement started up around her again, seeming to be twice as loud and bewildering as before.

'Shall we purchase something to eat, mistress?' Bess went on, obviously still concerned. She indicated a near by pie-vendor who was eyeing them with interest. 'You look a little pale.'

'Succulent pigeons in a coffin, ladies,' the man called, sensing potential customers. He gave an ingratiating grin.

Nell repressed a shudder and aimed a weak smile somewhere between Bess and the pie-vendor. 'No, I'm just a little tired, 'tis all. We'd best conclude our business and be gone.'

'Aye, 'tis a long walk back,' Bess agreed. She touched Nell's arm. 'This way, my lady. The old woman's booth is at the end of this row, near yonder trees. And let us hope we can slip away without those dolts noting our direction.' She glanced back as she spoke, frowning slightly. 'I don't like the way they've been following us.'

'They'll lose interest if we ignore them,' Nell murmured, hoping to heaven she was right. Dismissing the apprentices from her mind, she tried to remember the list of herbs and medicines she needed to buy. That was all she had to worry about, she told herself with grim purpose. Helping Bess's people. One especially.

The reminder sent another chill whispering over her flesh. For some reason a decision that had seemed so simple and right yesterday was becoming harder to contemplate.

'The last booth, you say?' she asked, determinedly fixing her gaze on a faded green awning set a little apart from the others. She quickened her pace, suddenly aware that, a mere fifty yards away, several men-at-arms were engaged in setting up butts for an archery contest later in the day. 'What is the woman's name?'

'Maudelin.' Bess lowered her voice, although at this end of the row of stalls the crowd had thinned considerably. 'But that's all I know. No one even knows where she lives. 'Tis said she appears at the castle, if she's needed, then vanishes back into the woods, though none have seen her go. And they say she has a pet squirrel that takes food from her lips.'

'She probably tamed it,' Nell muttered, still too busy battling with her own private demons to worry about the unearthly kind. 'But at this present moment I don't care if both she and the squirrel can fly.'

Bess looked rather awed at this reckless statement, but had perforce to remain silent. They had arrived at the front of the booth and Nell found herself subjected to a thorough scrutiny from the blackest pair of eyes she had ever seen, set like shiny little stones in a brown, wrinkled face. The woman staring at her looked as if the lightest puff of wind would blow her head over heels, but Nell didn't make the mistake of thinking the old dame was wanting in wits as well as substance. Those black eyes were shrewd and held the knowledge of ages.

'Meg is gone,' she said without any greeting and without taking her eyes from Nell. 'And you, girl, you want something special from me.'

'We want many things, Mistress Maudelin,' Nell answered with a calm she was far from feeling. Despite her brave words to Bess, the bent old crone was not the most comfortable person she had ever met, but she suspected that, like Beaudene, the woman respected those she couldn't intimidate. She made her tone brisk. 'To start, a lotion of comfrey or betony. Or, if 'tis not made up, then comfrey leaves, if they be freshly picked. Then, St John's wort and woundwort-cream. A little syrup of poppy. Horehound, coltsfoot, mint and bay—also in a syrup, if you have it, or steeped in spirit of wine. Mulberry leaves to make a paste for burns. Fennel and basil. And——' she took a deep breath '—some hyssop.'

Maudelin's black eyes narrowed, deepening the wrinkles in her lined and weathered face. 'So knowledgeable for a young lady,' she said, giving the words a slightly mocking intonation. 'But rash. Very rash, like all the young. You should try spitting thrice in a frog's mouth, girl. Or eating bees.' She laughed suddenly, a harsh sound that cracked in the middle. ''Tis safer for such a delicate creature as yourself.'

'I prefer something more certain,' Nell said, holding the dame's gaze. She didn't bother to correct Maudelin's assumption that the herb she needed was intended for herself. 'And I can pay you well.'

After another long minute of intent scrutiny, the woman shrugged. 'Then choose what you will,' she said, gesturing with a gnarled hand towards the bowls and flasks lined up at the rear of the booth. 'But later, choose wisely, girl. You think you are hard enough for the task, but there's a softness in you that few have seen. And remember, a deed once done may be regretted too late.'

Nell acted on the first statement and closed her mind to the rest, thankful that the old woman had turned her attention to Bess and was questioning her about

Meg. She did not speak again until her purchases were made and stowed safely in the willow basket they had brought for the purpose. Then she had Bess's curiosity to contend with.

'What was that all about?' the other girl pounced, the minute they were out of earshot. 'All that nonsense about frogs and bees. Does she doubt your knowledge?'

Nell shook her head and resisted the urge to look back. She knew Maudelin was watching her. She could feel that black-eyed stare boring into her back. 'Such people indulge in mysterious sayings to impress the ignorant and simple,' she retorted, while mentally crossing herself. Then she realised that this reply was hardly flattering to Bess. 'It matters not,' she tacked on hastily. 'If you are done here, we had best be off back to your camp. Creeping out before first light might have been easy, but saints know how we're going to explain such a long absence.'

And creeping out of the camp had only been easy because Beaudene had not returned to the hut, she added silently. The possible reasons for his absence had been one of the puzzles that had kept her awake long into the night.

'We'll tell the truth,' Bess said, with a blithe unconcern that had Nell staring at her in astonishment. 'What can they do except yell at us? We've already done what we set out to do.'

'Well, aye, but. . .' The words faded as Nell's mouth went dry. She had a sudden nerve-racking memory of Beaudene's reaction the last time she had roused his ire. And of the very different kiss that had come later. Somehow she didn't think he would waste a lot of time yelling; his retribution would be much more devastating. A devastation of her senses that was already beginning to tighten her nerves in half-fearful, half-tremulous anticipation. Sweet Lord, what was the man doing to her that she trembled with expectation rather than terror at the thought of his rage?

'But I think we may have a problem here first,' Bess added in an undertone that succeeded in breaking into Nell's dismayed thoughts.

She looked up to see that one of the town apprentices, obviously egged on by his fellows and a considerable quantity of ale, had planted himself in their path.

'I'm in the next wrestling match,' he announced in slurred accents. He waved towards the cleared space behind him and seemed to sway in the light breeze. 'And whatever wench cheers me on can spend the purse I'll win. For a small favour.' He leered. 'What say you?'

'Win!' Bess drew herself up to her full height, which was several inches below their inebriated swain, and glared at him. 'Your opponent will only have to breathe and you'll topple over. Out of our way, you drunken oaf, or I'll call the soldiers.'

Her clear voice carried for several yards. Amid an outburst of laughter from the passers-by the youth's companions began jeering and shouting out crude advice.

Under cover of the noise, Nell tugged at Bess's sleeve. 'We don't want any soldiers,' she hissed.

'Too late,' Bess muttered, as three men-at-arms abandoned their archery targets and began to push their way through the crowd rapidly gathering about the small scene. 'Don't worry,' she added. 'They'll cart the lot of them off and throw them into a cell until they're sober. You won't have to speak at all. Indeed, 'twould be better if you did not.'

'Give way there!' The first man-at-arms to reach

them plucked an urchin out of his path, looked at Nell and Bess, and puffed out his chest importantly. 'You ladies havin' trouble here?' he asked, and hiccuped.

'Oh, no,' groaned Nell. 'He's been drinking, too. What in heaven's name are we going to do?'

Every eye in the crowd turned to her. Too late, she realised why Bess hadn't wanted her to speak.

'A lady!'

''Tis a lady.'

'Dressed like that? Don't be an idiot.'

The comments rippled through the crowd like a breeze through the grass. Almost imperceptibly the mob shuffled closer. A hand reached out and touched Nell's gown, as if testing the stuff.

Nell slapped the hand away. 'Loose my gown, fellow,' she ordered in her haughtiest tone. If the damage was done, she thought, she might as well try to command her way out of their predicament.

Almost instantly she realised that it wasn't going to work. The murmurs rose higher on the air like the hum of a hundred bees.

'Now, mistress, you don't want to cause any trouble,' another man-at-arms began in portentous tones. He took her arm in a hard-fingered grip. 'You just come along with me and——'

'I have no intention of going anywhere with you.' Nell wrenched her arm free and glared at the soldier. 'If you had a grain more sense than those fools, you'd take *them* away and teach them not to harass common citizens.'

'That be no common citizen,' shouted a voice in the crowd.

'How would you know, Martin?' yelled another. 'You can't even see straight enough to tell what's female and what's not.'

There was a roar of laughter.

'Them be female enough to tease us all morning,' accused one of the apprentices. 'And if she be a lady, what's she doing here with only another wench?'

An ominous rumble of agreement rolled through the crowd.

Encouraged by this sign of public support, the youth pressed on. 'Who knows them? Who can vouch for them? More likely they're outlaws come to rob——'

He was promptly howled down by a merchant standing near by. 'They paid their money, like everyone else,' the man shouted, apparently taking up the cudgels of defence. 'Just because you louts follow anything in a skirt——'

He got no further. Carried away by the knowledge that at least half the crowd was on his side, the apprentice rammed his fist into the merchant's fat belly. The man doubled over.

'By our Lady!' A second merchant pushed through the crowd, grabbed the strutting youth with two beefy hands and shook him like a rat. 'Is this the sort of protection we pay good money for?' he yelled to his fellows as the boy's companions rushed to his rescue. 'Let's teach them some manners, lads.'

A second later, with what seemed to Nell like a concerted roar of approval, the field erupted into a seething mass of brawling men and crashing tables. Shrieking and yelping with dismay, women, children and dogs dived for cover behind the more solid booths.

'Saints deliver us!' Clutching her precious basket of medicines, Nell exchanged one horrified glance with Bess then looked around desperately for an escape. There was none. They were right in the middle of the madly swaying crowd, and, worse, she was staring directly into the grim face of a sober man-at-arms, who, wisely deciding against interfering in something he couldn't stop without considerable risk to life and limb, had already taken another firm hold of her arm.

'Oh, no, you don't,' he growled. 'You're coming up to the castle with me, mistress. Both of you can answer to the sheriff for this disturbance.'

'We didn't start this,' Bess protested indignantly. And before the soldier had any warning, she swung the length of wool she was carrying and caught him a blow to the side of the head.

'Run!' she shrilled as the man staggered back.

Nell, already trying to break free of his grasp, had to duck as a pigeon pie flew past her head. Her captor, equally determined to hang on was not so fortunate. Thrown off-balance by trying to avoid two more pies hurled in quick succession, which found their mark on his neck, he went down into the tangled sea of legs and feet, taking Nell with him. Her terrified scream was abruptly cut off as a large hand wrapped itself around her other arm and yanked her back to safety.

'God in heaven,' grated an exasperated male voice in her ear. 'Can't I leave you alone even for a few hours?'

CHAPTER EIGHT

BEFORE Nell could do more than gasp with thankful recognition, she was jerked behind her rescuer and released. The soldier leapt to his feet with an enraged yell, met Beaudene's clenched fist head-on and crumpled. This time he stayed down.

Rafe turned to fix Nell with an extremely annoyed glare. 'When this is over, princess, I'm going to take my hand to your sweet backside so hard you'll wish you *had* been dragged up to that castle.' He side-stepped a tun of wine as it hurtled past him and turned Nell none too gently in the direction he wanted her to go. 'Now, get over to those trees and see if you can stay out of sight!'

Using fists and feet with equal disregard for inflicting damage, he began to forge a path for them through the throng, then wheeled about to cover their retreat.

'They'll all kill each other,' wailed Bess as Nell grabbed her hand and they sped towards the shelter of the woods.

'Good!' Nell retorted through chattering teeth. She was still trembling and shaken from her recent fright, but she was also furious. How dared Beaudene threaten to beat her just because she had got into trouble while trying to help people?

'*Good*?' squeaked Bess. 'But Dickon is in there, too, and there's a price on his head. What if he's recognised?'

'It won't happen.' Nell reached the first of the trees

161

and stopped to look back. 'They're men! Far from getting into trouble they're probably enjoying themselves, and then they'll look forward to the pleasure of yelling at us. Never mind that we're the innocent parties here.' She had to pause for breath, then continued as furiously as before. 'Well, I, for one, am not going to let them lay this at our door. If we'd been dealing with rational beings we wouldn't have had to sneak away in the first place!'

'Oh, don't let them hear you say so, my lady. Look, they've reached those trees over there to our right, and not before time.' Bess pointed in the direction of the castle, where a score of soldiers could be seen descending the rise at a run.

The fairground itself had become a shambles. Enthusiasm for the fight didn't seem to have waned in the slightest. Men-at-arms, apprentices and tradesmen alike threw themselves into the battle without regard to station, sobriety or sense. Nell winced as a farmer sailed through the air and crashed into an archery butt. He got up, shook his head, and waded back into the fray.

'Idiot males!' she fumed. 'Numbskulls! They wouldn't have a brain between the lot of them.'

A twig snapped behind her. 'Precisely what I was going to say,' grated Beaudene. 'I thought I told you to get into the trees and stay out of sight, not take up a front-row stand.'

Nell's head whipped around. Beaudene was striding towards them with another man who, at first glance, looked startlingly like him. There was one rather obvious difference, however. The second man was laughing so much that he could hardly walk.

'Mistress Nell,' he gasped, sobering long enough to get the words out. 'My compliments. I swear I haven't had as much fun in a score of months. Nor has Rafe, probably, but he won't admit it. And judging by the look on his face he won't present me.' He bowed. 'Sir Richard Peverel, at your service.'

Rafe threw him a furious glance and stalked past him. Wrapping his fingers around Nell's wrist, he pulled her further into the wood. 'You can indulge your misplaced sense of obligation later,' he growled. 'We'd better get these two away, before those fools out there realise the perpetrators of the whole thing have vanished.'

'Perpetrators——!' began Nell, outraged. She was interrupted from an unexpected quarter.

Bess had turned away from the battleground and was staring at Richard as if she'd never seen him before. 'Sir Richard Peverel?' she repeated weakly. Then her eyes flashed blue sparks. One fist went to her hip. '*Sir Richard Peverel*!'

Richard eyed the roll of cloth in her other hand warily. 'Now, Bess, lass,' he placated her, 'I was going to tell you.'

'Don't you "now, Bess, lass" me,' Bess stormed. 'You let me think. . . You let me believe—How *could* you, when you knew what had befallen me at the hands of your kind?'

'Damn it, that's why,' Richard exploded, suddenly completely sober. 'Bess——'

'Come on,' Rafe murmured, yanking Nell out of her state of shock at this unforeseen turn of events. 'The horses are over here.'

'But what about. . .? We can't just leave. . .' She was towed inexorably onward.

'They'll follow. Richard will soon have your little friend calmed down.' He grinned at her, the expression so startling after the anger practically crackling in the

air around him that Nell nearly tripped over an exposed
tree-root in surprise. 'All the way here he was threatening to turn her over his knee, but I rather think he
may have just met his match.'

'You, I suppose, still intend to carry out your stupid
male threat to beat me,' Nell panted. It was difficult to
infuse the proper note of defiance into her voice when
she was being hauled through the forest by a man
whose strides were twice as long as hers. 'Even though
it wasn't my fault.'

His grin vanished. 'It damn well was your fault.
Little idiot! I should beat you within an inch of your
life. Mayhap then you'd learn not to throw yourself
headlong into danger every time my back is turned.'

'That shows how little you know,' she muttered. 'I've
spent the last three years keeping myself out of
danger—without the help of any man.'

They reached the horses and Rafe stopped, swinging
around to pin her with a dangerous stare. 'Is that so?'
he asked very softly. 'And just how did you manage
that, princess?'

Nell stiffened her spine and glared back at him. 'It
wasn't difficult. They didn't have any brains or sense
either. Like you, they saw what they wanted to see and
didn't look any further.'

His fingers tightened around her wrist. 'And you let
them see what they wanted to see, didn't you? Lan-
guishing sighs, sidelong looks, admiring glances. Not
to mention——'

'Admiring!' Nell broke in without ceremony. She
didn't have any desire to hear the rest of what was
undoubtedly a lengthy catalogue of her faults. 'If I'd
followed my natural inclinations, and laughed at those
preening peacocks, they would have turned into

extremely nasty small boys—except they had the strength of men.'

He was silent for a moment, his eyes intent. 'And you're too small and soft to defend yourself physically,' he murmured. 'Is that what happened, little one? Did you learn to use men rather than be used?'

Nell discovered that her heart was beating uncomfortably fast. All at once the gently enquiring note in Beaudene's voice made her want to give in to the impulse she had felt when she'd realised who had saved her from the guard. At that moment, she remembered, she had wanted nothing more than to throw herself into his arms and feel them close around her, strong and protective. Only the fight raging around them had stopped her.

For which she should be grateful, Nell told herself now, gazing up at him. Throw herself into his arms? She didn't even know if he was still angry with her. If his punishing grip on her wrist was anything to go by, any move to fling herself at him would probably result in an accusation that she was trying to use *him*.

'I don't use men,' she denied at last. 'I have no use for them.'

His voice went even softer. 'Indeed? Then you've never been made love to properly.'

'Love!' Now she could hardly breathe. 'What has love to do with the dealings between men and women?'

''Twas merely a manner of speaking,' Rafe said absently, intrigued by the signs of increasing female agitation. The almost imperceptible tremor in her voice was having a strange effect on him, smothering his anger beneath a growing need to hear his name spoken in that breathless, utterly feminine whisper. He took a step closer and saw her tremble.

What was she thinking? he wondered. Her chin was

up and her soft mouth set in a stubborn line, but her dark-lashed eyes were wide and, in the sun-dappled forest, appeared more green than hazel. She looked as if she didn't know whether he was going to beat her or kiss her.

But he knew what he wanted. He knew what he needed. His hand clenched around her wrist.

She didn't make a sound, not one whimper, but her lashes flickered and went still.

On the edge of dragging her into his arms and kissing her senseless, Rafe froze. His eyes narrowed on the sudden pain tightening her face and his grip shifted, his hand sliding down to clasp hers. Still holding her eyes with his own, he reached out with his other hand and pushed the long sleeve of her gown halfway to her elbow. A single glance was all he needed to see the bracelet of dark bruises circling the tender flesh of her wrist. He cursed softly.

'Did I do that?'

'No.' The faint whisper barely reached him. ''Twas the soldier. The one you hit.'

'I should have killed him,' he said, still staring at the discoloured flesh. 'He'd have deserved it.'

Her shaky laugh washed over his senses like a caress. 'For bruising me?'

'For that.' His eyes returned to hers and stayed. 'For frightening you.' He raised her hand to his mouth and pressed his parted lips gently to the inside of her wrist. 'For daring to touch you.'

Her hand quivered in his, as if she would pull it away. 'D-don't.'

God, if her voice trembled any more he was going to——

The thought stopped abruptly when his gaze lowered to the pulse beating wildly in her throat. Was it fear or——? The question hovered at the edge of his mind for a moment, then certainty hit him like a fist to the gut. And this time there was no doubt at all overlaying it. This time there was no trace of desire in her eyes, nothing but fear and—Rafe frowned—even a hint of tears.

Stunned, he released her. 'Nell?'

'I. . .I. . .' Nell closed her eyes briefly against Beaudene's searching gaze. 'I think I hear the others.'

It was a lie. She couldn't hear anything over the pounding of her heart. Then relief turned her knees to water as the lie became truth. A rustle of leaves and the cracking of a small branch heralded the arrival of Richard and Bess. Before they reached them, Beaudene turned quickly, shielding her.

'We'd better split up,' she heard him say to Richard. 'This forest will be crawling with men-at-arms before too long, and a double trail may serve to confuse them.'

Richard answered. Or, at least, Nell supposed that he did. All she was conscious of was the powerful, broad-shouldered back directly in front of her and the memory of the expression in his eyes just before he'd turned away. For the first time since she'd met him, she could have sworn Beaudene had been as puzzled and unsure as she was herself.

And she could hardly blame him, Nell thought. After the almost blatant way she had thrown her supposed past in his face, she was now acting like a terrified rabbit whenever he came near her. Worse. For a mind-numbling instant there, she had actually been teetering on the brink of telling him the truth. Of telling him everything. The longing to do so had warred so fiercely with her natural caution that she'd felt rent in two, and though caution had won it had left her feeling more alone than she had ever felt before. Alone and desperately uncertain.

She moved restlessly, trying to throw off the sudden feeling of vulnerability, and the vials in her basket clinked together.

Beaudene swung around, his gaze sharpening. 'What's in there?'

'Herbs. Medicines. What we came for,' Nell finished in a stronger tone, recalling Bess's earlier advice. She glanced towards the other girl, but Bess and Richard were already riding away. Nell seized the only other diversion available. She peered into the basket to check that nothing had been broken during her struggle with the soldier. 'They're all still intact, fortunately.'

'Give them to me,' he ordered, his voice curt. 'I'll hand them up to you when you're on Samson.'

This was not the time to protest his lack of gallantry in letting her mount alone. Nell obeyed without a murmur. Beaudene handed her the basket, gathered up the reins and swung himself into the saddle behind her. His arms came around her, guiding Samson away from the direction Richard had taken.

Nell nearly leapt straight back to the ground in panic. To be so close to him, caged between his arms, was more than her overwrought nerves could bear. Against her back he felt warm and hard, overwhelmingly large, reassuringly strong, a threat, protection. . .

Saints in heaven, she wouldn't last a yard riding like this, let alone several miles. The fragile hold she had on her emotions would crumble like so much dust, and she would do something completely stupid. Like burst into tears. Cling to him. Beg him to hold her and never let her go.

'Surely. . .' Her voice was a husky croak and she had

to start again. 'Surely 'twould be better if I rode pillion——'

'The way you attract trouble? I'm keeping you where I can see you.'

For one blissful second sheer disbelief had Nell forgetting everything else. 'By the Rood!' she exclaimed. 'What sort of trouble can I get into on the back of a horse?'

'You'd be surprised,' he growled, sounding distinctly menacing.

Nell turned her head to stare at him. It was a mistake. Her cheek brushed his shoulder and his mouth was only inches away from hers. The sight drew her gaze and held it, fascinated. Contrasts, she thought again, but vaguely. How could she think when she wanted to touch him, to trace the chiselled line of his upper lip, to press her fingers to the fuller lower one?

'Keep looking at me like that, princess, and I'll demonstrate just precisely what I mean. Is that what you want?'

The soft, suddenly rough tone yanked her back to reality with jarring thoroughness. Her head whipped to the front as if he had struck her. 'No,' she whispered, and knew she lied.

And if she didn't say something else—*anything else*—he would know it too.

'How did you get your scar?'

The air around them seemed to go cold in an instant. Nell felt Rafe stiffen behind her and held her breath. Dear God, of all the questions she could have asked, why in the name of——?

''Tis a long story.'

Nell blinked, hardly able to believe he had actually answered her. 'Good,' she managed, after another nerve-racking minute of silence. ''Twill pass the time.'

He muttered something that sounded suspiciously like, 'That's not such a bad idea.' Then he added aloud, 'And not very pleasant hearing. Suffice it to say that I tried to recover something that had been stolen from me before I was old enough to fight for it.'

'Someone robbed you when you were a child?' She felt as if she was poised precariously on the brink of discovery, longing to move forward, but afraid that one false step would see the treasure snatched away from her. 'And then. . .'

'And then he tried to rob me of an eye when I confronted him, yes. Not a very heroic tale, is it?' His tone was mocking, but Nell heard the bitterness and pain behind the mockery.

'You were a child,' she said gently. 'But what of your father? Could he not——?'

'My father died before I had any memories of him. But since he left everything in my mother's hands, even when he was alive, I doubt I missed much.'

''Tis not an uncommon thing if a man is often away from home,' Nell ventured. The feeling of being balanced on the edge of a precipice was stronger than ever. 'But 'tis difficult sometimes, for a woman alone. I'm sure your mother would have fought for you had she been able.'

He gave a short laugh. 'Before you start wallowing in sentiment, princess, I have to tell you that my mother helped the thief in his enterprise, and then, fortunately for her, died before I knew any robbery had taken place.'

Nell was silent. She wanted to speak, to tell him that she knew what it was to be betrayed like that, to feel the pain of that betrayal, but instinct warned her that Rafe would reject any sympathy with brutal despatch.

No wonder he mistrusted women, she thought

broodingly. And no wonder he had misjudged her, given the evidence at her farewell banquet. It sounded very much as if Rafe's mother had manipulated her husband to the advantage of her lover—for what other reason would a woman conspire to steal from her own son? It was also plain to the meanest intelligence that he considered both Yorkist and Lancastrian queens to be manipulative. And when Rafe had first seen *her*, she had been juggling men right and left. The realisation was unexpectedly lowering.

'You intend to fight this man again, don't you?' she murmured in an effort to lift the cloud of depression hovering over her. 'Was that why you were at Court?'

He laughed again, softly. 'I was right. You are a worthy opponent, little princess. Aye, my petition is one of the many piling up on Edward's table these days.'

'Will he grant your right to whatever it is?'

Nell felt tension stream through his body the instant before his hands clenched on the reins. His voice went flat and hard.

'Whether he does or not, I will take back what was mine. One way or another. I have sworn an oath on it.'

The cold promise of retribution in the words made Nell shiver. God send that such an implacable desire for revenge was never turned on her.

'Well. . . I wish you good fortune, my lord,' she said, with a brave attempt at the light chatter she had once used to such good effect. 'If my determination equals your own, we should both succeed in our quests.'

'If you're about to mention Wells again,' he promptly countered, 'let me save you the trouble. The answer is still no.'

An intense flash of annoyance surged through Nell. She was pathetically grateful for it. For some reason, annoyance was oddly reassuring. 'But last night you said——'

'I said we'd stay here for one day. That was the extent of our bargain, my lady.'

'In that case, I wonder you did not chase after me on the Wells road this morning,' she flashed. 'Instead of going directly to the fair.'

'There was never any doubt about that,' he murmured. 'You had given Bess your word. But if what you're wearing was meant to be a disguise, it failed dismally in its purpose.'

Totally forgetting the danger in looking at him while she was practically in his arms, Nell turned to stare upwards in utter amazement.

'I thought you hadn't noticed,' she finally said in a voice that betrayed all too clearly that he had succeeded in throwing her entirely off-balance. He trusted her word!

His mouth curved in a way that sent shivers rippling down her limbs. 'Oh, I noticed, princess. The problem is, so did every other man at that fair, as you discovered to your cost.'

'What? But—but—I changed my clothes so I wouldn't be noticed,' she spluttered. 'This dress is *nothing* like the one I. . .you. . .And it even has a surcoat over it!'

'That fits you like a second skin.'

Nell took several steadying breaths. 'Well, I can see there is no pleasing you, my lord. First you threw my headdress to the four winds. Yesterday you slew my new shoes. And now——'

'I didn't say I dislike the dress,' he interrupted. His eyes, narrowed and glittering, slid over her in a look of such intimacy that she felt suddenly, terrifyingly, naked. 'Your other gown was an invitation to look.' His voice lowered to a soft growl. 'This one makes a man want to touch.'

Every bone in her body seemed to melt in the heat that flooded her veins. Her breasts swelled and tingled. There was a strange fluttering sensation deep inside her.

She wanted him to kiss her again, Nell realised, horrified at the depth of her response. He hadn't so much as touched her, was even now watching her with that strange assessment she had seen last night—while she was quivering with anticipation.

'You forget yourself, my lord,' she got out at last, tearing her gaze away from his to stare sightlessly at the forest in front of her. 'You are supposed to be my bodyguard.' *She* had certainly forgotten that. 'Whatever your opinion of my clothes, my person or my. . . my actions, I will thank you to keep them to yourself.'

'And I,' he answered beneath his breath, 'am beginning to think that I don't know much about you at all, despite your clothes, your person or your actions.'

The rest of the ride was accomplished in a silence that stretched Nell's nerves to the limit. In an effort to distract herself she brooded for a while on the second discovery of the day—that her bodyguard clearly knew the outlaw leader well. The situation should have made her mildly uneasy, to say the least, and the fact that it didn't promptly led her back to the disturbing question of trust and another flash of the strange affinity she felt with Beaudene.

She trusted him with her life, with her safety, but he threatened her in ways she could only sense. He trusted her word, but still believed her to be wanton.

They had reached an impasse, she realised with a

little shiver of awareness. And, to overcome it, one of them would have to do something neither had done since childhood. Trust blindly.

She shivered again as the next logical question occurred to her. Why would she want to break such an impasse in the first place?

The task of caring for the wounded took up the rest of the day, with Nell dispensing medicines and advice and Bess following her instructions with strict attention. Nell had been grateful for the work. It had kept her mind from contemplation of a deed that had made her feel more cold and shivery inside with every passing moment, until now, with the sun hovering just above the horizon, a fine tremor had seized her hands and she felt sick to her stomach.

Bess had not seemed to notice her increasing pre-occupation, but had kept silent herself a good deal of the time. Nell wished she knew Bess well enough to mention the girl's liaison with Sir Richard, if only to offer comfort, but all she could do was brood on the inevitable result of a relationship between an outlaw girl and a knight of the realm—even if he did have a price on his own head.

Another woman at the mercy of some man, she thought angrily, even while knowing that her resentment might be misplaced. Bess was certainly capable of making her own choices, but Nell remembered the betrayal in the other girl's eyes and knew that she was in love with Sir Richard.

Holy Mother, she demanded silently, isn't there one male among them who can behave honourably when a woman is involved?

A fleeting memory of Beaudene at their first encounter, scornful and uncompromising, flashed into her mind. One, she admitted. One man. And he believes *me* to be dishonoured.

Pushing the thought aside with an effort, she paused outside the hut next to Bess's cottage and handed the basket of flasks and linens to her companion.

'There's nought to do here except dispense what comfort I may,' she said, calmly enough. 'You've been nursing the wounded day and night. Why don't you rest a while before we eat?'

To her relief, Bess nodded. 'An hour's repose would be welcome, indeed,' she said in weary agreement. 'But more importantly——' she touched Nell's hand in a shy gesture of friendship '—thanks to you, my lady, I'll sleep easier tonight knowing the children will live.'

Nell stepped into the dim, quiet hut with those words pounding in her head.

Children. Living. Laughing. All but one. A child who might not even exist, she told herself, stepping closer to the bed as her eyes adjusted to the muted light. She stood there for what seemed like a very long time, watching the girl who lay asleep on her side, her face turned away from the door.

Why did she hesitate? Nell wondered. Hadn't she known yesterday what needed to be done? Hadn't she already decided? The task was an easy one. Terrifyingly easy. The powder was prepared. All she had to do was mix the dose with a little syrup of wine, then waken the girl, hold the cup to her lips. She would drink before she was fully awake, unknowing, innocent of any wrong, free to live her life without the reminder of fear and shame and brutality.

Still she waited, shaking visibly now. And cold. So cold that she couldn't even feel the little bag of powdered herb clenched in her hand. She couldn't feel anything except the churning sickness in her stomach, the tightness in her throat.

There might not be a child, she told herself again. And if no child existed, there would be no harm done. No one would ever know what had passed here in any event. But if there was a child. . . If a babe lay snug in that fragile vessel, not yet living, but surely deserving of life; created by violence, but an innocent victim also; a soul belonging to God, but denied salvation——

'Oh, blessed Christ, I cannot do it!'

Nell sobbed aloud and clapped her hands to her mouth to stifle the sound. The bag pressed against her cheek and she lowered her hands again to stare at it. The sight of it made her almost physically ill.

'Dear Lord,' she prayed in a choked whisper. 'Help this innocent soul, for I cannot.' And it was not of her own soul that she thought in that moment. She simply couldn't kill.

Utterly unable to think beyond that fact, she groped blindly for the pouch still tied beneath her gown, and stuffed the little bag of herbs out of sight. Then, moving very carefully, she turned and opened the door.

Beaudene was standing not two feet away. It was the first time she had seen him since they had returned to the camp in silence.

'Bess told me you were here.' He hesitated, frowning at her. 'Come and rest now. You've been on your feet all day tending these people.'

Nell couldn't meet his eyes. She gave a jerky nod, gazing past him to the fire. Warmth. Heat. She needed it. Desperately.

'I'll sit by the fire,' she murmured. Her voice was husky and she cleared her throat, stepping sideways to go around him.

'Nell?' He stopped her with a hand on her arm. 'What's amiss?'

It was as well she still felt frozen, she thought vaguely. The note of genuine concern in his voice didn't affect her at all. But his hand was warm. Warm and strong and alive. She could feel the pulse beating in his fingers as they curled against the softness of her inner elbow. Or maybe it was her own pulse. . .or both. . .two hearts linked, beating as one.

'I'm just tired! That's all!' She pulled her arm free as she spoke and almost ran towards the fire, noticing too late that Richard was already seated there, sprawled against a log. She couldn't turn back. Beaudene had followed her and she didn't need to look at him to know that his intent, narrowed gaze was focused on her face.

Richard got to his feet and smiled. 'Mistress Nell,' he greeted her. 'Bess tells me you've saved the lives of our wounded. I hope you know that, if I can ever repay you, no service would be too great to ask of me.'

Nell shook her head. She didn't know if she could trust herself to speak, but unless she wanted the men hovering over her she would have to act as normally as possible.

'One man may yet die,' she warned, ordering her knees to unlock so she could sit down. She edged closer to the warmth of the flames, keeping her gaze on Richard as he and Rafe seated themselves on either side of her.

Rafe picked up the wineskin next to him and handed it to her. 'Here, have some of this. 'Twill put some colour in your cheeks.'

'No fancy goblets, I'm afraid,' Richard said, apparently feeling the need to excuse the rough amenities of the camp. He grinned. 'But the wine's good, and there's roasted suckling pig for our supper.'

'Roasted suckling pig,' Nell repeated valiantly, while her stomach roiled. She took a cautious sip of wine and put the skin down. 'Where did you get it?'

'Better not ask,' Rafe put in drily.

He was still watching her. She could feel his gaze like a physical touch. What was he looking for? Was there something in her face, some lingering hint of the terrible crime she had almost committed? And how was she to get rid of the herb without his knowledge? It was far too dangerous to be left in inexperienced hands. Though it could be useful in the treatment of chest ailments, too much could kill.

Disjointed plans scurried around in her head like mice in a cage. She would have to destroy the powder. But how? Burn it? Impossible to do that without being seen. Bury it, maybe? Aye, that was it. Bury it where no one would find it, and eventually it would lose its potency. She would have to slip away from the camp and——

'Rafe tells me you have to leave in the morning.'

'What?' Nell jumped, staring at Richard until the statement sank in. It seemed to take forever. 'Oh. Aye. If my lord says so.'

'Saints above! You must be tired. Such compliance.'

'Don't tease the poor girl, Rafe. 'Tis an uneven match at the moment. Do you need me to watch your back tomorrow?'

Rafe made a negative sound. 'If fortune favours us, they'll be ahead of us by now. Besides——' he paused and glanced at Nell '—we're going to Wells first.'

Nell's head jerked around so fast that she nearly lost her balance. 'What did you say?' She hadn't heard right, of course.

He smiled faintly. 'Are you forgetting your own strategy, princess? A detour to Wells will keep us from overrunning your family's heels, or meeting them on their way back.'

'Oh.'

A truly intelligent answer, she thought. But what else could she say? If she asked him why he had changed his mind, he might very well change it again.

'Aye. A fond family you have there,' Richard remarked. 'Hiring an assassin, by God.'

'He was assisted by a certain party who made a habit of frequenting the stable at midnight,' growled Beaudene, before Nell could answer.

She scowled at him. 'I went out there to say goodbye to my horse, if you recall.'

'An innocent excuse,' he conceded. 'On that particular night.'

'What is that supposed to mean?'

'It means, princess, that your relatives were very certain of your whereabouts. So, clearly you frequented the stable at that hour more than once.'

'Someone could just as easily have seen the candle I had left there earlier and assumed I'd slip out to see Chevette,' Nell retorted. 'They knew I was fond of her, and that I couldn't take her home.'

'Why not?' asked Richard, his gaze shifting from Nell to Rafe and back again like a spectator at a tournament.

They both turned to stare at him.

'Just an idle thought,' he offered meekly, but his lips twitched.

Nell flushed, and fought down her rising temper. It was useless to rant and rave or try to justify her actions to Beaudene, but at least she now felt a little better.

She wondered suddenly if that had been his intention in baiting her.

'My uncle said 'twas too long and hard a journey,' she told Richard. 'But——' She shrugged and dared a sideways glance at Beaudene. 'It hasn't been so bad.'

'More likely she was too steady a mount, if they were planning something during the trip,' he said with more than a touch of cynicism.

'I can't see Tom planning anything,' Nell said doutfully. 'He's a dolt and usually has his face buried in an ale-cup. Edmund, now, he's sharp and he's vicious enough, God knows, but——'

'He's too young,' Beaudene finished for her. 'I think you'll find 'twas your lady aunt who was the brains behind their ambition, princess. But don't worry, I'll get you home safely. You have my pledge on it.'

'Better beware,' Richard warned Nell with a grin. 'Every time he said that when we were boys I always got into some sort of trouble.'

'Boys. Aye. You know each other!' Nell exclaimed, abruptly reminded of her other grievance. She looked at Beaudene, her temper simmering again. 'You know each other well. That is why you didn't seem overly concerned about our capture.'

He merely shrugged. Just as if she hadn't been worried sick yesterday that he might have been involved, she thought indignantly.

'We were opposite numbers in the late, er, royal squabble,' Richard confided. 'Scouts sent out to locate the other army. Remember the day we came face to face when we discovered that bolt-hole at the same time, Rafe?' He laughed. 'We hadn't seen each other for years. I don't know who received the greater shock.'

'But you didn't betray each other,' Nell said with

great certainty. She sat back, content to let the conversation flow around her as she focused properly on Richard for the first time since their meeting. Apart from his grey eyes, his outward resemblance to Beaudene was still striking—both were tall, with the type of lean, powerful build that owed more to sheer muscular strength than bulk, and both were dark—but, as the two men began to talk of the war and their experiences in battle, she saw now that the likeness arose more from the hard-edged ruthlessness that characterised them than any similarity of physical feature. A ruthlessness, she mused, that was born of a close acquaintance with hardship and danger, and a way of life that forged a personal code as inflexible as it was honourable.

Perhaps Bess would be safe with Richard after all, Nell decided. If nothing else he would protect her, as Beaudene had sworn to do in her own case.

She cast a glance at him from under her lashes, her eyes tracing the scar at his temple as she recalled what he had told her earlier. As though sensing her regard, he reached out, without breaking off his conversation with Richard, and took her hand in his, enveloping it in a warm, strong clasp.

Heat spread through her, a sweet, melting tide of sensation that momentarily fogged her brain. She struggled free of it, unwilling to yield again to something she didn't yet understand. Something, she thought, almost panicked, that she *had* to understand if she was not to lose herself to the hidden mists of danger she had sensed today and last night. But she couldn't bring herself to pull her hand free. His touch was too necessary, too compelling. She needed it, needed to feel that strong, vital connection to him.

Had he known that? Had he sensed how cold and alone she had been feeling inside?

Nell looked away, gazing blindly into the fire as a new wave of confusion assailed her. Sweet saints in heaven, her earlier suspicions that Rafe had had something to do with their capture were nothing compared to the thoughts now whirling around in her head. Every time they talked, nearly everything he said only confirmed what he thought of her, and yet at the same time he could be so. . .so. . .

She couldn't think of just the right word. Kind was too tame. Nice was ridiculous. Gentle, maybe? Tender? But didn't tenderness imply a kind of caring?

Nell frowned as she struggled to make sense of her mental turmoil. It was almost as if Rafe sometimes forgot her supposed wantonness and treated her as if he actually liked her. Or perhaps. . .

A faint chill penetrated the protective warmth enveloping her. Perhaps the reverse was true. Perhaps Rafe was being gentler with her, despite his contemptuous opinion, because he wanted something.

The chill spread. Not that, she pleaded silently, not even knowing exactly what it was that she feared so greatly. Nor could she think clearly here, so close to him, touching him, his hand covering, enfolding, *caressing* hers. She realised in a sudden shocked awareness that his thumb was lightly stroking her palm.

Heat, cold, excitement, fear. The torrent of opposing sensations pouring through her was so swift, so violent, that she almost cried out from the force of the conflict. It was too much. She had to get away, had to——

'I. . . I think I'll walk the stiffness out of my legs.' the words tumbled out so abruptly that Nell didn't realise she'd broken into the men's discussion until they both turned to stare at her. Only then did she hear the silence. It seemed to surround her.

'I'm rested now,' she added, as if that explained everything. It must have explained something, however, because Rafe released her hand. Her fingers immediately curled inwards of their own volition, as though trying to hold on to his warmth. His eyes caught the small movement, then lifted to her face.

'I'll come with you,' he said.

'*No*! That is—' Nell scrambled to her feet. 'I won't go far. I just. . .'

She was rescued by Richard. 'Hell's fiends, Rafe. Let Mistress Nell have some privacy. There's a stream through those trees,' he advised her, waving a vague hand towards the eastern side of the camp. 'Go on. We'll eat when you return.'

'Aye. Thank you.' Nell fled, unable to look either man in the face. Her own was fiery red.

She didn't stop until she was completely out of sight and hearing of the camp and surrounded by the quiet sentinels of the forest. Then she paused, catching her breath. In the waning light she saw some small animal flit through the bracken and vanish. A bird twittered once and fell silent. A leaf drifted down in front of her, spiraling slowly towards the earth.

''Tis as good a place as any,' Nell muttered as she watched it land. Glancing quickly about, to be sure she was alone, she knelt and brushed away other leaves. Their dark gold hue reminded her of Rafe's eyes.

Rafe. When had she started calling him that in her mind? Why did he blow cold then hot? What could he want from her? So many questions. And only one answer she was sure of. He still believed her to be wanton, to be no better than her family. That was most likely why he hadn't presented her properly to Sir Richard.

Nell sat back on her heels, staring at the small hole she had made. The realisation that Rafe *hadn't* told his friend her full name struck her with painful force. Richard had addressed her as 'Mistress', not 'Lady Nell'. Although he had clearly been told of the danger her family posed. What was she to make of that?

Only the obvious, she concluded miserably. Rafe still disapproved of her, so, if he was being gentler, it was because he wanted something. And all she possessed was herself.

Dear God, not that, she prayed again. But knowing, this time. Knowing, somehow, that if Rafe wanted what every other man had wanted from her, and nothing else, it would destroy something in her. Because he was different. As different from those other men as the swift, hunting hawk was from the self-important, strutting bantam. She had known that from the start—instinctively then, with utter certainty now.

And just the thought of being alone with him again had her heart shaking.

With a half-strangled sound of impatience, Nell began to attack the hole like a small, ferocious harrier. This was what came of too much thinking. Hearts did not shake. Nerves, yes. And no wonder. She had nearly been dragged ignominiously before the local sheriff; she was bone-weary from nursing people all day: she was upset by her inability to help the poor abused child back at the camp, and she had still to inform her father that she could not marry the man he had chosen for her because. . .because. . .

Well, just because!

Several more frantic seconds of digging ensued. Determined to keep her wayward thoughts on one problem at a time, Nell shook loose dirt from her hands, then stood and lifted her skirts to untie the pouch. The light was fading rapidly; she dropped her skirts and began to grope for the herb. She had to hurry. If she tarried any longer, someone would come looking for her and——

She went utterly still. The hair at the back of her neck lifted. Her entire body tingled. He was coming. There was no sound, no warning, but she knew. She could feel him. Close.

The opened pouch fell unheeded to the ground. Nell turned, her heart in her throat, the little bag still clutched in one hand, and watched Beaudene come through the trees towards her, as big and dark and silent as the forest enclosing them.

CHAPTER NINE

THERE was nowhere to run. It was too late to hide. She could only stand there as he drew closer. Could only wait, trembling inside, as his hawk-like gaze pierced the shadows between them, sweeping over her tense face before dropping to the incriminating bag in her hand and thence to the hole at her feet.

'You were gone a long time.'

The words were very soft, very gentle, but when his lashes lifted Nell felt the impact of the questions in his eyes all the way to her soul.

She struggled free of the panicked urge simply to turn and flee into the forest. She had to think, to say something. He might be starting to trust her word, but that trust was fragile. If he even suspected the truth, she would be damned forever in his eyes.

A half-truth? Would it be safe? Men knew little of physics and potions unless they were monks or clerics trained to the work. And truth had carried the day once before, she remembered. For a price.

Her heart jolted at the memory, then began to throb in a slow, heavy rhythm. 'I'm sorry. I didn't realise. . . But I had to——I mean, I thought I would need this herb, but as it happens I don't and 'tis not safe, so. . .'

His gaze never wavered from hers. 'So?'

Nell swallowed. 'I thought to bury it.'

In the heavy silence that followed the trees themselves seemed to wait for his answer. Nell wished she knew what Rafe was thinking, but his eyes gave away nothing. She could only strain to hear the slightest change in his voice that might warn her of his mood.

'What is it, this herb that is unsafe rather than healing?' he asked.

'Oh, it can heal.' Ignoring the question, Nell rushed into speech again. ''Tis most useful for ailments of the chest, but the dose must be measured with great care and skill and I don't have time to explain all to Bess, so. . .' Once more she faltered to stop.

'Ah, I see. Its preparation must be learned over time?'

'Aye.' She nodded quickly.

'And, since no one here is suffering from aught but burns and the wounds of battle, you decided to forgo a lesson that must needs be hasty, though you purchased the herb?'

'Aye.' This time the affirmative was whispered.

Rafe held out his hand. 'May I see it?'

Nell's own hand shook as indecision gripped her. But it was just a powder, she reassured herself. A powder like any other. He would not know it.

She offered him the bag, praying that the waning light hid the tremor in her fingers.

He came closer and took it, his long fingers pulling the laces free so he could look inside. He lowered his head and took an experimental sniff. When his gaze lifted again to hers Nell felt the first cold knife-thrust of fear.

'What name has this herb?' he asked.

He would not know it, she repeated silently, as though reciting a magical incantation. He was a warrior. Even if he had a rough knowledge of the rudimentary treatment of battle-wounds, he would not know of internal cures. It was safe to tell him. Holy Mother of God, it had to be.

'Nell?'

'Hyssop.' The name passed her lips like the sigh of the wind.

And before she had taken her next breath, she saw it. Her mistake. His knowledge. Leaping to life in his eyes amid an explosion of rage so violent it made his former anger look like mild annoyance.

'*Hyssop*!' The word hissed between his teeth. 'By the fiend, it slides off your tongue as easily as the dose would slide down your throat. You don't even seek to lie.'

'My——? No. . .'

'How often have you used it, my lady?' He overrode her faint protest as if she had said nothing, his voice harsh, flaying her, stripping flesh scorched by his fury from nerves stretched beyond human endurance. 'How many times have you used the knowledge learned in your aunt's household? Once? Twice? Why throw such a useful herb aside now because you were mistaken in your reckoning? Save it for——'

'*Stop*! Stop it!' Nell flung up her hands, as though trying to ward off the relentless onslaught of words. 'You're wrong. *Wrong*! 'Twas not for myself. I didn't need. . . I've never. . .'

Rafe hurled the bag to the ground with such unrestrained savagery that Nell's protest ended in a frightened cry.

'God's teeth! Do you mean to tell me that you bought it for someone else? That you were going to use your whore's tricks on one of those sick women back there?' He half reached for her, his big hands flexing before they clenched and fell back. 'Does she know of your *kindness*, my lady? Or did she refuse to have her soul blackened for so foul a sin against the laws of God and man and——'

'The laws of man?' Her voice was low and shaking, but it cut across Rafe's tirade like a sword cleaving mist. His eyes were still slitted and violent, his powerful body rigid with barely contained fury, but she didn't care, no longer saw, felt only her own rage rising in a flood that swept over fear and guilt until she felt nothing else.

'Aye, you men! You men who make the laws, who stand so righteously before your women and point accusing fingers, who would condemn without hearing. Tell me what *you* would do when you look at a child. . . a *child*. . .who has been taken and used until she would rather perish where the vile creatures left her than return to her people. What good is your male honour then, my lord? Does it remove her hurt, her shame, her despair?'

'Another sin won't remove those things, either,' he roared. 'God damn it, Nell, I don't care what you learned in that accursed house, you must have known that at least.'

In the wild storm of her emotions, the sudden pain in Rafe's voice went unnoticed. 'Another sin?' she cried, anguished. '*My* sin? Is that all you can think of? Did you spare a thought for the terrible sin committed by men who do not have to live with the consequences? Do they suffer? No! Their lives continue without let or hindrance. *They* continue, sinning again and again, and women have no defence, no safety, no protection. . .'

Despair lanced through her again and she turned away, stumbling, blind to her surroundings, her arms held across her waist as if she had received a body-blow. 'And I couldn't do it. Oh, God save her, even knowing all that, I couldn't do it. I couldn't help her. I couldn't——' Her voice broke.

For a moment there was nothing but the tortured

echo of her own words in the silence, then strong hands cupped her shoulders from behind, holding her. 'Easy,' he said. 'Be easy, Nell. I didn't——'

'*No*!'

His sudden gentleness was too much. Screaming, Nell wrenched herself free, fighting him even as she whirled, striking out blindly, as frantic as a wild creature caught in a trap, too desperate to be free to take heed of any hurt.

Rafe rode the glancing blow she landed on his face, then in a lightning-swift move grabbed her wrists, pinned her hands behind her back with one of his and pivoted. Before Nell realised what was happening she was immobilised between the trunk of a giant beech and the weight of Rafe's body. His free hand pressed her head into his shoulder and his mouth lowered, brushing across her hair.

'Shhh,' he murmured, when a small, frantic sound escaped her. She was still trying to struggle and he tightened his hold, but carefully, so as not to hurt her. 'Be still. Be still, little one. Let me hold you.'

He kept his voice low, almost crooning the words, but renewed fury lashed him. God send a pox on that vicious family of hers. And on her father, who'd sent her to a place where innocence was undefended, and knowledge learned that would have destroyed what was left of goodness in anyone less strong than the girl in his arms.

She was quiet now, no longer fighting his hold, but her inner conflict still had her in its grip. The tension in her delicate frame as she struggled for control was so great he wondered that she didn't shatter like brittle glass between his hands. He fought back his own rage. There would be time enough to deal with her family, when he had her safe beyond their reach.

His head bent lower. 'I'll protect you, Nell. I'll keep you safe.'

He heard the words with a vague sense of surprise. How did she arouse such feelings within him? This tenderness. This need to protect. He didn't understand it, but knew beyond all doubt that he had made a vow that would never be forsworn, no matter who or what she had been in the past. It no longer mattered. He wanted her too much.

Wanted her with an urgency that was driving out his other violent emotions and increasing with each moment he held her in his arms. Not the urge to use her deliberately. He scarcely recalled that cold, measured decision to sate his physical need within her body until he was free of it and her. This was fierce, and hot, the force of it so beyond his control that as Nell abruptly softened against him, yielding to his strength with a shuddering little sigh, his body hardened in a rush that drew a harsh, agonised breath from him.

''Tis all right,' he said at once, knowing by the tremor that shook her from head to toe that she was aware of his response to her. 'You're safe. I want you, but I'm not going to do anything about it.' Not right now, anyway, he added to himself. 'You're safe with me, Nell.'

She was silent.

Very carefully he released her wrists. Her hands went at once to his chest, but she made no attempt to push him away. He flattened his hand at her back and began a gentle stroking movement. 'Do you believe you're safe with me, little princess?'

For a moment he thought she wasn't going to answer, then she stirred against him.

'Safe? Knowing you want what every other man has

wanted from me?' Her voice was low, and husky with unshed tears. 'When I can feel you——'

She stopped, appalled. But still unable to free herself, unable to trust herself to stand without his support.

His mouth curved in a smile against her suddenly burning cheek. 'Aye, a man's desire can scarcely be hidden, can it?' he murmured wryly. 'But I'll never force you, Nell. I want you to know that. I want you to know that in my arms you're as safe as you want to be.'

Nell was too exhausted to work that out. Too exhausted by the emotional battering she'd endured in the past hour even to wonder at her own responses since Rafe had rendered her helpless. She should have been afraid, but the instant she had stopped fighting him the heat and sheer male power of his body had poured over her, drowning her in sensations that had had her all but melting against him. She could have stayed in his embrace forever, safe, protected, savouring the strength of his arms, the heavy beat of his heart against her cheek, the tightly restrained force of his desire.

A ripple of uneasiness stirred her to life. If he had not spoken, if his desire had remained unacknowledged between them, would she have renewed her struggles or given in to the heat and power overwhelming her senses?

The fact that she didn't know the answer scared her more than the events of the past ten years put together.

'Let me go.'

His soft laugh held a note that sent excitement and fear combined shivering down her spine. 'If I did you would fall.'

For the second time in the space of a minute Nell's

face burned. He was practically taking her entire weight. She straightened so smartly that her head nearly clipped his jaw.

'There! I'm standing.'

His grip shifted to her arms, steadying her before he released her. 'That's good,' he murmured. One hand lifted to her face and he brushed her hot cheek with the backs of his fingers. 'I want you willing, princess, not weak.'

'What makes you think you'll have me at all?' Nell muttered, but Rafe only smiled darkly and bent to retrieve the sack of hyssop.

Nell decided not to pursue such a dangerous discussion. That smile had struck her like an arrow piercing chainmail. She felt shattered, as though something had been torn from her, some part of herself that had been locked away all these years but had now broken free, only to be captured and held by a man who made her want things she had never thought were possible.

'When we get back to camp I'll burn this.'

Shaken, she looked up to find him watching her, and the strange yearning increased, tightening the muscles in her throat until they ached. 'Aye.' Barely able to speak, she made a small gesture of repulsion. 'Do what you will. I never want to see it again.'

He nodded. 'You've never used it before, have you? Despite knowing its properties.'

At the note of certainty in his statement some of the tightness eased. 'No. Never.'

'Little fool,' he growled. 'Didn't you know the decision would tear you apart?'

'I refused to think of it until the last moment.' She laughed unexpectedly, a sound without humour. 'The witch was right. At the fair. . . Oh!' Her hand went instinctively to her crucifix as she spoke and a short, startled exclamation broke from her lips.

'What is it?'

The question was so abrupt that Nell almost jumped. 'N-nothing. That is, my. . . I must have dropped. . .' She began peering at the ground, conscious that Rafe's gaze had sharpened again. Well, he would just have to do without an explanation, she thought tiredly. Her mind was simply not up to the task of manufacturing one.

'Is this what you're looking for?'

Straightening, Nell watched Rafe bend and scoop up the half-open pouch. Even in the near-darkness she could see that several inches of jewelled chain had spilled from its hiding place and now lay across his hand.

'Aye.' She stepped forward nervously to retrieve her property. 'Thank you.'

He ignored her outstretched hand and opened the pouch so that the heavy gold crucifix was revealed. Nell's hand fell nerveless to her side as she watched Rafe examine the engraving on the solid bars of the cross. He weighed it in his palm.

'A valuable and unusual trinket,' he murmured at last, his gaze shifting from the jewel to her face. 'Where did it come from?'

Nell tried a careless shrug that felt more like a shudder. ''Tis mine, of course.'

One eyebrow arched. 'And you've been wearing it all this time?'

'Aye.' This time her voice was firmer. It was the truth, after all.

Then her nerves jangled all over again when he shook his head.

'You've been wearing it very well-concealed, in that case, princess. Why is that, I wonder?'

'Not because 'tis stolen,' Nell flashed, desperation and tiredness causing her to take refuge in temper.

To her utter amazement he laughed. 'You know, I'm beginning to understand how your mind works, little one. Stolen is exactly what this is, isn't it?'

'No! It belonged to my mother and now 'tis mine. At least. . .' Oh, why did everything have to go wrong all at once? Hadn't she had enough to cope with today? She felt her lower lip quiver and bit down hard.

Rafe reached out, tipped her chin up and stroked his thumb across her lip, freeing it from between her teeth. 'Tell me,' he coaxed, cradling her cheek. 'Trust me.'

'I—I do,' she stammered. 'I do trust you, but. . .'

'But?'

It wasn't her secret to divulge.

'I don't know you,' she almost wailed. Jerking her head back, she retreated a pace or two. 'I don't know what you'll——'

'You know more of me than anyone on this earth, bar three others.'

Nell drew a sharp breath. It was true. He did know what it was like to have something of value taken from him when he'd been helpless to prevent it. He knew what it was to be betrayed. 'The King, Sir Richard and the man who stole from you,' she whispered.

He nodded, his eyes intent on hers.

He would wait until he wore her down, Nell realised. And at the moment she had few, if any, defences against his will. She didn't even want to fight him.

The first words came out in a rush. 'My mother wore the crucifix all the time. It never left her possession. My father had given it to her, you see.' She looked away, gazing into the shadowed distance as memory took her back to a childhood that had been cut brutally short. And now that she had started, it was a relief to tell the tale.

'The night she lay dying she sent the servants out of the room and made me swear by my love for her to keep the crucifix close until it could be buried with her.'

'She didn't ask her priest to ensure it?'

Nell blinked, startled back into the present. 'No. She sent him away also. I don't know why. He was old. Perhaps that was. . .'

She shrugged and continued. 'She should have asked him rather than me. When the servants came back into the bedchamber my nurse took me away and I never saw my mother again. She died that night. The next morning Uncle Edward's steward arrived with an escort to take me to Langley. I wasn't allowed to attend my mother's burial, all the servants I had known were dismissed, and we left that very day. I found out later that my father had known my mother had not long to live. She had written to him, and the arrangements to take me to Langley Castle were already in train.'

Rafe frowned slightly. 'Has Langley never permitted you to visit Wells to fulfil your vow?'

'I wasn't even permitted to keep the crucifix,' Nell told him, remembered anger and frustration breaking through her weariness to give her voice an edge. 'There was no privacy at Langley. I didn't have a saint's chance in purgatory of keeping such a valuable object hidden. The moment my aunt laid eyes on it, she claimed it for herself and took it from me.'

A faint smile softened his mouth. 'Not without a fight, I warrant.'

Nell didn't return the smile. 'She has the marks to prove it.'

'Hmm. I can see why she was not overjoyed to welcome you into her household, princess. Why didn't you take your claim further if it meant so much to you? Not then, but later when you grew older.'

'To whom should I have taken it, my lord?' she asked softly. 'Three years ago King Henry had fled to Scotland and Margaret of Anjou to France to rally more supporters. Should I have taken it to Edward of York, perhaps?'

His eyes narrowed at her tone. 'Three years ago Edward had just been crowned King. Lending ear to a young girl's petition would have been just to his liking.'

'Aye. It was. For a price.'

Rafe's expression was suddenly very grim. 'And what price was that, my lady?' As if he didn't know.

'The price I expect he demands of every woman. Of course, I was only thirteen at the time, so he drew the line at holding a knife to my throat, but when I——'

'Enough!' *Thirteen*! God, he didn't want to hear any more. The stark violence of the emotions ripping him apart was stunning. If Nell said one more word, just one, he'd be able to think of nothing except avenging her.

And how was he supposed to do that? Rafe demanded of himself in silent mockery. Challenge his king because of a years-old encounter that had nothing to do with him?

With a vicious, barely-stifled curse, he stuffed the crucifix back into its pouch and shoved it out of sight in the pocket of his surcoat. Let it suffice that she had got the crucifix back. The sooner he arranged to have it placed in her mother's tomb the better.

'What's past is past,' he grated. 'We won't speak of it again.'

'But——'

He closed the distance between them with one swift, gliding stride and laid his fingers against her mouth. 'No more,' he ordered gently. And, removing his hand, he bent and kissed her.

It was the briefest caress, a fleeting brush of lips, no more, but Nell felt the impact of his tenderness in the deepest, most carefully guarded reaches of her heart.

'I'm taking you back to the camp,' he murmured. 'You need food and sleep or you'll never stay in the saddle tomorrow.'

'I've managed so far,' she felt obliged to point out, but it was a half-hearted attempt at best to regain control of her senses. She didn't want to argue with him. She was too tired, his gentleness too seductive. At this moment it didn't even seem important that she hadn't told Rafe the entire story. Or that he still had the crucifix. It was safe with him. She would ask him for it later.

He glanced down at her, the arm about her waist keeping her close to his side as they walked back through the trees. But there was no danger in him now, she thought vaguely. Only safety and protection.

'If we leave early we should reach Wells by mid-afternoon,' he said as the first of the huts came into sight. 'I'll take you straight to the Bishop's palace and——'

He stopped dead, his arm tightening around her. Nell looked up to see what had caused the sudden poised stillness in his body.

'It looks like the day isn't over yet,' he said very softly. 'Damn it.'

A few paces away, his back to them, stood Richard, confronted by what to Nell's startled gaze looked to be every man in the village. Then she saw that the crowd was divided. Three men stood a little apart from the others; the larger group included Simpkin and young Luke.

Richard half turned his head, as though he had heard Rafe's comment. 'I can handle this,' he said quietly.

Rafe moved closer, Nell still pinned to his side. 'What's going on?'

'I announced my intention to seek a pardon and turn honest,' Richard replied. 'The reception was rather mixed, as you can see, and I'm afraid the rogues who prefer a life of crime are blaming you.'

'Courageous of them. Perhaps they'd like to discuss the matter with me,' Rafe suggested drily. Neither man had taken his eyes off the sullen trio during the exchange.

'We only want fair treatment,' growled the tallest of the three. 'You promised us rich pickings and one last job will provide it.' From beneath a thatch of unkempt reddish hair, his eyes flickered over Nell and returned to Richard.

'What the hell does he mean by that?' Rafe asked in a voice that made Nell jump.

'I'm afraid someone overheard Mistress Nell telling Bess that you're her bodyguard.' Richard sent her a quick apologetic glance. 'They seem to think that a woman travelling alone with a bodyguard must be worth a considerable amount to someone.

'Aye, for her person or her whereabouts,' the outlaw spoke up again. 'We don't intend to hurt the wench, and there'll be a share in it for you if you like,' he added, nodding at Rafe.

Nell was certain Rafe hadn't moved, but menace was suddenly emanating from him in waves. His arm fell away from her waist. He took her hand and at the same time stepped forward a pace, so that she was half shielded by his body. His right hand rested lightly on his sword-hilt. Nell couldn't see his face, but his voice would have frozen fire.

'Is this how you repay my lady for tending your women and children?'

There was a low murmur from the rest of the men. It reminded Nell of the fair just before the fight broke out. She clung to Rafe's hand like a limpet.

'None of us have women here,' the trio's spokesman retorted.

'How very fortunate,' Rafe said softly. 'In that case there's nothing to stop you from leaving. Right now.'

'Not until we get——'

'You heard him,' Richard interrupted. 'Take your weapons and some food and get out.'

For several tense seconds the threat of violence seemed to hover over the settlement, as if awaiting a signal. Then the men glanced from Rafe and Richard to the silent group opposite, and Nell saw acknowledgement of their weaker position cross each face in turn.

'Come on, Ned,' one of the three muttered. 'No wench is worth getting cut up for.'

Ned apparently agreed. His mean little eyes still glared at Rafe but he backed up.

'See that they get their share of whatever money we have,' Richard instructed Simpkin. Then added quietly to Rafe as the rest of the outlaws dispersed, 'Take a bow with you tomorrow. There's no telling if those fools will take it into their thick heads to follow you, but they'll turn tail when they learn you don't miss what you shoot at.'

Rafe nodded. He didn't seem particularly worried about the possibility of having to pick off anyone foolish enough to follow them, Nell reflected. She realised she'd been holding her breath and let it out with a long sigh of relief.

He turned to look down at her. 'Come on, princess. You're almost asleep on your feet. You can eat in the hut.'

'Aye. Best keep her out of sight until I have those three escorted off the premises,' Richard agreed. 'I'll see you in the morning, Mistress Nell.' With a nod to Rafe he walked away.

'Believe me, I was in no danger of falling asleep during that little scene,' Nell said with great feeling as she followed Rafe across the clearing. She remembered the expression in Ned's eyes when he had looked at her and shuddered. 'Do you think I could have a bow, too?'

'No.'

The blunt, uncompromising answer took her aback. 'Why not?'

Rafe stopped outside Bess's hut. 'Because apart from the odd scar or two I'm still in one piece, and I'd like to stay that way.'

'Holy Saints! I'm not going to shoot you!'

'Good. I'm sure you'll understand that I'd like to be certain of that.'

'Well! Of all the——'

The rest of her indignant protest was smothered by his hand. 'I know you're not used to relying on anyone but yourself, princess,' he said very quietly. 'But you don't have to fight your own battles any more. I'll protect you.'

He removed his hand, but Nell didn't speak. His quick understanding had surprised her into silence. But of course he understood, she reminded herself. He had been alone nearly all his life, just as she had. Had been able to rely on no one but himself, had had to fight his own battles. She wondered what he would say if she told him how very alike they were.

And then she wondered at the sudden longing that swept through her to fight his battles with him, to stand at his side, to *be* with him.

'I don't trust easily,' she said slowly, carefully. 'But nor do you.'

'No,' he agreed. 'But sometimes. . .'

'Sometimes?' It was the merest whisper of sound.

He frowned, as though considering. 'I don't know. Sometimes, little one, just lately, I've wondered if trust can be learned.' He gave a short laugh and shook his head. 'A question for the philosophers, no doubt, not for a soldier.'

'No doubt,' Nell murmured.

'Tell me——' His voice was still quiet, still gentle, but Nell sensed the moment of fragile intimacy was over. He had withdrawn from her; the part of him that might never trust a woman had been closed off again. 'The camp was attacked only five days ago. This girl who was raped—you cannot know at this moment if there'll be a child from it.'

'I don't.' Nell drew a deep breath and tried to banish the strange wistfulness that had come upon her again. 'I would never have known one way or another.'

He nodded, his gaze holding hers. 'But you still couldn't bring yourself to make sure of it.'

When she didn't answer, he lifted his hand and tucked an escaped tendril of hair into her crespinette. His hand lingered, his long fingers tracing the line of her jaw to her chin.

'Soft little Nell,' he murmured. 'But don't fear that it makes you weak.' His hand fell away from her face. Don't fret about the girl. We'll look after her, whatever happens. Now, go inside. I'll bring you something to eat, then you should get some sleep.' He gave her a fleeting smile and walked away.

She was supposed to sleep after that exchange?

Nell entered the hut with innumerable questions battering at her brain once more. Had Rafe meant 'we' in the literal sense? Had he meant that they would care for the girl together? How could that be, when he would leave her once she was returned to her father? Unless——

No. What she was thinking wasn't possible. She was the last person Rafe would want to marry. And she didn't want to be answerable to a husband anyway.

But there was no longer any real conviction in that last reminder, and Nell knew it. For just a moment out there that 'we' had given her a glimpse of a future that beckoned irresistibly, that promised warmth after coldness, closeness to another after years of solitude. It was probably an illusion, Nell thought wistfully. Rafe had probably been speaking in general terms, but why not dream just once? What could it hurt? She was alone and tired and it would comfort her.

After all, an illusion couldn't harm her if she indulged it for only a little while.

Arms that were warm and strong enfolded her. Hands that were powerful but gentle stroked her hair, brushing sleep-tousled strands from her face.

Half-asleep, her eyes still closed, Nell made a small sound of pleasure and nestled closer to the warmth.

'Nell.'

She murmured wordlessly and burrowed her head into the firm pillow beneath her cheek.

'Sweetheart. Wake up.'

'No,' she mumbled. Loath to relinquish her dream to the insistent voice trying to drag her back to reality, she spread her fingers so she could cling tighter to the bed—and frowned. 'Furry,' she said.

'God damn it, woman, will you wake up? I'm not made of stone!'

The hissed command jolted Nell into full wakefulness within a second. Her eyes flew open to fasten on a sight that made her heart stand still. In the very faintest lifting of the darkness she could just make out the hut's interior. All was as it had been last night, except for one thing. She was no longer alone in the bed.

Not only that. She was lying all over the bed's other occupant as if she was glued to him, her legs tangled with his, her head resting on the hard pad of muscle on his shoulder, and. . . Dear God, her fingers were buried in the dark pelt covering his chest.

The only thing that stopped Nell from screaming in total panic was the realisation that they were still partially clothed. She in her shift, he in his hose and undershirt. The undershirt didn't cover much, however. Its front lacing was undone more than halfway to his waist.

'R—Rafe?'

'Who else were you expecting?' he growled.

Nell flinched and tried to move away.

'No.' His arms tightened and he tipped her face up to his. 'Forget I said that, princess. The past is over and the future is what we make it. Once we get out of this bed, that is,' he added wryly.

She hardly made sense of the words. His warm breath washing over her lips drove out every other awareness except how big and hard and *close* he was.

'Nell?'

'I—I don't think I can move,' she faltered. She didn't

want to move, but she had to. If she stayed in his arms any longer——

'You can't move?'

'No. I seem. . .that is, we seem to be all tangled up.'

Not as tangled as we're going to be in a minute if I don't get out of here, Rafe thought, trying to remember why he couldn't take Nell here and now. The reason seemed to be buried somewhere in a mind that could only think of one thing. The need that had been growing to agonising proportions since he'd woken to find Nell, soft and warm and tantalising, lying all over him.

He shifted slightly and felt her tremble as her thigh slid between his and was trapped there. 'Aye. I see what you mean,' he managed, his voice sounding rough even to his own ears. 'But don't worry, sweetheart. Fortunately, in a situation like this, I can do the moving for both of us.'

'What does that——?' Nell began, only to break off with a startled gasp. Powerful muscles bunched and surged beneath her and before she could even blink she was on her back.

And just as imprisoned as before. More so. Rafe lay on his side next to her, propped on one forearm, so that he was looking down at her. The heat and size of him held her completely enthralled.

Her gaze dropped to her hand which, inexplicably, was still attached to his chest. How could that be? she wondered dazedly. By all the laws of nature her hand should have fallen when Rafe turned her. But instead her fingers were threading through the dark whorls of hair as if they had a life of their own. She felt the small nub of a male nipple beneath her little finger and stroked it curiously.

His breath hissed between his teeth. 'You're playing with fire, princess.'

'Will it warm me?' she whispered. Her gaze lifted as he made a rough sound in his throat, her eyes widening as she took in the breadth of his shoulders, the beautifully muscled contours of his chest, the sheer *maleness* of him.

'Warm you?' he repeated, his voice shaking. 'God in heaven, 'twill burn both of us.' Thrusting his fingers into her hair, he lowered his head and took her mouth with his.

Oh, yes.

If Nell had been able to she would have moaned the words aloud. His mouth was hot and demanding, and she knew now that she had been wanting it, wanting this, since Rafe had kissed her two nights ago. Heat. Life. She needed it, needed his strength, his touch, his taste.

Her hands slid upwards and she wreathed her arms about his neck, clinging, needing him closer. And this time, this time, he gave her what she needed. He shifted, his arms going under her back to arch her into his body as he moved to cover her completely.

Nell made a soft, whimpering little sound of pleasure as she felt his weight crush her into the bed. The kiss changed, becoming hotter, deeper, his tongue stroking over hers again and again in a slow dance of seduction and retreat until she began to respond, shyly at first, with tiny, darting touches that made him groan softly and tighten his hold, until she was utterly lost in sensation.

He lifted his weight slightly and his hand began caressing her, moving over her back from shoulder to hip, returning upwards to trace the soft indention of her waist and the delicacy of her ribs. Heat bloomed and ran before his touch. Her breasts flushed, tingled, grew heavy. Nell moved restlessly, her mouth soft and yielding beneath his, wanting. . .wanting. . .

Then his big hand closed over one aching breast, his thumb finding and stroking the velvety tip, and she almost fainted under the torrent of pleasure that flowed through her body.

'God, you're sweet,' he whispered. 'So sweet, so soft.' His open mouth slid across her throat, nudging aside her shift, and she moved again, her hips lifting in an instinctive rhythm that echoed the throbbing deep inside her.

'Rafe,' she breathed, scarcely able to speak. She felt dazed, stunned by the force of sensations she had never experienced.

'I know.' He lifted his head, his eyes searching hers in the dawn light beginning to creep into the hut. 'I didn't expect this,' he said thickly. 'I didn't expect *you*.'

Nell trembled helplessly under the impact of the fierce desire in his eyes. Somewhere in a hazy distant corner of her mind a warning little voice was trying to make itself heard, but it was silenced completely when he pulled the ties of her shift free and opened it to her waist with one sweeping movement of his hand.

Nell felt his touch on her bare flesh for the first time and arched wildly, her breath splintering into mindless little cries.

But the sounds of her own response startled her, shocking her into an abrupt awareness of what was happening. This was passion, she thought wonderingly. This sweet, melting weakness; this breathless, mounting excitement; this need to give herself completely into Rafe's keeping, to trust him as she had trusted no other man, to let him lead her into the unknown world of desire. But there was something——

'Nell, sweetheart, I have to have you.'

The urgent words were muttered against her throat, his hands were kneading and stroking her breasts. Streamers of fire unravelled and spread to the soft hidden flesh between her legs, but now she was torn, confused. Wanting him, but wanting *more*.

Her head turned restlessly and she forced her eyes open, struggling to understand the sudden conflict within her. And in the ray of light streaming through the unshuttered window she saw Bess lying asleep on her pallet.

Heat and desire leached out of her body in an instant. She froze, just as Rafe's hand slid down her belly and into the soft nest below.

'Rafe, no——'

''Tis all right,' he said hoarsely. 'I won't rush you. I won't hurt you. Oh, God, you're so soft.'

'No! We can't. Stop!' She tried to shift his hand, tugging frantically at his wrist, but his fingers caressed her warm womanflesh and she gasped in shock at the intimate invasion.

'*No!*' Desperate, torn between embarrassment, fear and the pulsing of newly-aroused desire, she began to fight him in earnest.

'Blessed Jesu!' He lifted his head, the gold fire in his eyes clear now in the morning light. The weight of his body subdued her struggles without effort. 'You want this as much as I do,' he grated savagely. 'You can't deny it when I'm touching you like this.'

'I can't. . . Bess!'

He went still, his eyes blazing down at her for a searing instant before they flashed to the other side of the room. A single vicious word was bitten off, his teeth coming together with a snap that was audible. In a slow withdrawal that Nell felt in every shuddering nerve-ending he removed his hand. His powerful chest expanded with the deep, controlling breath he drew in, then he pushed away from her and got to his feet in one swift movement.

Bending, he snatched his surcoat and boots off the floor and strode to the door. He jerked it open and looked back, his gaze slicing down the length of her body in the second before Nell managed to grab the blanket and pull it over her semi-nakedness.

'A good thing you remembered we weren't alone, princess,' he said with biting coldness. 'But God help you if I get that close again and you stop me.'

The door was shut behind him with a restraint that was deadly, leaving Nell with her first taste of frustrated desire, and a desolation that went as deep as her soul.

CHAPTER TEN

BY MIDDAY the green forests and meadows of the Avon valley had given way to the foothills of the Mendips. As they travelled further south Rafe kept to the high country, avoiding the narrow valleys formed by the outcrops of limestone that reared skyward in craggy, bracken-clad splendour.

The scenery was magnificent, but at one point the land fell away so sharply that Nell had to avoid looking down at the valley floor far below her, its cool, green dimness scarcely touched by the pale grey light of the cloudy afternoon.

The dizzy heights didn't seem to bother Rafe at all. During the past couple of hours he had left her several times to seek a higher point where he could scan the land behind and around them.

Lost in thoughts that were none too happy, Nell hadn't noticed his vigilance at first—there was no sign of human habitation on these rocky, windswept crags, no villages or even solitary dwellings—but when he reined in yet again to sweep the hills and valleys with his narrowed hawk-like gaze, she, too, looked back, a ripple of uneasiness gliding over her skin.

The land seemed empty. And yet there was life and movement here on the uplands, she thought, tilting her head back and breathing deeply of the clean air. The brushing of the breeze through the gorse and bracken, the clatter of the jackdaws, the keening cries of two kestrels high above her as they rode the wind-currents in effortless soaring flight. Somewhere, nearby but invisible, water trickled over stone, and she heard the cough of a badger.

The kestrels shimmered and blurred and Nell squeezed her eyes shut, realising she'd been staring so hard at the sky that they were watering. Then saddle leather creaked close by and her lashes flew open again.

'Stay away from the cliff-edge,' Rafe advised her, nudging Samson into a walk. 'These hills are like a honeycomb, full of caves and hollows where the rock has given way.'

For a first remark after an enraged exit from the hut and an entire morning of silence, it was quite mildly delivered, Nell decided after a moment. Although Rafe hadn't seemed angry, she reflected, suddenly recalling the odd, considering glances she had intercepted from him during the morning. He'd appeared more lost in thought, as she had been.

The depression that had hung over her since they had said farewell to Bess and Richard seemed to loosen its hold on her mind a little. She brought Rufus up closer and tried a tentative smile.

'I remember my mother telling me stories of such caves. Caverns like underground halls and castles, where fairies ruled their kingdoms, and sailed their boats on magical lakes and rivers.'

He smiled faintly. 'Those stories live forever in these parts. Like the tales of Arthur.'

'But he truly lived, did he not? Some say that he will come again when England is in danger, and others have seen his hounds drinking at the well at Cadbury, before following the King along the ancient road to Glastonbury.'

'Hmm.' He watched as she glanced back with an involuntary shiver. 'Something tells me you preferred scaring yourself with tales of ghosts rather than listening to fairy stories when you were a child.'

'I confess that the possibility of ghostly hounds appearing on our path is not a comforting one,' she returned. 'Even in full light of day.'

The smile reached his eyes. 'That's why you have a bodyguard, princess. But if it makes you feel any better——' he reached into his surcoat pocket and withdrew her crucifix '—I'll return this.'

'Oh! Thank you.' She slipped the chain over her head. 'I'd forgotten. . .' Having had several other matters on her mind all morning.

He looked at her rather closely for a moment, and Nell fought to keep herself from blushing. Silence fell again, but this time she made no attempt to break it. What was there to say? Why were you in my bed in the first place? Why do I wish we were there still, and alone?

Holy Saints! She couldn't even control her own mind. Embarrassed heat suffused her entire body when she remembered the way Rafe had touched her, and her abandoned response in his arms. She gritted her teeth and fought it back once more. If Rafe was no longer angry with her she ought to be able to put the whole episode out of her mind, just as he seemed to have done.

Aye, and Arthur would reappear right that minute and dance a measure with his hounds.

A piercing yearning stabbed at her heart. She would never forget how it had felt to lie in his arms. Never forget the feel of his hands on her body. Never as long as she lived.

But would Rafe remember after he had left her? She looked at him, her yearning clear in her eyes. He had made arrangements with Richard for the others to meet him at his manor as soon as the wounded could travel, but for her it seemed that a dream and a memory would be all she would have. And it wasn't enough. It wasn't nearly enough.

The thought had no sooner crossed her mind when he turned and caught her gaze. Nell flushed and looked away at once, angry with herself. She had been staring at him like a love-struck——

'Nell?'

'I was just wondering why you've been looking behind us ever since we started riding over the top of these mountains,' she said with forced brightness. 'I see no sign of pursuit.'

'They're hills, and you wouldn't.' Without warning, he reined Samson in and reached out to catch Rufus's bridle when she would have ridden past him. 'Nell——' his voice was suddenly curt '—I'm sorry about this morning. I didn't mean that to happen.'

Hurt lanced through her, sharp and cutting. 'Well, I dare say it would *not* have happened if you hadn't climbed into bed with me. However, there is no need to apologise. I know only too well how easily men succumb to lust, and would suggest that tonight you seek your own——'

'I wasn't the only one succumbing to lust, princess,' he grated. 'And I was in your bed in case some of the other men took it into their heads to hold you to ransom. Or worse.'

'Oh. I see. You were there to protect me? Thank you. How foolish of me not to recognise——'

'God damn it, will you kindly shut up? You were so exhausted last night you wouldn't have known I was there at all if I hadn't woken up to find your hands all over me!'

'*What*?' She went so red with outrage and embarrassment that she thought her skin would peel right off her flesh. 'I was asleep!'

'Unfortunately, knowing that didn't help.'

'Well. . .well. . .' Excuses tumbled wildly around in her head. 'You could have kept your shirt laced.'

'It *was* laced when I fell asleep,' he said through his teeth. 'But it didn't stay that way for long when your little fingers got busy.'

Nell wondered if anyone had ever died of shame. The possibility that she was about to do so seemed all too real.

'I didn't know. . .' she stammered. Holy Mother of God, she had never undressed a man when she was *awake*. How, in the name of all the saints, had she done it while asleep? Did she have the instincts of a courtesan, after all?

When she thought of Rafe's probable answer to that, it took every ounce of resolution she possessed to force herself to look at him. 'My lord, you must believe——'

'Hush.'

'What? But——'

'Shhh!

Belatedly, Nell realised he was no longer looking at her. His eyes, fixed and intent, were focused on a point beyond her. She turned her head. Nothing moved in the rugged landscape except for the wind's constant ruffling of the bracken and wildflowers growing along the cliff-top.

'Do you see those horsemen on the road below us?'

She didn't see a thing, but thankfully the question successfully diverted the conversation away from the early hours of the morning. Then, as her eyes narrowed against the distance, she at last made out a group of riders, appearing then vanishing as the road snaked through the valley.

'Do you recognise any of them?'

She frowned. ''Tis too far to tell. I don't——' Her breath came in with a rush.

'Your uncle's stallion,' Rafe said at the same time. His tone was grim. 'With Tom on his back. Your cousin must be more of a dolt than you thought, princess. He should be at least thirty miles ahead of us by now, not bringing up the rear.'

'Unless he's going straight to Wells as you said he might,' Nell suggested nervously. So much for her brilliant idea of avoiding pursuit, she thought. Rafe had been right all along.

'The same thing applies. If Wells was his destination he should have been and gone long ago. 'Tis more likely that he's stopped at every town and inn along the way to make enquiries, but even so——'

'If he did that,' she observed thoughtfully, 'he would have stopped long enough for a drink. Several drinks.'

'God's teeth! I know you said he was a sot, but——' He broke off with a sharp, dismissive gesture. ''Tis no use bemoaning the fact. Whatever he stopped for, yesterday's fair would have been right in his path, damn it!'

'Why? Do you think——?'

'I don't think. I know. Richard sent a man out at dawn to make sure Ned and his fellows had made themselves scarce. He tracked them as far as the town, and what do you think was the main topic for gossip this morning, princess?' He fixed her with a narrow-eyed stare. 'The mysterious lady who caused several of the town's good citizens to spend last night in the castle cells.'

'Oh.' Nell bit her lip. Obviously there was no end to her crimes.

'Yes, oh. I'm glad you're finally beginning to comprehend the seriousness of the situation. Even Tom can figure out that if he's so close to us after the lead we had, it means we're probably in Wells or near by.'

'But we're not. At least, not yet. Couldn't we let them pass us and then——?'

Rafe shook his head, his gaze returning to track the group of riders. 'Possibly, but once he's in Wells he has enough men to send them in any direction to pick up our——' Again he broke off, this time going very still. 'God damn their renegade souls to hell,' he swore softly.

Nell's flesh went cold. 'What is it?'

Without answering, Rafe drew the bow Richard had given him from its deerhide cover and reached over his shoulder for an arrow. 'Get ready to ride as if all the fiends of hell are on our tail, sweetheart,' he said, nocking the arrow and taking aim at the point where the horsemen were gradually reappearing.

He waited, not moving, keeping Samson still by the sheer pressure of his thighs alone. Then, as the last man came into view, he gently released the arrow and watched it find its mark seconds later.

'Ride!' he yelled, and slapped Rufus on the rump.

Clinging with hands and knees, Nell obeyed, urging Rufus into a gallop. Behind and below them she could hear faint shouts and knew they'd been seen, but she didn't look back. Beside her, Rafe kept pace, riding easily, with one hand guiding Samson and his bow in the other.

'Where are we going?' she gasped, the wind nearly whipping the words from her mouth.

'We have to get off this cliff while they're scrambling for cover and wondering what's happening,' he shouted back. 'There are only one or two paths safe enough for the horses. If they get to them before we do, we're stuck, but if we reach lower ground we can dig in and fight.'

'*Fight*! But they didn't know we were up here,' she shrieked. 'Why did you——?'

The way suddenly became steeper as the land dipped, and she had to concentrate on keeping Rufus's head up as he slithered on his hocks.

'Easy,' Rafe commanded. 'We'll make it. See that formation of rocks yonder, where the valley opens out? That's where we'll wait.'

'And then what?' She was still yelling, fear and anger combining to shred any attempt at control.

'Then we see if our chances have improved. That was Ned I shot. Without him, the other two might back off and we'll have only seven to cope with.'

Only seven?

Nell fixed her eyes on the rocks several hundred yards distant and halfway up a sloping hillside, and rode as she had never ridden before in her life. She would worry about fights and how the outlaws had come into the picture later.

They hit level ground and Rafe urged Samson to a faster pace. Rufus followed gallantly, but by the time they came to a plunging, snorting halt both horses were breathing hard from the final uphill run and Rufus's sides were dark with sweat.

Rafe leapt from the saddle, yanking his sword free of its scabbard before he had hit the ground. 'Get the horses over there between those two standing stones,' he ordered as Nell dismounted on shaky legs. 'Then come back here and keep your head down.'

She obeyed, fuming.

'Do you mind telling me why we're doing this?' she demanded when she returned to Rafe's side. He was waiting, half-hidden by a stone that stood shoulder-high, and they were surrounded by others of varying shapes and sizes, piled one on top of the other. Several more boulders were scattered about the hillside, the crest of which stretched in a long ridge that joined the cliff on the other side of the gorge.

Rafe's dark brows were set in a frowning line as he examined the crest and the narrow entrance to the valley.

'Well?'

'No, 'tis not well at all,' he answered. 'I can pick off the first two, maybe three men to come through that gap in the hills, but the others will dive for cover. We'll be safe from fire from that direction, but there's nothing to stop one or two of them from circling around on the other side of that ridge. You'll have to watch the rocks behind us, princess, and yell the second you see anyone.'

Nell barely heard the instructions. She ground her teeth. 'That isn't what I meant.'

He shifted his gaze from the valley entrance and looked at her. 'For God's sake, think, Nell. You've been alone with me for two full days and three nights. What do you think your cousin will do to you if you fall into his hands?'

'There was little danger of that before you fired that arrow and announced our presence,' she retorted, not answering his question.

'That might have been true if Tom hadn't met up with Ned and the others.' He went back to watching the gap, half leaning against the boulder, an arrow ready nocked but pointing earthwards. His sword was propped beside him, its naked blade gleaming silver in the afternoon light. 'I'd wager Tom or his men heard the talk about the fair and started asking questions, and Ned was none too happy about losing a leader who helped him to easy money and then told him to leave. Put those circumstances together and what do you get, princess?'

This time she stayed silent.

'I'll tell you,' he continued inexorably. 'You get a dissatisfied outlaw who knew when we were leaving the camp and where we were going. And you get him meeting up with a man who was very probably offering money for any information about you. Not only that — ' his eyes flashed swiftly to hers '— Ned knew the location of Richard's camp. He could have betrayed him.'

Nell's breath caught. 'Do you think he has already?' she asked, suddenly appalled as his words sank in. She slumped against the nearest boulder, feeling sick. She was to blame for all this. If anything happened to Bess and Richard and the others it would be her fault.

'I only went to the fair because I wanted to help,' she murmured brokenly. 'I didn't mean. . .'

Rafe crossed the small space between them with one long stride, captured her face with his free hand and kissed her, quick and hard. 'No, I don't think Ned went that far,' he stated, looking into her startled eyes for a moment.

He returned to his post and took up his watchful stance again. 'Ned had a price on his head, too, sweetheart. 'Twould have been safer to seek revenge against us by joining up with your cousin than by betraying Richard.'

'But now he won't do either.' Nell looked at Rafe, standing so still, the bow in his hands. Relaxed and yet alert, waiting like the predator he was. 'Will you kill the other two?'

'Aye.'

And that was all she needed to know. He would kill

her cousin and his henchmen, also, if it was necessary to keep her safe.

'I'm glad I'm with you,' she whispered.

He smiled at her then, a swift, slashing, dangerous smile that hit her like a bolt from a crossbow. 'Don't worry, little one. I've been in worse corners than this. We'll be all right. If I can wound your cousin we'll be rid of the danger for good.'

The words had barely left his mouth when Nell heard the thundering hoofbeats of several horses. The riders burst through the valley entrance and reined in sharply, milling about as they looked over the apparently empty land.

Why didn't Rafe fire? she wondered impatiently. The men were little more than a hundred yards away, well within range of his longbow, and were obviously arguing about their next course of action. She craned further around the base of her rock and spied Tom in the middle of the group. One of the men pointed to the rocks and said something, and she ducked back again.

'Those two outlaws are still with them,' she observed, trying not to sound terrified.

'So I see. Your cousin must have offered them a substantial reward.'

For some reason this calm answer pulled her already straining nerves tighter. 'I thought you said outlaws take care of their own.'

'Aye. Well, apparently Ned and his cohorts have never heard of that particular philosophy. That's right,' he crooned before she could respond. 'Just a little closer. Another step and——'

Rafe straightened, brought the bow up and fired in a movement so fast it was blinding. A scream of pain rent the air. Before it had died away, he had sent three more arrows after the first.

Stunned by his speed, Nell could only crouch in the grass, listening to the confused sounds of yells and the neighing of panicked horses as their riders leapt for whatever cover they could find on the exposed hillside.

'Fiend seize it!' Rafe wheeled back behind the boulder and reached for another arrow.

'What happened?'

'I killed one of those outlaws and hit two of your cousin's men, but Tom managed to flee back to shelter.'

'Leaving his men?'

'Don't sound so shocked. Did you think a man who hires assassins to do his work is anything but a coward? Stay down! Three of them have bows. When nothing else starts flying from here, we're going to have a hail of arrows falling around us.'

Several of the missiles went whistling overhead even as he spoke.

'Damn!' Rafe scowled after them. 'I could wish their aim was better.'

Nell stared at him, wondering if she was losing her mind. Or perhaps she was living in some crazy nightmare and would soon wake up. 'You want us to be *hit*?'

'Of course not. I want more ammunition.'

Dear God, that was why he had stopped firing when Tom had retreated. He couldn't afford to loose an arrow unless he was sure of it finding its mark.

'We could sit here for hours,' she realised aloud. Dismay had her voice shaking. 'No one out there is going to move just so you can shoot him.'

'I think Tom's patience will run out before too long,'

Rafe answered with a brief, reassuring smile. 'As for his cowardice, it might work in our favour.'

'How so?'

'Men won't risk their lives for a craven who has shown he'll abandon them to save his own skin. Not only that. He still has a man with him behind that entrance, but he hasn't given any order for covering fire so the others can retreat safely.'

That left six men out in the open, Nell thought, two of whom might only be wounded, not dead.

'What are we going to do?' she asked.

'Wait. 'Tis all we can do for the moment. Except to pick off anyone foolish enough to show himself.'

'And if those men out there crawl closer without making a target of themselves? What then?'

He grimaced. 'I was hoping you wouldn't think of that, princess. Let's just say I'll need more arrows than I have to pin them down and persuade them to change their minds.'

'*Nell*!'

Rafe's head whipped around as Tom's voice bellowed across the space between them. He risked a quick glance past the boulder to make sure the men flattened in the grass hadn't moved.

'Nell? Can you speak? Can you answer me?'

'Nice touch,' Rafe growled sardonically. 'Puts the idea in his men's minds that I have you under duress.'

'But won't they learn our exact position if I answer?'

He shook his head. 'They saw me when I fired at them, sweetheart. Answer him, but keep your eyes on those rocks above us while I watch the front. This could be meant to distract us.'

She nodded and took a deep breath. 'I'm not a prisoner, Tom,' she shouted. 'So you might as well go back home. I don't need you.'

From the corner of her eye she saw Rafe grin. 'Good girl,' he said. 'Make him angry enough to forget caution.'

She certainly seemed to have done that. Tom's voice when he yelled out again had a distinct edge to it.

'Nell? You're a fool if you stay with Beaudene. He's a killer, a murderer. He killed the man my father hired for extra protection.'

'You mean the man your father hired to kill me!' Nell shouted back. 'I saw the cut rope, Tom.'

''Twas Beaudene's plan to use the horse, but when it didn't work, he decided to make some money out of you. Why do you think he let those outlaws capture you? They're his friends.'

She flicked a quick glance at Rafe, then went back to examining the rocks. He wasn't smiling now. His eyes were narrowed, his face tense. Did he think she would believe anything Tom said? she wondered vaguely.

'Ned told me what happened,' Tom went on when she didn't answer. 'How you nursed them. He was going to the sheriff to free you when he found me instead.'

'You're the fool if you think I'll believe that,' Nell cried huskily. Her voice was getting hoarse from all the yelling and she cleared her throat. 'I was there. I know what——Rafe!'

Her warning scream was still echoing around the rocks when Rafe turned and fired. The shadow that had suddenly loomed above her wavered then became a man. He pitched forward, hit the rocks and bounced off to roll down the hillside.

At the same moment, a series of battle cries told Nell that the others had taken advantage of the situation to try to pin Rafe down so they could rush his cover. She heard him cursing steadily as he returned their fire, but her eyes were fixed on the body that had come to rest against a boulder some distance below them. The man didn't move. Beside him lay his long-bow, and a deerhide quiver.

She glanced back at Rafe. The hail of arrows had stopped again, and there was a raw graze along his jaw.

'You were hit!'

''Tis nothing. Stay where you are.'

'But——'

'The arrow was spent, Nell. It rebounded off one of the rocks and just caught me. 'Tis not even bleeding now.'

He was right, but——Once more she fought down rising fear. 'Did. . .they get any closer?'

'Aye.' His tone was still terse. 'Damn their eyes. I think I hit one or two, but I couldn't get a clear shot without getting killed myself. Still, your cousin is now alone behind that cliff, so they can't try that particular diversion again.'

But they might try something else, Nell thought. She looked at the arrows in Rafe's quiver. There were five. Not enough to stave off another attack. Not even to kill each man singly if the wounded could still fight.

She bit her lip, her gaze returning to the body wedged against the rock. From where he stood, Rafe couldn't see it, but it was only about fifty feet away. If she moved very fast, she could reach it, grab the quiver. . . She wouldn't think about getting hit. It was her fault they were in this mess, and if Rafe was wounded or killed because of her she wouldn't be able to bear the pain and guilt.

Taking a long, steadying breath, she got to her feet. 'I'm going after those arrows,' she said quietly.

He didn't turn his head. 'Don't be an idiot. They're scattered all over the——*Christ Jesu!*'

Nell was already racing down the hill, staying as low as she could. Cursing, Rafe leapt into the open and fired arrow after arrow, his aim so deadly that one man jerked and went still and the others flattened themselves even further.

'Run!' he roared as she grabbed the quiver and turned back. He caught her arm as she reached him and flung her behind the rocks, hurling himself after her.

Nell lay gasping for breath. 'They didn't shoot back,' she panted. 'I thought they would.'

He came up on one knee beside her, wrapped his hands around her upper arms and shook her furiously. 'By God, I ought to——' He stopped, crushed her against him and held her hard. A second later she was free. With one searing glance from blazing gold eyes, Rafe got to his feet, shrugged off his empty quiver and snatched up the one Nell had retrieved.

'What are you going to do?' she gasped, more breathless from his anger than her own exertions.

His mouth set hard. 'Finish this.' He turned away, nocked an arrow and took careful aim.

But not at the men still trapped in the open, Nell realised suddenly. She scrambled to her feet to watch. The arrow soared high, seeming to touch the clouds, then plummeted to earth just short of the place where Tom was hiding.

'Curse it!' Rafe fired again, and again the arrow soared skyward. 'Come on, you bastard,' he muttered. 'Fly!'

'What——?' Nell began. She was cut off by a startled yell and a horse's angry squeal. Tom's stallion burst into the open, plunging and bucking, completely out of control.

'You hit it!' she exclaimed, incredulous.

'Not at this range, when I couldn't even see it.' Rafe's voice was tight with grim satisfaction. 'But that shot was obviously near enough to panic the brute into running, which is what I wanted.' He fired again, sending the next missile straight past the horse's face just as Tom got its head up.

The stallion reared, pawing the air, then put his head back down and went into a frenzy of bucking. Tom managed to hang on for a few seconds before he was sent flying. He landed with a sickening thud and lay still, one arm at an odd angle.

'Stay here,' Rafe commanded. Picking up his sword, he sheathed it and strode out of their shelter, readying his bow as he went.

Nell waited until he was several yards ahead, then followed.

The men on the ground had scrambled out of the stallion's path when the horse had bolted after throwing Tom, apparently considering the greater risk lay in being trampled rather than shot. They now watched Rafe's approach with varying degrees of wariness.

He stopped a few feet away and looked them over, his eyes cold. Two appeared unhurt, one had an arrow through his leg, another was unconscious but breathing, and Tom was doubled over, groaning. The rest weren't going to move again short of a miracle.

'On your feet,' he ordered the two uninjured men. 'Leave your bows on the ground. You've got five minutes to pick up your dead and wounded and start back to Langley. And make sure you don't turn around. If I even think you're following us, there'll be no one left to see that Master Tom gets home in one piece.'

'Bastard!' spat Tom. He struggled to sit up, his eyes bloodshot and glaring. 'You won't get away with this. My father will go to the King and——'

'Let him,' Rafe interrupted without ceremony. 'You gave yourself away the minute you mentioned that stallion in connection with the rope. Something you wouldn't have known if you hadn't planned it, since the rope in question is in my possession.'

'We only intended to delay Nell's journey,' Tom muttered, turning sullen. 'But the stubborn jade had the devil's own luck. 'Twas her father's fault. He shouldn't have taken her from us. And now my arm's broke. I can't ride. How——?'

Again Rafe cut him off. 'A pity it wasn't your neck. 'Twould be no more than you deserve after ordering your men to open fire at the risk of hitting a girl to whom you no longer have any rights.'

'More rights than you, Beaudene, as you'll discover.' Tom's mouth twisted with spiteful satisfaction. 'My father sent a rider direct to Hadleigh. How do you think fitzWarren will react when he learns his precious daughter has been alone with you all this time? She'll be marked as your wh——'

The vicious word was never uttered. With no compunction whatsoever, Rafe drew back his foot and silenced Tom with a brutal kick to the jaw, knocking him nearly senseless.

There was movement to his right and he wheeled, bringing the bow up. 'Don't even think about it,' he said, eyes slitted with menace.

The men backed off. Looking as sullen as their master, they got to work rounding up horses. They were ready to depart just after the five minutes was up, a very groggy Tom being the last to be helped into the saddle.

Rafe looked at him, not bothering to hide his contempt. 'Tell Langley that if you, or he, or any other member of your family comes near Lady Nell fitzWarren again, I will assume 'tis with the intent of doing her harm and I will act accordingly. Is that clear?'

Tom glared blearily back at him. Nursing his jaw, he opened his mouth to reply, then glanced past Rafe and shut his lips on whatever he'd been about to say. Nodding stiffly instead, he gave his men the signal to start.

Rafe watched them go, thankful the process had been so easy. He had taken a risk, assuming that the men wouldn't fight if Tom was taken out of the reckoning, but they still could have turned on him. There had been three men capable of using a bow—or a knife, come to that. He hadn't left them entirely weaponless to face the journey back to Langley.

Then he turned and saw the other reason why his adversaries had decided to be so amenable.

Nell was waiting motionless in front of the rocks. She had retrieved a dead man's bow and an arrow, and was standing ready to fire, the weapon aimed steadily at the place where Tom had been.

Something unbearably poignant tightened inside Rafe as he took in the sight of her. She looked like a young Viking queen, ready to fight at the side of her warriors. Her crespinette had fallen off when he'd grabbed her and hauled her behind the rocks again, and her long hair flowed free in the wind, a bright chestnut banner against the green of her surcoat. She stood slightly side-on to him, the bow held in a grip that was practised and sure. His throat tightened again when he saw that the weapon was at least half a foot too long for her. And yet, despite that, despite the strain and fear she had to have felt, she had been willing to fight with him, to risk her life to help him.

He walked slowly towards her, knowing that with every step he moved closer to a destiny he no longer wanted to question.

She wasn't looking at him. As he drew nearer, he saw that her eyes, huge in her delicate face and darkened to the shadowed green of a hidden woodland pool, were still fixed on the point where the arrow was aimed. He made his voice low, so that he wouldn't startle her, but tension was gathering, racing through his body like wildfire out of control.

'You can put the bow down now. They've gone.'

Nell blinked, and looked at the weapon as if she'd never seen it before. Carefully she eased her hold on the drawn bowstring and let the arrow fall. 'A good thing I didn't have to use it,' she murmured. ''Tis heavier than I'm used to.'

She felt strange, unsettled, as if not quite sure what to do or say next. Nor could she look at Rafe, although she sensed his gaze hadn't wavered from her face. She mustn't let him see her eyes. That was the only clear thought in her head. If he did, if he looked into her eyes, he would see the sick terror that had seized her when he had walked into the open, thinking Tom beaten.

But he hadn't known her cousin as she did. Tom might have been hurt, but he was vicious and stupid, a combination as volatile as it was dangerous. Rafe could have been killed.

Dear God in heaven he could have been *killed*.

''Tis over,' she whispered, as though reassuring herself. 'We're safe.'

'Over?' Rafe's tone was suddenly so harsh that Nell jumped, her gaze flying involuntarily to his. 'Safe?' The bow was wrenched from her grasp with such speed she barely registered its absence. Rafe flung it to the ground and thrust his hands at her. They were shaking.

'Look at that!' he ground out raggedly. 'I've been like this since you made that insane, suicidal dash for those arrows, and knowing you're safe isn't stopping me thinking about what could have happened to you.'

Nell started to shiver deep inside. His eyes. Those fierce hawk's eyes were filled with emotions that were primitive, savage, all restraints of civilisation gone.

'Rafe,' she breathed. Just that, his name. She took a step towards him, her hand lifting to touch the graze on his jaw, and something else flashed in that burning gaze. The ruthless purpose she had sensed before, unleashed at last, and unstoppable.

He reached for her, sweeping her up into his arms without warning. Then, his eyes holding hers, he turned and carried her back into their shelter among the stones.

CHAPTER ELEVEN

NELL was trembling when he laid her on the grass and
knelt beside her, but she could no more have stopped
him than she could stop the frantic rhythm of her heart.

He didn't love her. She knew that. It was only
passion, a primitive urge to couple, born of danger and
the threat of death, but she would take it. She would
have this moment. She would have this to remember
when he was gone; the way he touched her face with
his fingertips, as if he didn't trust himself with a firmer
caress, the fine tremor still in his hands as he swiftly
unlaced her surcoat and then her gown and shift. The
almost agonised expulsion of air as he parted the fabric
and watched the rosy tips of her breasts peak in the
cool air.

Just for a moment shyness threatened to overwhelm
her, a ripple of trepidation at the awareness that she
was lying half-naked beneath his gaze. But then his
long fingers closed over her soft mounds and fire
streaked through her, drawing a whimpering sound of
pleasure from her throat. Her head went back and she
wanted to close her eyes, to abandon herself to the
clever, knowing caress of those powerful hands, but
now something apart from shyness held her back,
something deep within her that clamoured for
acknowledgement.

His face. It was in his face. Hunger. Desire. But more.

She forced her blurred vision to clear, struggling to
understand, and shivered uncontrollably when she saw
the fierceness in his eyes, the sharp-edged mask of

passion tautening his face. Men had looked at her with desire before today, but this. . .this *intensity*, this utterly focused need was terrifying. He would demand—*take*—everything she was.

And in that moment she knew with mind-shattering clarity that there was nothing he would demand that she wouldn't give. Willingly, passionately. Somewhere, some time in the past few days, she had fallen in love with him, with his fierceness, his moments of gentleness, the vulnerable boy he had once been, the strong man he had become. Her body, her heart, her very soul were his. Absolutely. Irrevocably. For all time.

'Rafe,' she said again, and this time there was full knowledge, trust, love.

He made a rough sound in his throat and came down over her, his mouth hard and urgent on hers, his tongue plundering deep, deeper, until she was kissing him back as frantically, her arms around him, small hands probing the powerful muscles of his back, learning him, savouring his strength.

She couldn't think any longer, couldn't speak or breathe, but it didn't matter. He had stolen everything, but she was alive as she had never been before. While he kissed her, caressed her, awakened her body once more to his touch, she lived only for him. He groaned against her mouth and she felt the vibrations of sound echo all through her body.

'You're mine,' he said hoarsely. 'Mine! I don't care who. . .'

He swept her skirts upwards as he spoke and his words ceased to make sense. She cried out when his fingers found her, touched the soft, melting centre of her womanhood, stroked, circled. She was mindless, drowning in exquisite sensation, almost sobbing with pleasure.

Rafe tore his mouth from hers, wanting to see her, wanting to watch her as he touched the sweet heat between her thighs, but the lure of her parted lips, swollen and moist from his kisses, defeated him, tormenting him with images of the deeper possession to come. He couldn't wait. He was burning, aching, shuddering uncontrollably with the need to have her.

Dimly he realised that he could be endangering them both by taking her here and now, but instincts, wild and savage, were driving him. He had to take her, make her his, brand her with his body until she remembered no other man but him. He lifted his weight slightly to free himself of his clothing and it was like tearing his own flesh away to be apart from her for even that brief moment.

His arms closed around her again and he pressed her legs wider, groaning harshly as he felt the silky warmth of her body begin to enclose him. He buried his face in her hair, fighting for control. She was so small. Small and tight. 'Oh, God, I can't wait. I can't wait. Nell, I have to——'

Her sharp cry tore through the mists of passion as he thrust into her with the full force of his body. Rafe froze, his breathing hoarse and broken, hardly able to believe the evidence of his senses.

'Nell? My God!' He raised his head, his fingers spearing into her hair to hold her still for his shocked scrutiny. She gazed up at him, her hazel eyes luminous with tears that she instantly blinked away.

'It doesn't matter,' she said urgently. And he felt the truth of that in the sudden pulsing of her body around him. 'It doesn't. . . . Oh, Rafe. Don't stop. *Please* don't stop.'

A ragged sound that could have been a laugh or a groan was torn from him. 'Stop? God, I couldn't stop now if there was a loaded crossbow at my head. Nell, sweetheart. . .' She was innocent! She was *his*! The thought nearly drove him over the edge. Only the knowledge of her innocence, and the feel of her, soft and fragile beneath him, gave him back the will to leash his strength, to take her slowly. For her he could be gentle. Only for her.

He felt her tremble, felt the involuntary tensing of her body as he withdrew slightly, and touched her face with a tenderness he hadn't known he possessed. ''Tis all right, sweeting,' he whispered. 'I won't hurt you again.' He began kissing her, easing her back into passion with gentle stroking movements of his body. 'Relax. Just relax for me.'

Relax? When he was seducing her so gently, so sweetly. When all her senses were filled with him, overwhelmed by him. She had never imagined such closeness. She felt bound, linked to him forever by the unbreakable chains of this most intimate act, her will gone, her very self merged with his, no longer separate.

And the sweet, pulsing ache grew and grew until she couldn't bear it any more. He began to move more forcefully, and tension coiled tighter within her. Impossibly tighter. It was like being caged by fire and yet she had no desire to be free. The unrestrained force of his hunger was too powerful, burning away everything but the need to belong to him. Her heart raced so fast it must surely burst; she heard her own voice almost sobbing, pleading, felt her body arching helplessly beneath his and wondered distantly how he could do this to her. If she hadn't trusted him so deeply the total loss of control would have terrified her.

Then his arms tightened around her with crushing strength and she felt the edge of his teeth against the side of her throat.

'Nell. *Nell*. . .'

The sensation was too much. She barely heard the anguished sound of her name. The tightening coil of tension seemed to spring open and a torrent of voluptuous pleasure flooded every part of her body. She was helpless. Blind. Deaf. Exquisite sensation blotted out everything, throbbing through her in wave after wave of ecstasy, until, gradually, the waves became ripples that drew his name from her with every sighing breath she took.

Sound came back first. The wind moaning softly through the rocks, the twitter of a bird, the faint restless movements of the horses.

Nell lay motionless, listening to the sounds of reality as her heartbeat returned to normal and the delicious sense of utter relaxation that had enfolded her began to fade. And in its wake came tension, coldness, dread. Ice touched her skin, a creeping chill that spread from her head to her heels as the realisation of the completeness of Rafe's withdrawal seeped into her consciousness.

She was alone again. He had straightened her clothing while she had lain almost senseless with bliss, covering her against the autumn wind, but she no longer felt the wonderful weight of his body, was no longer protected by the hard strength of his arms, no longer engulfed by the fire of his passion. He had withdrawn from her totally, was no longer touching her at all, although she sensed he was near.

One of the horses stamped and snorted, making harness jingle, and Nell turned her head in that direction. Rafe was lying on his back beside her, one arm flung across his eyes. His other hand lay clenched in the grass at his side.

The longing to reach out and touch him, to entwine

her fingers with his, to hold on, *somehow*, to that feeling of being one with him, was almost overwhelming. But the way he was lying. . .

Could he not bear even to look at her?

All at once she felt sick with nerves. What in Christendom was she supposed to say? What *could* she say when she had just given herself to a man whom she'd met only three days ago? Three days! And for most of that time he had considered her to be a nuisance at best. Holy Mother, what was he thinking, lying there so still and quiet? Did he regret what had happened?

Aye, of course he would, she answered her own question immediately. He didn't love her. He didn't even trust women in general. He had thought her experienced and was probably now cursing her for deceiving him. She wouldn't be able to endure it. His resentment. His disgust. Even if he blamed himself, in part or entirely, the knowledge of his regret would burn through her memories of this one time together until there was nothing left but ashes and heartache.

Nell clenched her own fists as determination flowed into her. She would not have this spoilt. She would not be made to feel shame because she had given herself to the man she loved, even if he didn't want or know of her love.

She sat up, and with shaking hands began to lace up her gown. Her crucifix gleamed up at her from the grass. Rafe must have removed it, she thought, slipping it over her head, and in the heat of their passion she hadn't even noticed. Beside her, he stirred as if he'd felt her movement, and she knew he was watching her.

'The wind blows cold,' she observed, with a composure that Edward's notoriously ice-cold queen would have envied. 'And 'twill be dark soon. We should be going.'

He came up off the ground as if propelled by a catapult, taking her hands and pulling her to her feet in the same movement. 'Don't,' he said, taking her in his arms and pressing her head into his shoulder. 'Just. . .don't.'

Nell stood quietly within his embrace but she didn't soften against him. Let him apologise for this, she thought grimly, and I'll hit him.

She felt his head bend to hers. 'Are you all right?' he asked, very low. His hand began stroking her back in a movement that was probably meant to be soothing, but only succeeded in pulling her already straining nerves tighter. Concern for her physical comfort was the last thing she needed.

'Of course I'm all right,' she muttered, lying through her teeth. 'Why wouldn't I be? You. . . We. . .' Her courage quailed at the thought of describing the incredible pleasure he had given her.

After a moment of silence he gave a short laugh. 'I don't wonder you find it impossible to describe. I went at you like——' His breath hissed out and he held her tighter.

Sudden awareness hit Nell like a bolt of lightning. He was regretting the *way* he'd taken her, not the act itself. At least. . .

Oh, blessed Lord, let it be so.

'Like a man who had just seen us through a very real threat to our lives,' she murmured, lifting her head so quickly that she took him unawares. The piercing intensity in his eyes almost made her falter. Shy colour tinted her cheeks but she looked up at him unflinchingly. 'You didn't hurt me.'

When he raised a disbelieving brow, her colour deepened. 'Well, only for the veriest moment.'

His hands shifted to cup her shoulders, his eyes watching the movement as his fingers caressed the delicate bones beneath her clothes. 'But you're so small and I was—— Sweet Jesu, Nell, I must have scared you witless.'

'Witless, indeed,' she muttered, lowering her gaze to stare fixedly at his surcoat as she remembered her utter abandonment to ecstasy. 'But not from fear.'

In the deafening silence that followed, Nell wished she could be struck mute. When was she ever going to learn to guard her unruly tongue? 'I. . . I mean. . . I might not have been as shocked as you would expect because. . .well, at Langley. . .'

'Aye, Langley.' He released her shoulders and took a step back.

Nell risked one fleeting glance upwards and almost shrivelled inside at the sternness in his face. Now she had made everything worse. 'A girl could hardly remain ignorant there,' she whispered.

'No.' His agreement was cool, giving nothing away. 'But knowledge is not experience. You were innocent. God's *teeth*!' he exploded suddenly, turning away and raking a hand through his hair. 'Everything pointed to you being——'

'What you thought me,' she finished.

He stood with his back to her for a minute, then wheeled about and wrapped his hands around her arms. 'You never denied it,' he accused, giving her a little shake. 'From the moment in the stable when I asked the whereabouts of your lover, you didn't deny a thing. Damn it, Nell, you answered me as if there *was* a lover. That first night on the road you taunted me with your supposed lovers. And then there was the

hyssop. I thought. . . God, at that stage I didn't know
what I was thinking, but when I discovered your
knowledge of the herb any uncertainty I had about
your past was gone, even though you'd never used it.
Why else would you need such knowledge? I thought.'

'How did you know of it?' she asked abruptly,
curiosity on this point momentarily diverting her.

His eyes were hard for just an instant. 'My mother
used it,' he told her flatly. 'I was very young but I can
remember her taking it, the odour of it. Eventually it
killed her.'

Nell's breath caught in her throat. How was she ever
going to overcome so much distrust and bitterness
learned at such a young age? The immensity of the task
overwhelmed her—before she remembered that she
wouldn't have to worry about it. Rafe would be gone
after he delivered her to her father.

'And what was I seeing that night in your uncle's
hall?' he went on, as if the detour in their discussion
had never taken place. 'What did I hear?'

Nell sighed, the sound soft and a little sad. 'A lie,'
she said quietly. 'A lie I enacted from the night the
King tried——' She broke off and shook her head.
''Twas the only way I could protect myself. It worked
but 'twas becoming harder. I had to watch, all the
time. Never to be alone with a man, but to bestow a
smile here, a few words there. Even a kiss, if 'twould
get rid of. . .' she faltered, shuddering, and let the
words fade away, but Rafe wasn't finished with her.

'Edward,' he said. 'Why didn't you tell me the truth
then, Nell? When you told me about the crucifix.'

'I tried,' she retorted, her chin coming up as indignation lent her strength. 'You wouldn't let me finish.'

He smiled slightly in wry acknowledgement. 'Your
dislike and contempt for Edward were so great I

thought 'twas because he must have forced you to trade your virtue in exchange for your mother's crucifix. I couldn't listen to the rest. If I had I would——' he gave a short laugh and shrugged. 'I don't know. Throttled him, maybe.'

Nell smiled, too, but faintly. 'A good thing I escaped the King's attentions, then,' she said. ''Twas when Edward was visiting my uncle. He did try to force such a bargain from me, and when I refused he became angry and tried to use force of another kind, until I shamed him by pointing out how spoilt he was, that because no woman had ever refused him he thought he could even rape with impunity.

'I was so angry, so. . .*distressed* that a king would behave so, that I went straight up to my aunt's chamber and stole the crucifix back from her. Then I marched through the hall in full view of everyone and made a hiding place for it in the stable.'

'That's why you were out there that night?'

She nodded. 'Aye. If I had stopped to think about any of it, I probably wouldn't have succeeded, but no one noticed anything amiss. They were too drunk, as usual, and Aunt Maud never wore the crucifix; she just took it from me for spite.'

'But she might have noticed its disappearance any time these past three years, which means you've lived with the risk of discovery as well as everything else. Because you had a vow to fulfil.'

She made a small gesture of assent, but when she would have turned away at the finality in his tone he reached for her and drew her close again. 'Nell,' was all he said, but in the murmured sound of her name she heard regret and understanding, and something else she couldn't recognise.

He held her like that for a heartbeat of silence. Nell

thought his lips brushed her hair once, before he released her and stepped back.

'We really do have to reach Wells before dark,' he said, his voice deep and husky. 'I'll get the horses.'

Nell watched him turn away, then bent her head and finished lacing her surcoat. She shouldn't feel so lost and desolate because he hadn't said anything about the future, she scolded herself. He might have regretted taking her maidenhead, but why should he feel anything else for her? She hadn't expected him to.

But she had! Merciful saints, deep down she had! Despite everything she had told herself—that she'd known he didn't love her, that she had only wanted one moment out of time with him—she hadn't expected his indifference to hurt so much. She hadn't known. In her innocence she hadn't known how much more devastating it would be to see him walk away after they had been so close.

He led the horses over to her and she carefully kept her expression blank. It took a considerable effort, and for the first time she was grateful for the years spent learning control. Not that she felt shamed by what had happened. She had no intention of marrying the man her father had chosen for her, or marrying anyone else come to that, so the loss of her virginity didn't matter, but——'

'Come on, princess, up with you.'

The command broke through her preoccupation. Nell blinked and found herself confronted by Samson's solid bulk. Rafe lifted her into the capacious saddle and mounted behind her before she could question the arrangement. She looked back as he nudged Samson into a walk, to see Rufus following on a makeshift leading-rein.

'Why——?'

'This will be more comfortable than riding astride for you, sweetheart,' he murmured, and bent to brush his mouth across her cheek. 'Are you very sore?'

Nell felt herself flush bright scarlet all the way down to her breasts. She jerked around to face the front. Holy saints, she had blushed more in the last hour than in her entire life. If only Rafe wouldn't keep taking her unawares with such embarrassingly intimate questions.

Then she remembered the heart-shaking intimacy that had led to the question, and her control tottered as an echo of sensual pleasure hummed through her.

'No,' she gasped in a hopelessly breathless voice. 'I told you. . .you didn't hurt me.'

His arms tightened around her and he settled her more closely against him. ''Twill be better for you next time, little one, I promise you. Much better.'

Nell's eyes widened. She only just managed to stop herself turning to stare at him. Better? There was better than that sweet, melting, utterly thrilling—— Next time!

Her heart stopped beating, she was sure of it. Next time? He was going to. . .? Did he mean to. . .? What in the name of all the saints was he. . .?

Her thought process shattered. She didn't dare ask for clarification, but if she didn't ask *something*. . .

'What. . .what shall we do when we get to Wells?' she stammered, practically unable to recall why she had wanted to go there in the first place. 'You said something. . .last night. . .about the Bishop's palace.'

'Aye. We'll find accommodation for the night in the guest dorter and I'll arrange for you to visit your mother's tomb in the morning.'

'Thank you,' she whispered, truly grateful. A measure of sanity returned and she closed her hand protectively around the jewel beneath her surcoat. 'I wish I didn't have to part with this,' she confided. ''Tis all I have left of my mother, and though, as I grew older, I thought her weak for loving my father so blindly, she loved me also, and I her.'

'Is that why you set your face against marriage, Nell? Because of your parents?'

'That and what I saw at Langley.'

'Well, I can hardly wonder at that, but don't fret, princess. You're far from weak, and if that taste of you I had was any example, I'll never give you cause for tears because I've gone to another woman.'

She hadn't heard aright. Either that or she had left her wits back there at those rocks. 'I beg your pardon?' she asked in a very polite, very small voice.

'We're getting married,' he explained calmly. 'In fact, before we worry about accommodation or anything else, we're going to hunt up the Bishop or one of his priests and have our betrothal vows witnessed.'

The only thing Nell could think of to say to that pronouncement was that he hadn't asked her to marry him. Which was so absurd that she dismissed it immediately.

'Why?' she finally produced, and decided she really had lost her mind.

He seemed to hesitate, and she felt him go very still against her for a fleeting second before he relaxed again. 'The usual reasons. I've been considering marriage for some time. Every man needs sons, and they need their mother to be honourable and strong as well as their sire. You are that, Nell. 'Tis a rare quality in a woman, and one I value.'

The words made her heart melt, but some perverse demon was still driving her, goading her to probe his reasons for wanting to marry her.

'I don't know your situation,' she began, choosing

her words as carefully as he had seemed to do. 'But I
am an heiress. My father may well object, since he has
already chosen a husband for me, and if I disobey him,
you could find yourself taking a pauper to wife.'

'You don't have to concern yourself with that,' he
answered curtly. 'I'll handle your father, and in any
event, I'm not in need of a wealthy wife.'

While she was still considering that, he added, 'You
needn't try to think up any more objections. We're
getting married.'

Indignation stiffened her spine, even as she longed
to agree. 'Are we?'

'We are. Make up your mind to it, princess. Apart
from any other cause, I could have got you with child.
'Tis reason enough.'

And a reason she hadn't even considered until now.
Her hand went to her belly in wonder at the thought of
a small being within. Rafe's child. Her baby. His. Part
of them both.

It was no less prosaic a reason for marriage than the
others Rafe had given her, but did it matter? She knew
her hesitation was only caused by the last remnants of
her distrust of men, her fear of being so vulnerable, of
virtually becoming a man's property. But this was Rafe.
The man she loved. Hadn't she already realised that
one of them would have to trust blindly?

Aye, she thought, and like her mother, like most
women, she would take that risk for love. And,
mayhap, one day in the future, Rafe would learn to
trust her also. Even. . .one day. . .if she loved enough,
he might love her in return.

'All right,' she said at last. 'I'll marry you.'

'Many thanks,' he returned drily. Then, when she
giggled suddenly, he bent to nuzzle her hair and she
felt his lips, warm and seductive, on her throat.

'Don't be afraid of me, sweeting. I know you felt pleasure before, but 'twas only a ripple compared to the pleasure you gave me. I couldn't even——' He lifted his head, strain and a certain puzzlement clear in his voice. 'I've never lost control like that with a woman. Never! Holy saints, we were still clothed; I barely touched you, barely took enough time to prepare you——' He took a deep breath and held her hard for a moment. 'It won't be like that again.'

'You knew I. . .' Nell hadn't even heard the rest. She was blushing wildly yet again and knew he could see the hot colour staining her face.

He laughed softly and stroked a finger down her cheek, leaving more fire in his wake. 'I could feel it,' he murmured wickedly. 'And I can't wait to feel you around me again.'

Nell decided, rather belatedly, that it was a great deal safer to remain silent until she was no longer sharing a saddle with her betrothed. Otherwise, if the conversation continued on its present deliciously dangerous path, Rafe would also feel the half-nervous, wholly-thrilling shivers of anticipation coursing through her.

But she nestled closer within the circle of his arms and laid her head on his shoulder, and, for the first time in ten years, allowed a warm little glow of hope and tentative happiness to light the depths of her heart.

CHAPTER TWELVE

LATE the following morning, Nell stood in the graveyard beside the cathedral at Wells, blinking a little
after the taper-lit gloom of the vault where generations
of her maternal ancestors lay at eternal rest, and
wondered what Rafe was doing.

Since their arrival in Wells on the previous evening,
and the exchange of betrothal vows before they had so
much as rested after the rigours of the day, they had
spent very little time together. While Rafe had been
closeted with the Bishop, regaling that shocked cleric
with the tale of Nell's treatment at the hands of her
family, she had been shown to a guest-chamber, where
a girl fetched from the town had waited upon her.
Then, after a meal and a blissful hour's soak in a tub
of hot water, she had had only enough energy left to
tumble into bed.

She had slept the sleep of the exhausted, not stirring
until her maid had knocked on the door with the news
that Father Simeon, the priest assigned to escort her,
was waiting in the ante-chamber and would be at her
disposal all morning.

The good father had turned out to be an elderly,
plump little individual, whose greying tonsure and
faded blue eyes belied a sprightly nature. He had heard
her confession—couched in very vague terms; pronounced a penance—negligible—and had accompanied
her to Mass in the cathedral. He had also been of
considerable help in other ways.

Nell turned on the thought as the clunk of the vault's

lock sounded behind her. Father Simeon met her gaze with a smile.

'Is there somewhere else I may escort you, my lady?' he enquired politely. 'A walk in the cloisters before dinner, perhaps? Or, if you prefer a moment of prayer now your task is done, the Lady Chapel is quiet at this time of day.'

'Thank you, Father.' Nell returned the smile warmly. 'I fear I have kept you from your duties overlong, but I could not have managed without you. You have my heartfelt gratitude, especially for your kindness in finding that little casket in which my mother's crucifix could be sealed.'

''Twas a small enough service, dear lady,' Father Simeon demurred.

But Nell shook her head. ''Twas more than that. I confess I was not looking forward with any pleasure to the prospect of having the tomb itself opened.'

'Departed souls deserve their privacy,' agreed Father Simeon comfortably. 'And your lady mother will surely rest easier now her final wish has been granted at last.'

'I'm glad 'tis done,' Nell sighed. 'I thought I would miss having something of hers, but now 'tis gone I feel more relieved than anything.'

The priest nodded. ''Twas not an easy task to lay on a child. And now. . .?' He paused, enquiring again.

'And now I may just sit here awhile, if 'tis allowed. The morning is fine and——' she coloured slightly '—my lord will know where to find me.'

'Ah.' Father Simeon smiled with cheerful understanding. 'And 'tis not my company you'll be wanting when he does,' he said, a most unpriestly twinkle in his blue eyes. 'In which case I had best hie myself off to the meeting in the chapter-house. God bless you, dear child.'

'Thank you again, Father.' Nell watched as the little priest hurried across the grass towards the imposing bulk of the cathedral.

He turned to wave before he vanished through a door and she waved back, feeling more at peace than she had done in years. And with the peace was a growing sense of anticipation. For the first time the future held promise, and she couldn't wait for it to begin.

Suddenly restless, she walked across the graveyard and around to the west front of the cathedral. Here, carved in tier upon tier on the façade of the building, were statues of the saints, fashioned with painstaking diligence and detail. Here also, she could watch for Rafe while affecting a fascinated interest in the statuary above her. He had said he would see her on the morrow and the day was already half done. Surely he would be here soon.

What would he think of her? she mused, looking down at herself with purely feminine concern. Her hair was in neat braids but bare of any headdress to lend elegance to her appearance. She still wore the dusky rose gown and moss-green surcoat. They had been brushed, and her shift and hose had been laundered, but the outer garments were still travel-stained, and as for her shoes. . .

Nell lifted the hem of her skirts and contemplated the sight of the tips of her toes peeping from her decapitated footwear. The interlude by the stream seemed to have happened a long, long time ago.

'Something else amiss with your shoes, little princess?'

Nell yelped and jumped about a foot in the air. She whirled around to find Rafe grinning at her—and forgot all about scolding him for creeping up on her again.

Somehow his height and powerful build always managed to take her breath away. He was wearing his black surcoat again. The sombre colour should have made him appear unobtrusive, at least, but the stark severity of the garment seemed rather to emphasise the leashed strength beneath it. And now, in full daylight, Nell could see the subtle gleam of the fine gold thread at his wrists, on the high collar, and outlining the white rose badge.

Her widened gaze travelled slowly upwards again. Like her, he was bare-headed, his midnight-dark hair ruffled by the breeze. The strong, masculine contours of cheeks and jaw were more starkly revealed with the disappearance of several days' growth of beard, the outline of his mouth both clean and sensual. The scar on his temple made him look hard and dangerous, but in his golden eyes she saw memories that sent little darts of fire winging through her body.

'You'll have to stop doing that,' she said weakly.

His smile was slow and infinitely disturbing. 'What's that? Wanting you?'

'No,' she gasped, nearly strangling on the knot of nervous excitement building in her throat. She swallowed hard. 'Creeping up on me. If you intend to make a practice of it, my nerves will be shattered before the year is out.'

Or a lot sooner if he didn't stop looking at her as if they were. . .and he was about to. . .

'Well, at least you weren't talking to yourself, princess. That's a start.' His smile flashed again, then he released her from the sensual spell of his eyes, shifting his gaze to the cathedral.

'I thought I'd find you inside, studying the more humorous carvings, rather than contemplating these saintly figures,' he went on, saving her from having to think of a response that would have been hopelessly incoherent at best.

But the remark set her to gathering her scattered wits. Not for anything would she admit that she'd stayed outside to watch for him.

'I saw them many times as a child,' she murmured. 'My favourite was the carving of two dragons biting each other's tails. But, best of all, my mother used to bring me here to watch the clock strike the hour. I would wait and wait, it seemed like forever, and then the four knights would at last come charging out to knock each other off their horses. I never tired of it.'

'Aha! So that's what you were waiting for.'

Nell kept her expression serene with an effort. 'Isn't it amazing that a clock made more than one hundred years ago can show the phases of the moon as well as days and hours and minutes?' she observed chattily.

'Amazing,' Rafe agreed, the lines of amusement deepening around his eyes. 'And if you will accept my escort, my lady, we may go and marvel at such a wondrous invention.' He offered her his arm,

Nell regarded him suspiciously. 'Are you laughing at me?'

He came a step closer, took her hand and tucked it into the curve of his arm. 'Considering where we are, it seemed safer than kissing you,' he said softly, beginning to stroll with her towards the cathedral entrance.

'My lord——' the protest was faint but valiant '—you should not speak so. We are in a church.'

'Not quite, but you're right about one thing. 'Tis far too public a place for what I have in mind. Next time I kiss you, little one, I intend to make sure we won't be interrupted for a long time.' His voice lowered and went dark. 'A *very* long time.'

She had been right that first night also, Nell decided, hoping her suddenly trembling legs wouldn't collapse under her. Lord Rafael Beaudene was a dangerous man. Extremely dangerous. She just hadn't known in what way until it was far too late.

'I must thank you, my lord,' she began, determined to put a stop to his nerve-racking style of conversation before he discovered just how weak she was where he was concerned. She wanted his complete trust and love before that happened. ''Twas kind of you to arrange for Father Simeon to accompany me this morning.'

He paused just inside one of the entrance arches and looked down at her. 'I thought you would rather have a priest with you.'

'Aye.' Nell smiled shyly and began to relax. She should have known better.

'So, sweetheart, now that your vow is fulfilled, do you think you might trust me enough to tell me the true reason why your mother was so insistent on taking that crucifix with her to the grave?'

'I. . . I. . .what. . .?' Her brain seemed to freeze.

'Did she never tell you? Did you not investigate?'

'Investigate? I don't know what you mean,' she faltered. 'My mother only. . .'

He glanced around quickly, then released her hand and framed her face with both of his. 'We're already lovers,' he urged gently. 'I'm going to be your husband. Trust me with this.'

She had to, Nell thought despairingly. She had to trust him, and by her trust hope to draw him closer.

'I don't know what you mean by investigate,' she repeated more surely. 'I was only a small child when the crucifix was given to me, and all I remember is my mother telling me that it must never fall into the wrong hands. Then, later, I did wonder if it perhaps held something. The cross itself was. . .different.'

'Go on.' He was watching her intently, as if he would draw the rest from her by sheer will alone.

'That's all. I didn't want to see if it opened. Not that I had a lot of time to search for a latch or a clasp, but it didn't matter. If the cross indeed held a secret I thought 'twas probably something to do with the wars between York and Lancaster, and if my father had behaved dishonourably, which seemed all too likely from what I knew of him, I didn't want to know of it. I would not have agreed with my mother's desire to shield him, but I had promised her.'

He nodded slowly and took his hands from her face, touching the tips of his fingers to the sides of her throat. His thumbs lightly traced the delicate line of her jaw and met just beneath her chin.

Heat burst inside her, flowing all the way to her toes. 'Rafe? Do you. . .?'

'Aye,' he said instantly. 'I believe you, and you're right. It no longer matters. We have to——'

Footsteps hurrying along the path beside the wall interrupted him. There was something urgent in the sound, Nell thought vaguely. Then, just as one of the Bishop's servants skidded into the arched entrance where they stood, Rafe stepped away from her.

'Oh, my lord, my lady, thank the saints I found you.' The man paused for breath, then bowed low to Nell. 'Your pardon, my lady, but you must return to the palace at once. Your father has arrived and requests your presence immediately.'

'You were not surprised by my father's arrival,' Nell observed as she and Rafe approached the bridge across the moat surrounding the Bishop's palace.

Nor had he hurried her. Whatever urgency had sent

the servant searching for them in such haste, Rafe had seemed singularly unimpressed.

'I had warning,' he explained. 'Your uncle sent a rider express to Hadleigh with what tale we can only imagine. But it makes no difference, Nell. fitzWarren has no power over you now. We've said our betrothal vows before witnesses, and 'tis as binding as any marriage. A fact your father knows full well.'

She nodded, looking pensive. 'And what else did Tom say to you? I meant to ask before, but. . . Why did you kick him?' she amended hastily, remembering just how thoroughly she had been distracted at the time.

Rafe slanted an amused glance down at her. 'He said something I didn't like.'

The bland answer had her frowning at him indignantly. 'Well, that was patently obvious, but what?'

'Nothing important.' He stopped walking and raised the hand he held to his lips.

Nell steeled herself. 'Nothing important? You nearly broke his jaw over noth—— Merciful saints.' Her knees went weak. He was brushing the backs of her fingers across his mouth, over and over, and now he was pressing them closer, tasting the line between each finger with the tip of his tongue. She was going to faint. She was going to collapse and melt right here on the bridge.

'Stop that,' she said weakly. ''Tis not fair. Every time we argue about something, all you have to do is touch me or kiss me and——Oh, no!' she groaned in mortification as she realised where her nervous babbling was taking her.

But Rafe dropped her hand, turned her about and propelled her rather abruptly through the open door of the palace. 'You certainly pick the most inconvenient times to rouse a man's baser instincts, princess,' he growled. Then, as she looked back at him, he grinned wickedly. 'But don't worry about it. I'll remember what you just said.'

Her pulse was still racing like a fleeing hare when they stepped over the threshold of the solar where her father was waiting.

She wasn't sure what she had expected, Nell thought a second later, but it wasn't the obese, pallid man, clad in an ankle-length tunic of dark grey wool, who remained seated by the fire, watching them cross the room towards him.

The solar was a cosy apartment, with woven rugs on the floor, tapestries depicting scenes from the religious life on three walls and a fireplace set into the fourth. Two tall, arched windows let in the light, and there were tables and chairs aplenty, but Nell was blind to these comforts. Her gaze remained fixed on her father's face while she searched for a reason why her mother had loved this man so completely.

He had probably been handsome once, she conceded, and standing he would be almost as tall as Rafe. But his height and the piercing regard of his hazel eyes were the only traces left of the young man who had charmed women so easily. Everything else had softened, gone to seed. The lines about the mouth were dissatisfied, the cheeks flacid, the once-firm jaw slack. Deep pouches of dissipation pulled at his eyes and his skin had an unhealthy parchment hue. A life of self-indulgence had taken its toll.

'Well, girl, you don't favour your mother much,' he remarked as she and Rafe halted on the other side of the fireplace. His voice was strained, as though it was an effort to speak. 'Not in colouring nor meekness, if I'm any judge. I notice you don't curtsy.'

'I owe you nothing, least of all meek, unthinking respect,' she returned, meeting his cold stare with one equally as indifferent. 'As for my mother, I wonder you even remember her.'

Her scorn was evident, but the words were spoken without heat. He's nothing, she realised, and suddenly the anger and bitterness she had harboured towards her father seemed to have vanished, gone for good. She didn't need it, didn't need to pray that divine retribution would overtake him one day. The man sitting in front of her had destroyed himself.

He made a noise that betokened mocking agreement and looked at Rafe. 'You'll have your work cut out breaking that spirit, Beaudene. I'm surprised you still want her.' His thin lips twisted in a parody of a smile.

'Lady Nell will tell you she is mistress of her own fate,' Rafe said coolly. He stood, half leaning against the chair opposite her father's, his hand still clasping hers. 'I have no intention of breaking her spirit.'

'Hrrmph. New-fangled nonsense, but I haven't got the time to argue about it. Have to get ready to meet my Maker.' He glanced briefly at Nell, and frowned. 'Since 'tis obvious she's taken no hurt, despite the Canterbury tale that fool from Langley poured into my ear, we can dispense with her presence.' His mouth twisted again. 'No doubt you'll want to discuss the marriage contract with me, Beaudene.'

'Your concern for your daughter is touching, fitzWarren, but, aye, we do have something to discuss.' He smiled down at Nell and gave her hand a gentle, reassuring squeeze. ''Twould be best if you return to your chamber, my lady. Have your maid bring you something to eat.'

The gleam in his eyes belied the formality of his address, but Nell didn't return the intimate smile. Something was wrong. Something had jarred. She wasn't sure what it was. A remark? A certain tension in the air? Nothing in the conversation struck her as wrong or strange, given her father's disposition, and yet she felt this definite sense of unease, almost of dread.

'Rafe, I. . .' She half turned towards him, keeping her voice low so as not to be overheard, but he forestalled her, pressing a finger quickly to her lips.

'Hush, sweetheart. Let me handle this. 'Twill be all right, I promise you. Trust me.'

Nell sighed. He trapped her with that every time.

Worried, her stomach full of butterflies, though she knew not why, she nodded acquiescence and freed her hand. She looked once at her father, who was watching with a cynical expression on his face, then, without a word to him of acknowledgement or farewell, she turned and left the room, pulling the door closed behind her.

And halted before she had gone a dozen paces.

'I'm surprised you still want her.'

Still want her.

Still. . .?

Why still? She frowned, trying to pin down the elusive source of her unease. It wasn't the word itself— her father had most likely meant to pass comment on her defiance, although he must have known that Rafe couldn't break their betrothal, short of a papal dispensation, even if he had taken a sudden, instant dislike to her behaviour.

Could the 'still' have meant a longer time-span? That was impossible, surely. And there had been mockery, too, in her father's tone. What if it hadn't been meant as a subtle jab at her manners, but a direct strike at Rafe?

Her hands began to tingle as though a thousand pins were piercing her flesh. Nell tucked them under her arms, hugging herself, her eyes staring blindly ahead as certainty hit her. It had not been mockery she had heard. It had been malice. Her father had made that remark as if he had *known* Rafe would still want her. As if he was sure Rafe would want her had she been pock-marked, shrewish and devoid of any manners whatsoever. As if. . .

She went cold all over. As if Rafe would still want her had she been the wanton he'd first assumed her to be.

Without even thinking about it, she spun on her heel and retraced her steps to the door. She had opened it a little more than an inch when her father's raised voice had her hand freezing on the latch.

They hadn't heard her over the angry tirade. Nell managed to unclamp her fingers from the latch, but that was all she was capable of doing. Unable either to step forward into the room or retreat, she listened.

'If you hoped to force my hand in this by betrothing yourself to Eleanor before you returned her to me, you're a fool, Beaudene. I don't take well to threats of scandal. A lesson I thought I'd taught you nine years ago.'

'You gave me this scar nine years ago, fitzWarren.' In contrast to her father's, Rafe's voice was calm, and as cold as ice. 'The only lesson I learned from that was to wait until I was in a position of sufficient power before going against an adversary who was without honour.'

'You arrogant bastard, I——'

'Oh, I'm no bastard. You of all men should know

that. My father was still alive when you seduced his wife, if you recall. Any bastards my mother might have borne were killed by the same evil means that took her life.'

'Alise made her own decisions,' fitzWarren blustered. 'You can't blame me for her death.'

'No. I suppose even a sewer rat like you drew the line at outright murder, but it didn't stop you and my mother forging the deeds that gave you title to Hadleigh Beaudene.'

'Fiend seize you, I *had* right. Who do you think helped your mother run the place after your father died?'

'That's easy,' Rafe said. 'The man who posed as her paid seneschal, but was really her lover. The man who couldn't marry her because he was already wed to another. The man who used lies to banish me from my birthright after she died, leaving me with nothing except the clothes on my back.'

'I could hardly help being wed to another,' fitzWarren muttered sullenly. 'Until Eleanor was born, I thought the woman was barren. But, curse it, she was still my lawful wife. What could I do?'

'You could have divorced her on the grounds of her inability to bear children. But you didn't want that, did you, fitzWarren? A wife in the background left you free to dishonour other women without the threat of having to marry them. On the other hand, you had already wasted your wife's marriage portion, and most of her inheritance, so you had to look around for another source of easy wealth.'

'Don't run away with the idea that Alise was a young innocent, Beaudene. There she was with a husband twenty years older who expected her to produce a brat every year. That wasn't for her. She was a ripe plum, waiting to fall.'

'And you made sure you caught her.'

'A man has to grasp opportunity when it presents itself.' Her father made a scornful sound, as though suddenly more confident. 'But why drag this up again? Nothing's changed. When Henry was put back on the throne nine years ago your claim was thrown out, because you'd sided with York. And 'twill be no different now that Edward's in power.'

'You think not?'

'I know not, Beaudene. For the simple reason that you have no proof of forgery, and never will. Our last meeting was conducted without witnesses and so is this one. 'Tis your word against mine. Edward's father might have picked you out of the stews of London where I. . .shall we say. . .mislaid you, but he couldn't help you when I held title free and clear, and nor will Edward. He wants a peaceful kingdom, an end to lurking threats from the red rose. He's not going to hand Hadleigh Castle back to you, leaving me with an excuse to help finance Lancaster's next rebellion. That's why he sent you to Langley to look Eleanor over. That's why he suggested you marry her to settle any dispute. And though I agreed at the time, I'm not so sure. . .'

'Don't stop there, fitzWarren,' Rafe encouraged silkily. 'Take as much rope as you want.'

Her father laughed. 'As you wish. You see, I haven't made up my mind to the match yet. You're not much more than the adventurer I was. That estate York deeded to you is smaller than Hadleigh, and you can't have amassed a fortune putting down rebellions for Edward. No. Now that I see how Eleanor's grown to be a beauty, I might look for a better alliance.'

'You forget what I just said about positions of power, fitzWarren. The balance has shifted. I'm no longer a homeless seven-year-old child, or a fifteen-year-old youth burning too hot over past injustice to fight successfully for his future. You can look all you like for another match, but 'twill avail you nought. You see, 'tis not merely your honour at stake here—a commodity you don't possess in any measure—but—'

'You're bluffing, Beaudene.'

'But your immortal soul,' Rafe continued relentlessly. 'How do you feel about burning in hell for all eternity, fitzWarren?'

She was going to be sick. She couldn't listen to any more. She had to get away, before someone came into the hall and found her standing there, ashen and shaking.

Somewhere in the distance Nell heard her father shouting again, but she was concentrating too hard on backing away from the door for the words to have any meaning. She couldn't think, could scarcely breathe for the vice-like fist clutching at her throat. Her heart felt as if a sharp dagger had been plunged into it, and the knife was twisting. . .twisting. . .

Oh, God, the pain was terrible. She could hardly move. The effort of putting one foot in front of the other was agonising. The stone staircase leading to her chamber appeared before her and she had to put a hand on the wall for support while she dragged herself upwards, moving slowly, like an old woman.

When she finally reached the haven of her chamber one hand was pressed to her breast, as if to stop her heart from shattering. Her breath was coming in sobbing gasps, and she could barely focus her burning eyes enough to close the door.

There was still the small ante-chamber to cross, but

she couldn't go any further. Leaning against the wooden panels at her back, Nell let herself slide downwards until she was crouched on the floor, doubled over in silent, unrelenting agony.

Rafe had lied to her. *Lied*! Asking all those questions about her inheritance, showing concern for her safety, but only because he needed her alive to regain his lands. Knowing all the time that he was the husband her father was considering, passing judgement on her—looking her over. Oh, Holy Mother save her. *Rafe*.

The knife twisted cruelly and she whimpered. How long would it last? This anguish. This terrible sense of betrayal. Surely pain this crippling would have to ease. People didn't die because their hearts had been torn apart from loving someone who intended to use them. She would have to go on living. She would have to function.

But not yet. Dear God, not yet! She wasn't capable of returning to the hall, of facing Rafe and acting as if nothing had happened, as if happiness was still possible. She had to think. Her brain felt almost as shattered as her heart, but she had to think.

Her father! What had he done?

Nell covered her face with her hands, blocking out sight in an attempt to clear her mind. If she had heard aright, he had caused his lover to betray both her husband and son and after her death he had taken that son—sweet Jesu, a child of seven—and abandoned him to fend for himself; he had stolen and lied and committed felony after felony for his own gain.

Her father was the thief Rafe had faced as a boy, the man who had stolen from him, who had almost taken his eye when confronted by the victim of his crimes. Her father was the man Rafe had sworn to defeat, his first step being his petition to the King. And Edward's answer had been to 'look her over'.

She was nothing more to the man she loved than an instrument of revenge and justice. The daughter of his bitterest enemy. The one woman he would never be able to love.

Her hands fell from her face and she slowly straightened so she was sitting against the door. Through the half-opened doorway to the inner chamber she could see a corner of the curtained bed and the table beside the window, flanked by two high-backed chairs. A flask of wine and a trencher of bread and meat had been laid on the table, and Nell quickly averted her gaze. Even the thought of food made her feel sick, but she took a shuddering breath, clenched her hands and forced herself to her feet.

She would not grovel on the floor any longer, bemoaning her fate. An anguished little sound escaped her and she almost doubled over again. Her fate? That was a jest. Rafe had probably laughed himself silly when she had declaimed that she was mistress of her fate. And then, without a second's hesitation, without so much as a hint of anything permanent between them, she had melted in his arms.

She cringed inside when she remembered how easy had been his conquest. He hadn't even had to go to the trouble of seducing her. He had looked, reached out, touched. And she had given herself completely.

Had he ever really wanted her? *Her*. Nell. Or had physical desire been another weapon wielded cold-bloodedly to further his plans? Had she been more correct than she knew when she had described his loss of control yesterday as a reaction to the danger they had faced? And had he then turned it to his advantage?

Giving her all those reasons for marriage when all the time——

Knuckles rapped imperatively on the wood at her back, ripping through the tangled web of questions and making her heart lurch violently. Nell wheeled, backing away from the door as if a spectre from hell loomed on the other side. She didn't want to see anyone, she didn't want to——

'Nell?' Rafe, his voice sharp with command. 'Open the door.'

She shook her head, as if he could see her, and continued backing into the other room, trying to remember if she had locked the door. She couldn't face him. Not like this. Filled with pain and the agony of betrayal. Torn apart by hurt pride, understanding, rage, love. She had to think. She had to decide what——

The door crashed open under the impact of an impatient hand on the latch and Rafe strode into the ante-chamber. He took one look at her face, slammed the door shut and locked it, then reached the solar in three long strides.

Nell went utterly still, freezing like a hunted animal in the presence of danger.

He stopped just clear of the doorway, his face set hard, eyes blazing with implacable determination. 'How much did you hear?' he demanded, and slammed the second door shut with the flat of his hand.

CHAPTER THIRTEEN

NELL backed away so rapidly that she was up against the window before she knew it.

'How. . .did you know. . .?' Her voice was raspy, choked with unshed tears. She hadn't expected the sight of him to affect her so badly. She needed to be calm to survive this, but hurt was welling up within her, battering at her defences, crying to be free. She wanted to scream, to throw herself at him, clawing and kicking, to relieve the awful pressure of pain and rage and despair building inside her.

'The solar door was open.' He had halted as soon as she'd retreated and now stood watching her, big and dark and immovable, framed by the grey stone arch behind him. 'You're the only person who would open it again and not come into the room, and the only reason for that would be if you'd overheard enough to upset you.'

'Upset me?' She laughed, a shrill, brittle sound that had her biting her lip in an effort at control. 'Aye, you could say I'm somewhat upset. Being lied to does that to me.'

'I have never lied to you,' he said harshly. 'I may not have told you the whole truth, but——'

'Is that not a lie?' she cried, unable to maintain her calm in the face of his denial. 'Right from the start you've lied by omission. From that first night when you said you were there to escort me home. 'Twas the truth, aye, but you forgot to add that your other

264

purpose was to look me over, didn't you, my lord? Why was that, I wonder? Afraid I would refuse you?'

His tawny eyes bored into hers. 'As I recall, you were planning to refuse regardless of who the bridegroom turned out to be, but I didn't say anything then, because there was no need for you to know my reasons for considering a union with you.'

'No need!' Her voice soared and nearly cracked. 'That was the rest of my life we were talking about. I had every right to know why I was being *looked over*!'

'Will you stop throwing that phrase at me?' he yelled suddenly. He clenched his fists, and his eyes shut briefly in a visible bid for patience. 'Neither Edward nor I used it, no matter what your father said.'

'I don't care what phrase was used!' she screamed back. 'The intent was the same.' And, without warning, words were pouring from her in an uncontrollable stream as her frail shell of composure shuddered, cracked and was rent asunder. 'But you didn't like what you saw, did you? No wonder you were so angry that night. 'Twas because you were being forced to marry a woman you despised to have your birthright restored to you. Nor was that the only time you lied to me. You said my father had promised to renounce his allegiance to Lancaster if the King would confirm his title. Sweet Lord, why didn't I suspect then? All those quetions you asked about Hadleigh, and what would happen in the event of my death. Did you think I would be so grateful for your efforts in keeping me alive that I wouldn't care if 'twas in your own interests?'

She laughed again, wildly, mockingly. 'What a predicament for you. Faced with the same situation as Tom. Both of you trying to put me in a position where I would be forced to marry you, without getting me killed in the process. But you had more to lose, my lord. You even said so. One of the few times you told me the truth, I expect. My aunt *is* close to the Queen, and had Uncle Edward counter-petitioned to marry me to Tom, your revenge might have received quite a check. Especially since you believe the Queen is capable of bending Edward to her will, manipulation of males being such a dangerous female trait. What were you planning to do in that event? Seduce me?'

Something flashed in his eyes and Nell almost staggered back against the wall, gasping as if she'd received a mortal blow. 'You did,' she whispered in horrified comprehension. If he had admitted it aloud she would not have been more certain. 'You did! That was why you were. . .gentler. Why you let me help Bess. . .why you. . .'

She couldn't go on. Her protective rage had been torn from her by the shocking realisation that Rafe had, indeed, made such a cold-blooded plan.

'Are you done?' he asked with ominous quiet, when she didn't say any more. 'I hope so, because I'm only going to say this once. No one was forcing me to marry you. Nor have I ever lied to you. fitzWarren did petition the King, exactly as I told it, and 'twas that which prompted my own action, though I'd hoped to have more time to find the witnesses I needed to call fitzWarren into court. Edward then suggested the marriage to both your father and I as a means of protecting you, so you wouldn't be left destitute, but if for some reason I didn't want to marry you, he would have backed me in a civil claim.'

She just looked at him, disbelieving, her eyes dry and burning in her white face, pain crouching like a wild beast inside her, snarling, merciless, waiting to spring free the moment she let down her guard.

He must have seen it, seen her disbelief at least,

because his voice softened and he took a step towards her. 'Nell, use your common sense. Of course our marriage will make everything quick and tidy, but, if worst comes to worst, there is nothing to stop Edward rejecting your father's petition and restoring title to me on the simple grounds that fitzWarren fought on the side of Lancaster.'

'Nothing to stop him?' she echoed, incredulous. 'No, only his bride of four months. Apart from any other consideration, she was the widow of a Lancastrian, and is known to favour her family and friends beyond measure. You said yourself that Edward will do anything for her. No——' she looked away, speaking almost to herself '—marriage to me was your only sure way. There were too many risks otherwise. Elizabeth's influence on behalf of my father or my uncle, the fact that you had no proof, no witnesses. . .' She paused, vaguely struck by the word. 'Witnesses?'

Rafe gestured impatiently. 'Old serfs who had been at Hadleigh Beaudene when your father first arrived there. 'Twould have been unlikely, however. He was very careful to be rid of anyone who posed a danger to him.'

'Even the child of his dead mistress,' she whispered, raising stricken eyes to his. 'The rightful heir. Oh, Rafe. . .'

The beast inside her stirred, a claw reaching for her heart, and she forced it back, praying he hadn't heard her. 'Well, it doesn't matter any more. None of it matters. Indeed, this whole discussion is unnecessary and——'

'At least we agree on that,' he muttered. 'Nell, little one——'

She flinched visibly at the endearment and he stopped dead, his eyes narrowing.

'Don't,' she begged. 'I understand why you planned as you did. I do, truly. But you don't have to be. . .be nice. . .any more. You can take my father into court and win your lands back that way. You don't have to marry me.'

His brows snapped together. 'What?'

'Take my father into court,' she repeated, her voice beginning to shake. 'You have your witness. Me. I heard what was said between you. Hadleigh is yours by right of birth. You don't have to marry me for it.'

'I already know that,' he grated. ''Tis what I've just been telling you. What you heard doesn't change anything. It doesn't make any difference to us, Nell.'

'How can you say that?' she cried, anguished. Pain shuddered through her again and she barely suppressed a whimper. Didn't he understand what she was trying to do? Didn't he know how impossible this was for her? 'I'm the daughter of the man who wronged you so grievously he can never be forgiven, and to regain what you've lost you intend to ally with him—your worst enemy, a man you despise. Do you think I want to look at you one day, when I am no longer a means of revenge and justice, and see hatred or resentment in your eyes?'

'God damn it, I have never thought of you as a means——' He stopped abruptly, and the sudden flash of memory in his eyes struck Nell like an open hand to her face. She turned whiter still, the sudden roaring in her ears almost drowning out her own choked words.

'No, you can't deny it. The same way you can't deny that you planned to seduce me.'

'That,' he said through his teeth, 'was a separate issue entirely. And I ceased thinking of you as an instrument of revenge days ago. As for justice, it can be achieved through other means. In fact——'

'Then go ahead and achieve it through those means,' Nell shrieked. She couldn't bear it. She couldn't take any more. The pain was too much. Claws raking at her heart, tearing, rendering. . .'Prove you didn't lie to me. Prove you didn't intend to use me. *Prove it*!'

'All right,' he said very calmly.

She went still, staring at him.

'We'll go to Edward. You can give him your deposition, he'll pass judgement in my favour and that will be the end of it.'

Nell's eyes widened. She couldn't believe he had said that, and yet. . .

'Do you mean that, in all honour?'

'If you insist on it. But before you make your decision, princess, think on this. The minute the wax has set beneath the King's seal, I'll have us wed by the nearest priest.'

'Married?' She hardly dared breathe the word.

'That's right.' His voice was still calm, chillingly so. 'We can waste all that time so you can prove to yourself that I'm as easily manipulated as any other man, and end up just as wedded as if we'd been married here in Wells without any trouble or unnecessary delays at all.'

'I. . . I can't. . .' She frowned and put a shaking hand to her brow. She was getting confused. Somehow Rafe had turned the tables on her and she was no longer sure of anything. Manipulate him? She had wanted only to right the shameful wrong her father had done, without destroying herself. Was that so terrible?

'Aye, put like that, your objections do sound like the rantings of a hysterical female, don't they, Nell?' he said, obviously mistaking her long silence. 'Which is why we're not going to do it that way.'

'What do you mean?' she whispered, suddenly

afraid. His glittering eyes held an expression that made her mouth go dry and turned her limbs to water.

This was not the passionate lover of yesterday, nor even her fierce protector, but the man she had met at Langley. Cold, hard, ruthless.

He started slowly across the room towards her, his fierce golden eyes locked on hers. 'I'm sorry you had to find out about your father the way you did,' he said very softly, 'but I'm not letting his crimes disrupt our lives any longer. When you calm down, you'll know I'm right.'

'No! Wait!' Eyes wide, completely unable to move, Nell clutched the top of the nearest chairback with quivering fingers and watched his slow advance.

'We don't have time to wait.' He stopped less than a foot away from the chair she was clinging to, and his voice hardened. 'There's still the possibility of a child, if you recall, my lady. Doing things your way could take several months, and no child of mine will be born a bastard.'

It wasn't pain that hit her this time, but a healthy bolt of rage. She was trembling so violently with it that the chair shook.

'And you call women manipulative! My plan to save us both from a marriage of cold necessity, if indeed I ever had one, pales in comparison to your own to trap me into such a situation. Is that why you took me in such haste yesterday? To ensure my agreement to an immediate wedding? Well, it won't work. You can——'

Her tirade was abruptly cut off when he reached out, yanked the chair out of her grasp and tossed it aside as if it weighed no more than a feather.

Nell barely noticed the crash when it landed. Jerked off-balance by the force with which he'd pulled the chair out from under her fingers, she staggered forward against the unyielding wall of his chest with an impact that drove the breath from her lungs. Before she could recover, she was trapped in his arms, held so tightly that she could feel every hard male inch of him pressed to her softer frame.

She lifted her head to protest and her throat closed up. His eyes were savage, slitted, molten with fierce intent. They stared down into hers, blazing even hotter when her lips parted.

'Don't say another word,' he snarled, his voice so hoarse she would hardly have recognized it. 'Not one word, princess. I know yesterday was a shock to you, and over too damned soon, but I thought you knew I wanted you, at least. Obviously I was wrong, and——' he bent, swinging her up into his arms with a swiftness that shocked her '—you still need convincing.'

Nell stiffened, trying to hold herself rigid as Rafe carried her over to the bed. But her pulse was racing so fast she thought she might faint, and she began to shiver, even as the intense heat of his body wrapped around her.

'You're going to force me?' she got out, unable to believe he would actually go to such an extreme. 'You know I'll never forgive you. Never! Is that what you want? For me to hate you?'

Just for a second his face tightened with an emotion too fleeting for her to recognise. Then he laid her on the bed and came down over her, the weight of his body keeping her pinned there.

'No,' he murmured. 'No force.' And this time there was no anger in the voice rasping over her nerves, only gentleness. His big hands framed her face and he looked down into her eyes as his mouth lowered slowly to hers. 'There's too much passion in you to make force necessary, sweetheart.' His lips brushed hers. 'What do you think is tearing you apart right now? You're hurt and angry, I know, but there's more between us than cold necessity. I'm going to show you. . .'

She would not succumb, Nell vowed fiercely as Rafe began kissing her more deeply. Nor would she fight him. He would get no pleasure from this, neither conquest nor willing surrender. She would be as cold, as unfeeling, as passionless as the stone statues on the cathedral.

The vow lasted all of ten seconds. Rafe's mouth moved on hers with a gentle cherishing that crushed every vicious claw piercing her heart. Rage didn't have a chance; hurt reached out to be healed. He had never kissed her like this. As if kissing her was all. As if he needed. As if he *craved*.

Her lips softened and parted and she was powerless to stop the gentle, insistent invasion of his tongue. He filled her mouth, tasted, possessed. Her blood warmed, slowly. . .slowly. She put her hands to his shoulders, intending to push him away, and the solid strength beneath her fingers made her moan silently instead. Somewhere her mind was screaming. Not like this. *Not like this*! But he was warm and strong and she loved him. *Loved* him.

When this kiss ended it was so gradual that for a moment Nell lay dazed, her breathing light and fast. Then her lashes lifted and the brilliant gold of his eyes slammed into her with a force that left her senses reeling. Triumph, desire, sheer male determination to claim his woman. She read them all, and a silent cry of despair welled up inside her.

He had won. He would take her, and she would

marry him, regardless of his reasons, not knowing if he would ever return her love.

Oh, he wanted her. She believed that. But for how long?

She gazed up into his eyes, searching desperately, forgetting in her distress that he would not trust his heart easily, and saw only the reflection of herself lying helpless in his arms. He would win this particular battle every time, for she could never withstand him, never leave him. She needed to be close to him in the only way he seemed to want, and he would only have to touch her.

And, dear God in Heaven, he had known that. Oh, weak fool that she was, she had told him so herself not an hour ago, and he had, indeed, remembered.

It was too much. Defeat shrouded her in utter misery. She had tried to fight for the future she wanted and had been betrayed by her own body, and as Rafe bent his head to kiss her again the first hot tears seeped from the corners of her eyes and ran down to the pillow.

'You're mine,' he whispered against her trembling mouth. 'Mine! Say it!'

But she couldn't speak. Couldn't respond to the fierce urgency in his command. She felt his mouth touch the wetness on her cheek, felt him lift his head, and she tensed, turning her face away, closing her eyes and pressing her cheek into the pillow. But the silent tears were coming too fast to be hidden, and she knew he could feel the tremors shaking her body.

He went still for the space of a heartbeat, then caught her chin in his hand and swiftly brought her face around to his again.

'Nell? Oh, God, sweetheart. . . Don't. . .

Taking her face between his hands, he began pressing frantic little kisses to her eyes, as though trying to stop the flow. 'Don't cry. Darling, please. I didn't mean. . . I only wanted to show you. . . I *had* to show you. We belong together. I can't let you go. Anything else you want, I'll do, but not that. Not that!'

Somewhere through the jagged edges of pain the anguished sound of his voice reached her, but she still couldn't speak. Her throat was too tight. He was kissing her too desperately—her eyes, her mouth, her cheeks. Words of need, of love, poured over her as if he had wanted to say them forever.

'I know you don't love me yet, but you will. You will! I'll make sure of it. Oh, God, don't cry any more. My darling, my heart. I love you. . .love you. . .'

His mouth, hard and shaking, salty with the taste of her tears, covered hers, and with a wrenching sob Nell started kissing him back, her arms clinging around his neck until she couldn't breathe for the emotions filling her heart. The transition from despair to shock to tremulous hope was simply too rapid, too frightening. She wrenched her mouth free, buried her face in his shoulder and wept uncontrollably.

The storm didn't last long. Rafe held her against him as if he was afraid she would be torn from his arms at any minute, murmuring to her over and over, until finally she was calm.

'I'm sorry,' he said hoarsely. 'I'm sorry. I never wanted to hurt you, but you said we didn't have to marry and I panicked. I knew it was true that I couldn't force you and I panicked.'

Nell tried to find her voice. 'You? Panic?' was all she could manage in a husky croak.

He turned her gently on to her back and leaned over her, his fingers threading through her hair, brushing tear-drenched tendrils aside.

'Nell, look at me.'

Hesitant, still afraid to believe that Rafe had said he loved her, she raised her eyes to his face. And then she had to believe. The depth of emotion shimmering in her eyes made her heart stand still.

Aye, shimmering, she thought in wonder. This man who had been forced to survive the streets of London at a horrifyingly young age, who had grown into a warrior as ruthless as he was honourable, was showing her a vulnerability she had never even guessed at.

'I can't lose you,' he said urgently, holding her gaze. 'You mean too much to me. You're the one woman I didn't think existed. The other half of myself. My heart.'

At the deep note of tenderness in his voice fresh tears welled in Nell's eyes. She blinked them back, smiling shakily up at him, and he bent to kiss her, his possession of her mouth slow and gentle and deep.

'My little princess,' he murmured minutes later. 'How could you have doubted after the time we've spent together? Don't you know yet how very alike we are?'

If she had any doubts remaining after his kiss, those words would have dispelled them forever. 'I've known that for days,' she whispered, her heart mirrored in her eyes for him to see. 'Oh, Rafe, I love you so. Why do you think I agreed to marry you? Why do you think I let you. . .yesterday. . .?'

She broke off, blushing rosily when his hard mouth curved in a smile as wicked as it was tender.

'Let me? My innocent little darling, you didn't *let* me make love to you yesterday. I didn't even give you a chance to say yea or nay. You were practically in shock, and as for me——' his smile turned rueful '—an entire army of villainous cousins wouldn't have stopped me. I'd just seen you risk your life to help me, and all I could think of was making you mine in every way possible.'

'You would have stopped,' she said with absolute certainty. 'If I had truly wished it.'

'You have a touching if misplaced confidence in my control when I have you in my arms, sweetheart.'

'In your honour,' she corrected softly, putting a hand up to his face. ''Tis the first side of you I fell in love with. After that, the rest was inevitable.'

His eyes flashed with a sudden blaze of emotion, desire and tender love combined, and his arms tightened convulsively. 'Oh, God, Nell, I didn't know until yesterday how much you meant to me. I'd wanted you since the moment I saw you, but when you went racing after those arrows——'

He stopped, shook his head and added in a low voice, 'If you had been so much as bruised I would have killed every one of those men, including your cousin. I knew then that what I felt was more than desire, but I'd never let a woman come that close, never wanted to protect her with my life or trust her with my honour. I wasn't ready to call it love, until I realised what you'd overheard. Then I knew. Sweet Jesu, how I knew! I couldn't get up here fast enough to see how much damage had been done, and when I thought I'd lost you, I just went mad. All I could think of was holding on to you, showing you how it could be between us, when what I should have done was shown you this.'

He sat up as he spoke, drawing Nell up with him and taking a folded sheet of parchment from his surcoat pocket. She could tell by the deep creases in the paper that it was very old.

'You found that in the crucifix,' she whispered,

knowing immediately what had happened. 'So it did conceal something.'

'Aye. After you left it with me the other night, I found the hidden catch. This was inside the cross.' He handed the document to her. 'Read it.'

She took it with some reluctance, looking up at him, troubled. 'Rafe, I don't need to know what secret this holds. I trust you. I didn't mean all those terrible things I said. I know you wouldn't lie for your own gain, or try to trick me into marriage. 'Twas just. . .hearing all the dreadful things my father had done. . . I couldn't imagine how anyone would *not* want revenge and. . .'twas just too much.'

'Or not enough.' He leaned forward to brush her lips in a fleeting gesture of reassurance. 'That's why I want you to read it, love,' he said gently. 'At first I didn't want you to be hurt by the truth about your father, but, since you heard some of it, you should know it all. We should start on equal footing, you and I. We should *both* know I'm marrying you because my future is meaningless without you beside me.'

A warm glow spreading through her at that last remark, Nell spread the parchment open and began to read.

''Tis a confession,' she said, amazed, a few seconds later. 'My father's confession, in his own hand, of all he did to rob you of your lands. The forgery of transfer of title from the Beaudenes to the fitzWarrens. The way he dismissed the long-time servants when your mother died so his way was clear to eliminate you. Merciful saints, he even hopes for redemption because he didn't kill you outright. And then he finally remembers to tack on his unfaithfulness to my mother.'

A disturbing thought occurred to her. 'Do you think

my mother knew of this?' she faltered, frowning worriedly up at Rafe.

'No,' he said, with such assurance that Nell believed him instantly. 'fitzWarren told me he wrote this confession when he moved your mother to Wells a year after you were born, as can be proved by its date. He told me all, in fact. Did you know that you and your mother never lived at Hadleigh Castle, but at the manor she had inherited from her father? He used to visit her there after my mother died, and probably before, if the truth is known.

'Then, after years of a barren marriage, his wife was suddenly with child, and in the expectation of a son of his own he took me to London, and conveniently mislaid me in one of the meanest parts of the city. Apparently he regarded the birth of a daughter as divine punishment for his sins, and when no more children were forthcoming he decided to protect his soul by concealing that confession in the cross he gave your mother. He told her it had to do with his support of poor, mad Henry and that since the Duke of York was protector of the realm at that time, his life would be endangered if the document ever came to light.'

'Holy saints!' Nell exclaimed weakly.

'Aye. I don't think the man has ever told the truth in his life, except now, with the threat of death looming over him.'

'What will you do with him?' she asked. 'Accuse him publicly?'

Rafe shook his head. Taking the confession from her, he tossed it on the floor, propped his back against the carved bedhead, and settled Nell close to him again. 'I might have needed revenge once, sweetheart, but not any more. That document is just to keep your father from troubling us. As for his punishment, 'twill

come soon enough. The man is ill. If he sees the year
out 'twill be a miracle. I've given him two days to
return to Hadleigh, clear his trappings out of the place,
and move as far from us as possible. Oh, and before he
leaves Wells, he is to send your uncle's man back to
Langley for your baggage and Chevette.'

'Chevette! Oh, Rafe.' She raised shining eyes to his
face. 'You're going to ask my uncle for Chevette? Oh,
thank you.'

He grinned down at her. 'Might as well blackmail
everyone into giving us what we want while we can.
Anything you'd like from the King when I inform him
he's not to come near you again unless I'm with you?'

Nell smiled, so happy she would have forgiven the
entire world its sins. 'I don't want revenge either,' she
said. 'As long as I have your love, I have everything I
need. Although——' She stopped suddenly, remembering something she had wanted to do—holy saints!—
was it only four days ago? 'There is a *little* thing. . .'

'Name it.'

'You will have to let me go first,' she said demurely.

He looked at her. 'For a minute. If you're lucky.' He
opened his arms.

Nell rose on her knees beside him and let her gaze
travel over his face, from the quizzical expression in his
tawny eyes to the amused set of his hard mouth, and
then lower to the width of his shoulders and chest. She
remembered how her breasts had felt, crushed against
the powerful muscles beneath his surcoat, remembered
the strength in his arms, the intimacy of his touch.

With an inward shiver, she reined in her wayward
thoughts. There would be time later to touch, to savour
his strength, but first——

Her gaze returned to Rafe's face and she lifted her
hand towards him. The amused expression had van-

ished from his eyes. Nell shivered again, hesitating when she saw the smouldering heat that had replaced it. 'May I——?'

'Anything,' he said at once, his voice a low growl deep in his throat. 'Whatever you want.'

She edged closer and her hand touched his cheek, but the position threatened her balance. His eyes on her face, Rafe took her free hand and placed it on his shoulder, so she could brace herself. The muscle beneath her fingers was as hard as steel.

Her lips parted slightly as the heat from his body surrounded her. Love, desire, tenderness—all swirled within her. All for Rafe. Her hand touched his cheek again, and with the tips of her fingers she traced the scar on his face, from his brow to the short curve below his eye. Then she leaned closer and retraced the path with her lips.

'I'm so sorry,' she whispered. 'So very sorry.'

His arms closed around her, holding her against him with a fierce strength that was yet heart-meltingly tender. 'It doesn't matter any more. My little darling. You won't regret marrying me. You won't regret trusting me with your love. I swear it. We've both been scarred by the past, even if all the marks don't show, but the future is ours.'

He moved suddenly, with the unexpected swiftness that always managed to surprise her. Before Nell had taken her next breath, she was flat on her back, gazing bemusedly up at him. 'Starting now,' he growled, and lowered his mouth to hers.

'But. . .the Bishop. . .'

It was the only protest Nell managed to utter before Rafe was kissing her with the same intensely focused need she had felt in him before, kissing her until she was soft and melting inside, until she couldn't remember why she would ever want to protest.

His hands moved over her, even as she surrendered to the magic of his kisses, unlacing, shifting, sweeping their garments aside until she lay naked in his arms for the first time. Felt the burning heat of his body enfold her, felt the softness of her breasts crushed against the deliciously abrasive hardness of his chest. And, like his mouth, his hands cherished, worshipped, aroused.

Shyness intruded just once, when he raised himself slightly on one forearm to let his gaze move slowly down the length of her body. Nell murmured softly as warmth tinted her cheeks, and he bent swiftly to her mouth again.

'Hush,' he whispered. 'You're so beautiful. So beautiful, my darling. My princess. Let me love you. Let me. . .'

His dark voice was so strained and hoarse that it would have startled her had she been thinking clearly, but his hands started to trace the path his eyes had taken, and she could only feel. His long fingers found and circled her breasts, shaping their soft contours, teasing the rosy buds that responded to his touch in a tingling rush that sent lightning flashes to every quivering nerve-ending.

Leaving her wanting more of the thrilling caresses, his hand moved lower, flattening on the gentle curve of her belly, pressing and kneading lightly in a movement that was both sensual and possessive. Nell's hips lifted in a response she couldn't control, and a small cry of longing shuddered through her. He had given her pleasure yesterday, but this. . . She was drowning in sensations never before imagined.

'Shhh,' he soothed, trailing tiny kisses along her jaw,

then moving to the soft flesh beneath her chin. 'Slow, this time, sweetheart. Slow.'

With lips and tongue he tasted her throat, her neck, the delicate bones below, moving with nerve-racking slowness towards her straining breasts. His tongue curled around a velvety nipple, teasing over and over, making her writhe beneath him in frustrated need. Then, just when she thought she could not stand the sweet torment any longer, his mouth closed hotly over the throbbing peak, and at the same time his fingers parted the soft curls between her legs to stroke her body with earth-shattering gentleness.

Ecstasy burst inside her almost immediately. She arched, an almost soundless cry parting her lips, no longer herself but a pulsing, throbbing creature of fire and pleasure.

It went on forever. He gave her no rest, no respite, but with mouth and hands took her from peak to peak until, when she was almost senseless with pleasure, when she thought there could be no more, he raised himself above her and, with a look of love so intense she could hardly bear it, he filled her body with his. Took her heart. Gave her his own.

It was a joining so complete that she no longer had any awareness of two separate beings. Every breath, every whispered word of love, every heartbeat was theirs, shared. Every touch, every meeting of lips, of hands, of warm, naked flesh was a link binding them more closely. And when the final release came, when his life-force merged with hers, their souls met for one single, timeless moment of shared ecstasy.

Two weeks later, wrapped warmly against the brisk autumn wind in a sable-lined mantle of dark gold velvet, Nell stood in the courtyard of the inn near

Wells where she and Rafe had been staying since their marriage, and watched the last of her chests being loaded on to the baggage wagon.

A few yards away Samson and Chevette, already saddled, awaited their riders. Next to the bay's huge bulk Chevette looked more like a child's pony, but she didn't seem to mind the close proximity of the larger horse, even though Samson was standing with his head arched over her withers.

Indeed, if anything, Nell mused, suddenly realising that Samson had been assuming that particular stance since the little palfrey had arrived three days ago, Chevette looked rather smug.

'Are you ready to depart, sweetheart?' Rafe asked, coming up behind her. He didn't stop walking until he was close enough for her shoulder to brush his chest. 'They're expecting us at Hadleigh before the supper hour.'

Nell smiled up at the hard face of her warrior husband, and marvelled at the softer light that filled his eyes every time he looked at her. That, and his need to be within touching distance of her whenever they were together, had her utterly enthralled.

Of course, it had its disadvantages also, Rafe had informed her only last night. She was now so sensitive to his presence that, much to her glee and his pretended disgust, he could no longer creep up on her.

He looked down at her now and his eyes lingered, narrowing thoughtfully. 'Why are you smiling like that?'

The smile grew. 'Do you see anything familiar?' she asked, glancing to the side.

His gaze followed hers. He was silent for a moment, then, 'You don't have withers,' he muttered. 'And I don't *hang* over you.'

Nell giggled. 'Of course not.'

Rafe continued to watch the horses. 'Poor old Samson,' he observed, with patently false gloom. 'Another warrior brought to his knees by the female of the species.'

'Indeed?' Nell bent a minatory look on him. 'I don't think I've ever seen you——'

But Rafe wasn't listening. 'On the other hand, if he's going to be distracted. . . Euan,' he called to his young squire, who was contemplating the unenviable task of separating Chevette from her protector. 'Leave the palfrey's reins tied. I'll take my lady up before me on Samson for the first few miles. You can stay with the baggage wagon.'

'Aye, my lord.' Relieved of duty, the boy scampered off to fetch his own mount.

'But I was looking forward to——' Nell began, only to be stopped by a gleam in her husband's eyes that she had no trouble in recognising.

'Do you recall that I once promised to show you how much trouble you can get into on the back of a horse, my lady?' he murmured in the dark velvet voice that never failed to make her knees go weak.

And to think she'd just been picturing the interesting spectacle of her erstwhile bodyguard on *his* knees. A mind-numbing suspicion suddenly occured to her. Surely he didn't mean to. . .? On a *horse*? He couldn't! She wouldn't!

But, when Nell looked up into those intensely glittering hawk's eyes, she knew that if he could, she would.

'Do you know something, my lord?' she asked, her frown promising dire retribution even as a deliciously wanton shiver of excitement coursed through her. 'I am not precisely sure how or when it happened, but somehow I seem to have ended up no longer mistress of my fate.'

'Of course not. Do I look like a fool?' Rafe grinned at her, his expression wicked and very male. 'But never mind, little princess. You can be mistress of my fate instead. Console yourself with the reflection that 'tis a lifelong occupation.'

Nell tilted her head and pretended to consider. 'That,' she finally pronounced, 'will do perfectly well.'

And with a smile of dazzling brilliance she launched herself into Rafe's arms and into their future.

A years supply of Mills & Boon romances — absolutely free!

Would you like to win a years supply of heartwarming and passionate romances? Well, you can and they're FREE! All you have to do is complete the word puzzle below and send it to us by 29th February 1996. The first 5 correct entries picked out of the bag after that date will win a years supply of Mills & Boon romances (six books every month—worth over £100). What could be easier?

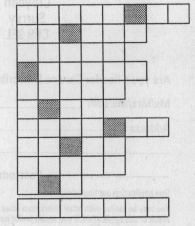

GMWIMSIN

NNSAUT

ACEHB

EMSMUR

ANCOE

DNSA

RTOISTU

THEOL

ATYCH

NSU

MYSTERY DESTINATION

Please turn over for details on how to enter